The Monkey Idol

Decker & Callie Adventure
Book One

K.D. McNiven

Book cover: Temple Ruins
Illustration by Jared Shear

Special thanks to my husband, David for his support and encouragement to follow my dream. Thanks to Ryan and Brit McNiven for their help editing and for being my cheerleaders, and to Sarah Thomas for the many hours of computer work she put in figuring out all of the nuts and bolts of publishing in order for me to accomplish this work.

Prologue

Honduras 2016

Leonard Romero bounded down the staircase, stopping abruptly at the bottom and peered around the corner. Under his arm he carried a wrapped package tied with heavy string. Satisfied that there was no one lurking in the marbled reception area, he stepped out from the shadowed nook and made his way to the counter.

"Would you make sure this is mailed today?" he asked, handing the package over to the hotel desk clerk, a pleasant Hispanic gentleman that Leonard had come to know quite well over the past months.

He nodded. "Si, Señor Romero. I'll make sure it does."

Leonard was hopeful the package would find its way quickly into the hands of his wife, Holly. In hurried strides, he made his way out of the hotel lobby where his jeep was parked. His two guides, Pedro Gonzalez and Basilo Suarez were already there waiting for him. They had come highly recommended and had led numerous expeditions into the Honduran jungles. Leonard could not have managed without their expertise.

He tossed his rucksack into the back, packed tightly with the equipment they'd need for excavation, along with plenty food supplies. His plan was to return to the La Mosquitia area—the darkest, most primitive land he'd ever ventured.

One day later, they were paddling their pipante, a long, slender boat, up the snaking Río Plátano River. The diverse vegetation ranged from four-foot grassy marshes to long trailing vines knitted together to form thick walls on either side of the river. Slim fingers of golden light filtered through the thick umbrella overhead, lending an eerie cast that made it seem as if they'd stepped from one world into another.

As they continued their trip up river, they noticed another boat following close behind. Fishermen and adventure seekers alike frequented the river—and unfortunately, drug runners and poachers as well. Leonard only hoped it was a couple local fishermen heading back to one of the villages located along the banks.

It was midday when they pulled the pipante and the rubber raft carrying their supplies, out of the current and onto the rocky shore. Pedro dragged the hollowed-out boat from the muddy surge and was banking it when a shot rang out, seemingly from nowhere. Instantaneously, Pedro's body crumpled into the river, the rushing water swirling around him. His splayed body bobbed over the river's peaks as he drifted away.

Both Leonard and Basilo bolted into the thicket, though not soon enough for Basilo. There was a loud crack, and his body collapsed in a lifeless heap. Another shot split the air, whizzing past Leonard's ear. His heart raced with fear. He dashed forward, briars and tree limbs raking his face and bared arms as he frantically ducked through the thick foliage. His breath was ragged. His mind spun with confusion. But he continued battling his way through the matted vegetation. His pulse quickened as he anticipating the next shot.

Gripped with fear, he realized he'd lost his bearings and could no longer determine where he was. It was strange where a person's thoughts could go when under duress, Leonard pondered. Gruesome stories began flashing through his mind about explorers who'd stumbled onto decaying bodies in the jungle because they'd gotten lost in the maze of undergrowth. He shuddered involuntarily.

He pressed forward into a slick trough of mud and fought desperately to find his footing. It was near impossible to get traction in the spongy, water-soaked ground cover. The thick sludge enfolded him, wrapping him in a warm blanket. Feverishly, he grappled at the slimy banks, clawing like a madman. He dug his heels deep into the mire and struggled to push himself to his knees and then to his feet.

It was enough that he had to cope with the slick terrain, but now he had to face a torrential downpour. The rain pelted against his face with stinging intensity and within minutes the ground turned into a surging watercourse. The force knocked him down once again, and he grunted when his face struck against a stone. His arms quaked as he dragged himself back to his feet, knowing that if he didn't, it would be certain death. Blood trickled into his eyes and dripped off his chin to mingle with his mud-caked shirt.

In a daze, he reeled forward, his instincts shouting at him to follow the stream back to the river so could regain a sense of direction. Behind him, he could hear brush crashing and snapping, and realized with dread, that whoever was trying to shoot him was gaining ground quickly.

Leonard didn't see the tree branch until it was too late. His feet got caught up on the rotting wood, and he tumbled headlong into the gurgling stream. Fatigue had overtaken him, and he barely had enough life-force in him to move, but desperation drove him. His arms flailed at the water, and he managed to push himself back onto shaking legs. He lunged forward when another shot tore through the dark jungle…

Chapter 1

Holly Romero grabbed clothes off hangers and in rapid fire tossed them carelessly into the opened leather suitcase. Her heart was pumping so fast, she thought it would leap out of her chest. She had to keep reminding herself to slow down her breathing to keep from hyperventilating.

In her haste, she found it difficult to determine what items she would need to take. It was inconceivable her life would take such a frightful twist and that common everyday life would be turned upside down. She was filled with uncertainty, and yes, fear. That was the emotion plaguing her right now—gripping fear. The slightest noise, like a dog barking or a car rumbling by, made her nerves snap with anxiety.

From the closet, she moved to her dresser and began sorting through her belongings. She continued to glance at her watch, praying Decker Hayden would return her call. She knew him and his wife, Callie, were vacationing because Garrett, Decker's father, had told her as much when she'd called, but she was desperate. Even though she'd always been independent, she was painfully aware that she could not manage this nightmare alone.

It was not as if she knew Decker and Callie all that well. The first time they met was on a dig in Montana when she had insisted on tagging along with her husband, Leonard. Even though Decker and Callie were leading the team, and were quite busy, Holly still managed to get acquainted with them. On one of the evenings they had gone out for cocktails, and another time they simply sat around the campsite to discuss the day's events.

Decker had also dropped in a couple of times over the years to go over some archaeological details with Leonard, and she had spoken with him a couple of times on the phone after that. What she was certain of was that Leonard had held Decker and Callie in high esteem. He trusted their expertise, as well as their friendship. Presently, in the midst of her confusion and angst, Holly was mindful that she had nowhere else to turn except to the Haydens.

Life was not supposed to turn out this way, she reasoned. Leonard was within one year of retiring—or so he would say. She gave an abject snort, concluding that Leonard would never have been able to settle down and give up archeology. It was buried deep within his soul. How she missed him already—the stories he had shared with her, the disappointments he had experienced and the undeniable thrill of discovering an artifact. There were times when she had been jealous of his passion for unearthing old relics because of the incredible amount of time it had taken away from them. But, that was who he was, and she would never have considered asking him to give it up.

She prepared to leave the bedroom when her eyes caught sight of their wedding picture. It stopped her dead in her tracks. With trembling hands, she grabbed hold of the photograph, pressed it to her heart, then opened the suitcase and placed it safely between the layers of clothing. Presently, she was uncertain of where to go or what would become of her.

As she walked out into the living room, the horror she'd experienced minutes before struck her smack in the face. The room was in shambles. Dresser drawers were pulled out and thrown onto the floor. Papers were scattered from the entry hall all the way to the adjoining rooms. Lamps were toppled over, and several chairs were lying on their side, insinuating that whoever broke into her house had been in a great hurry to find whatever they had been looking for. With Leonard's sudden death, and now this dreadful intrusion, Holly felt nauseous and alone.

She jumped with a start when the doorbell rang. She stood frozen to the spot, and then with great effort, she choked out the words, "Who is it?"

"Mail, Mrs. Romero, I need your signature."

On wobbly legs, she moved towards the door and peeked out of the security hole. Relief filled her when she saw that it was indeed the mailman. She cracked the door and forced a weak smile for his sake. Quick as her quivering fingers could, she sprawled her name out. "Thank you," she said, closing the door behind her.

Her heart was still racing as she examined the package in her hands. It was a heavy box wrapped in brown paper. It was from Leonard, postmarked from Honduras. Anticipation shook her very core. Carefully she peeled back the wrapping, lifted the lid and stared disbelievingly at an odd-looking artifact. It was a rather small statue that had deep grooves chiseled into it. By appearance, it resembled a monkey. Holly was stunned. It was apparent Leonard had sent the package from Honduras before he was murdered. Her mind whirled with confusion. Why? Was Leonard trying to smuggle the artifact out of the country? She knew him well enough to know he would never do anything illegal. Even she was aware that antiquities had to be registered with the government. The trafficking of any artifact was prohibited to protect the cultural heritage in other countries. She shuddered even to consider that he might do something so unlawful. Now, more than ever, she needed Decker and Callie. They would know what to do.

Her legs felt like jello, as she sagged against the wall for support. Her eyes remained locked onto the statue, her mind a vortex of unanswered questions. The sound of a car door slamming drew her attention. She peered outside and saw two men coming up the walkway in hurried strides. Both men looked intimidating and up to no good. The tall one had a scar deeply embedded in his shallow cheek. Stringy light brown hair brushed his shoulders, making him a rather foreboding figure. The other man walked with a notable limp, his coffee-colored face was leathered and deeply wrinkled, reflecting a hard life. His dark brows were woven into a menacing scowl.

The silhouette of a third man could be seen seated in the black vehicle parked on the street, though she was unable to make out the man's face. Filled with fear, she rushed out of the room to snag the artifact and frantically placed it back into the box, then stuffed it into her oversized purse. Hurried steps took her to the back door, panic overwhelming her. Heart racing, she raced across the lawn, through the back gate.

The only thought in her mind as she sprinted down the alley was to get away and find help. When she heard a man's voice yell, she twisted her head to see them dashing across the backyard, heading in her direction. She was an avid runner, which today was useful.

There were several stores lining the street and Holly ducked into a quaint dress shop, looking for a rear exit. The bell above the door jingled, and she caught sight of the two men as they rushed in. They stood still for a time, their eyes surveying the surroundings. One turned to the left, the other to the right, and they began a slow search of the store.

The store clerk glanced up. "May I help you?"

"Did a woman come in here?" The tall one inquired.

There was an edge of danger in his squinted eyes, and he glared at her menacingly.

The store clerk noticed a revolver tucked into the waistband of his jeans. Yes, she had seen the woman who had come in, but she was reluctant to tell him. Nervously, she replied, "I didn't see anyone."

Right then, Holly took the initiative and made a mad dash out the back door. Her heart felt as if it would explode as she headed back into the alley. Even though she did not turn back, she heard the back-door slam behind her. She merged with a side street where she was able to blend with the steady foot traffic on the sidewalk.

The pastry shop! Holly knew one of the waitresses there whom she had worked with for several years. With any luck, her friend would be on duty and would be willing to hide Holly from her pursuers. When she burst through the door, she nearly cried to see her friend Jeanette standing behind the counter.

Jeanette jumped with a start by the abrupt entrance. Her face went ashen seeing the ghost-white woman rush in, looking on the verge of hysteria. "Holly, what the…"

"I don't have time to explain, Jeanette. I need a place to hide!" Holly's face was stricken. Her entire body shook uncontrollably. "Please, Jeanette!"

Jeanette grabbed her arm and led her into the back room. "Stay here," she insisted. In a flurry of emotion, Jeanette headed to the front of the bakery. She flipped off the light switch, turned the lock on the door, and turned over the "*Sorry, we are closed*" sign. No sooner than she'd locked up the place, she spied two men dodging inside and out of some of the stores. Though Jeanette didn't know the present circumstances, she sensed these men were trouble. Jeanette hurried to the back room where Holly was hiding.

Holly's face twisted with fear, and she slowly slithered down the wall to curl into a tight ball, her entire body trembling.

Jeanette stooped down and dropped her hand on Holly's shoulder comfortingly. "Here," she offered her hand and helped Holly to her feet. "Take a deep breath. Now, what's this all about, Holly?"

Pent up tears began coursing down Holly's cheeks. Weeks of pain surfaced, and she could barely stop the flood long enough to speak. "You heard Leonard was murdered?" she sobbed.

Jeanette nodded her head, affirming she had read about his death in the newspaper. She realized that Holly was having to cope with her husband's murder, and at the same time, having to deal with these men chasing after her.

"I don't know what's going on; truly I don't. I came home this morning from shopping, and my house had been ransacked. Apparently, these men think I have something that they want because they returned a while later trying to find me. When I saw them, I snuck out the back of the house, and here I am."

"What can I do, Holly? Do you want me to call the police?"

Holly looked stricken. "No!" she blurted out. "I have to think this through. No police. Not yet."

"Would you like to stay at my house for a couple of days?" Jeanette offered. "You can't stay here. It's nearly shift change, and the store will have to be opened up. The men are not around here at the moment, but if they came back twice intent on looking for you, then you aren't safe going back home."

Holly didn't want to bring the police into it yet. Not until she knew what this whole situation was about. The last thing she wanted to do was draw attention to Leonard. She knew deep down that Leonard had sent the artifact in an attempt to keep it safe from someone. Possibly the two men who were after her. And she couldn't be sure there weren't others involved. Whatever the reason behind all of this, someone was willing to murder for it.

"That would be great, Jeanette," she agreed. "I'm waiting for some friends to call me and advise me what to do."

Jeanette squeezed her shoulder to reassure her. "I'll go get my car and drive it to the front. When I'm sure those two men aren't around, I'll motion for you to come out. Flip the lock on the way.

I'll call Nora Lang and explain what's going on. She'll be here in a half hour."

Holly nodded her head and tried to keep herself from falling apart. She stood and followed Jeanette out of the room and stayed close to the door until Jeanette drove her car around. Shortly, she saw Jeanette wave her hand that it was clear and she was safe to come out. Flipping the lock, Holly dashed out to the red Nissan and sank deeply into the seat.

During the drive, Holly remained silent. Thoughts whirled around in her head, many thoughts that had no answers. She cracked open her purse to confirm the statue was still tucked safely inside. Presently, it seemed to be the one thing that kept her connected to Leonard. So long as she had it in her possession, she realized her life would be in grave danger. Even so, she would protect it in every way she could.

"Holly," Jeanette's voice broke the silence. "What make of car were the men driving?"

"Why?"

Jeanette glanced in the rear-view mirror nervously. "There has been a black Toyota Land Cruiser following us for quite some time. Maybe I'm being paranoid?"

Holly's face drained of color. "That's what they were driving, Jeanette. Can you take an off ramp and see if they follow you?"

After they had driven a quarter mile down the road, Jeanette slipped across lanes and onto an off ramp. She looked in her mirror, and her heart picked up a beat. The Land Cruiser was close behind. Jeanette had never tried to shake someone from her tail, but instincts took over, and she accelerated, weaving her way through traffic, her heart pounding fiercely in her chest.

The Land Cruiser was coming up fast. The Nissan didn't have the power of the Land Cruiser, and Jeanette knew that they were losing ground fast. The Land Cruiser whipped into the other lane, then gunned the engine, and within seconds, they were side by side with the Nissan.

Holly leaned over instinctively when she saw a gun pointed at them. The driver, the one with the scar, cranked the car's steering wheel and smashed into the side of the Nissan with a vengeance. The Nissan shuddered and lurched right, but Jeanette managed to keep it from going off the road. Again, the driver of the Land Cruiser crashed into the side of their vehicle, causing Jeanette to lose control and the Nissan began to slide, then spin out, narrowly missing oncoming traffic. Their screams filled the interior of the car.

When the car came to a stop, they ended up facing the opposite direction. What made matters worse, the car sputtered and then died. Jeanette and Holly were in a panic. Traffic horns blasted as cars were barreling toward them, forced to swing wide to miss slamming into them.

Their pursuers swung around and came back after them. Jeanette's heart pounded as she turned the key. There were a couple grinding sounds, but the car wouldn't turn over. Once more, she twisted the key and pumped the gas. "Come on," Jeanette screeched. One last crank and the engine roared. She managed to get the car turned back in the right direction, nearly hitting an oncoming car. The sound of their horn resonated in Jeanette's ears. Sweat dripped off her brow as she shifted down and slammed the pedal to the floor. The smell of burning rubber filled their nostrils. Half a mile down the road, she whipped the Nissan down a side street and headed toward Los Angeles, the Land Cruiser still tailing her.

Looking over her shoulder, Holly saw they were gaining on them. "Faster Jeanette," her frantic voice blared. "They're behind us!"

Her car slid into the guardrail as she veered off the roadway and tried to maneuver the car onto a sharply curved ramp. The sound of shredding metal grated in their ears. The Nissan, even with the bumper dragging and the sides crushed in, miraculously kept going. If they made it through this alive, Jeanette

14

determined she would keep the Nissan for eternity out of gratitude.

She yanked the wheel sharply to the right, and the rear end fish-tailed but Jeanette managed to hold the Nissan to the road. Pushing the pedal still further, the Nissan picked up speed. Ahead, the light was turning red. "No!" Jeanette yelled, slapping her hand on the wheel in frustration. She knew if she stopped they would overtake them. That in mind, she punched the pedal to the floor and raced through the light barely missing a blue Impala that was pulling forward.

A loud bang resounded, and the back window of the Nissan crumbled. Glass bits sprayed across the seat, a few slivers raking against Holly's cheek. She raised her hand, and when she brought it back down, there were specks of blood on her fingertips. "They're shooting at us!" Holly cried out.

Frantic, Jeanette again torqued the wheel forcibly left, and the car spun out at the intersection where they remained, unable to go any farther. The magnitude of their situation weighed on them. As if in slow motion, they watched in awe the events that followed.

The driver of the black Land Cruiser slammed on the brakes trying to avoid the oncoming traffic, but not soon enough. Their vehicle rammed violently into the side of a white van, and the Land Cruiser flipped into the air, then dropped with a turbulent crash, rolling three times before coming to a dead heap.

The collision gave Jeanette enough time to gather her wits and get her vehicle back on the road. She gunned the Nissan and whipped onto a side street, a sense of relief washing over her. For a brief moment, both she and Holly cried and laughed, their emotions overwhelming them. They had survived!

Even though they knew the Land Cruiser was beyond recovery, they made multiple turns onto back streets to make sure they were in the clear. A half hour later, they found themselves pulling into Jeanette's driveway, and into her garage.

Waves of relief crashed over them. Both were silent. They dropped their heads back against the vinyl seats with a loud sigh and closed their eyes. They took in a moment to replay everything that had transpired.

Jeanette turned to Holly, her face pale. "You don't think they have my license plate number, do you?"

Holly didn't miss the terror in Jeanette's eyes. She shrugged. "I pray not, Jeanette. I'm so sorry that I got you involved in all of this."

"And what is THIS?" she stressed, her voice tight and shrill.

Holly shook her head. "I don't know. I only know that it has something to do with Leonard's discovery and why he was murdered. You should find somewhere to stay for a couple of weeks until I get this whole ordeal figured out. It wasn't my intention to get you involved, but now that you are, your life is in jeopardy. We both could have been killed."

"What about you, Holly? What will you do?"

"I don't know. My hope is that some acquaintances of mine, who are archaeologists, will return my call and help me sort through all of this." Holly looked somber. "If not, I guess I'm on my own."

Once they settled their frayed nerves, Jeanette motioned for Holly to follow her into the house. "Try and call your friends again. They probably have no idea how desperate this situation is. You can't do this alone Holly. You've seen what they're capable of."

"You're right. I need to call again. Look, Jeanette, I'll pay for your car and the expense of a place to stay. I can't in good conscience leave you in this mess."

Jeanette touched Holly's arm and gave it a gentle squeeze. "No worries. This isn't your doing either. I don't know what Leonard was mixed up in but it has to be something big considering someone murdered him and now they're after you.

Whatever he discovered has great significance and is worth a fortune."

"Do you have a place to stay?" Holly's concern for Jeanette was apparent. After all, Jeanette was an innocent bystander, and Holly had inadvertently gotten her drawn into a beehive of danger.

"My aunt lives south of here in San Diego. I know she would love it if I went to visit for a couple of weeks," Jeanette told her. "You will keep in touch?"

Shaking her head, Holly replied, "Of course I will. When I get the answers, I'll keep you informed. It's the least I can do. And if there's any way I can make this right for you, please, don't hesitate to ask."

"Look, it's nearly midnight. Let's try and get some rest— we'll figure it out in the morning," she comforted as she grabbed a couple of blankets from the hall closet. "Here," she said, handing the bundle to Holly. "I'll get you a pillow."

Holly stayed overnight on Jeanette's sofa, though it was impossible for her to sleep. She jumped at every tiny noise and figured Jeanette was having the same issue. How could she sleep when her world was spinning out of control? She couldn't stop wondering if the men had gotten Jeanette's license number and if they had the capability of gaining access to her address?

When they awoke, she and Jeanette discussed what their next move would be. Jeanette had secured a flight to her aunt's house in San Diego where they both agreed she'd be safe. She'd leave the following morning. It wasn't Jeanette they wanted after all; it was Holly.

Thankfully, the two women were close to the same build, and Jeanette found some clothing for Holly to wear, as everything she owned was back at her house, and there was no way she would risk going back there. Presently, Holly had nowhere to go. Her only hope would be if Decker and Callie agreed to help her and find her a safe place to hide until she could figure out what she was facing.

A crack in the curtains allowed a spear of sunlight to filter through. Holly pushed herself into a sitting position and brushed her dark hair back from her olive-colored face. Every muscle in her body rebelled. At least they had made it through the night without further incident. She had also managed to get an hour's sleep, but her eyes were swollen, and her head was pounding.

She shuffled off to the bathroom to brush her hair and teeth. The shadows circling her dark brown eyes exposed the grief she had suffered over the past two weeks and there didn't appear to be an end. She scarcely had time to mourn Leonard's death. She splashed cold water on her face. It helped to refresh her somewhat.

"Holly?"

As Holly stepped out from the bathroom, Jeanette's facial features relaxed. "I'm all right. You?"

Jeanette sighed with relief. Anxiety welled up in her when she hadn't seen Holly on the couch. "A bit stiff after our car chase, but I'll survive. I thought you'd slipped out when I didn't see you," she replied feebly, rubbing her neck.

"Nowhere to go."

"Let me cook us up something to eat. I know you probably aren't thinking about food, but it'll help get you through the rest of the day. I have some eggs and toast if you like."

Holly nodded. Jeanette was right, the last thing on her mind was food, but she hadn't eaten since the day before, and she wasn't sure where she'd find herself for the next few days. Eating breakfast and getting a cup of coffee down made Holly feel a little better and she appreciated that Jeanette was so kind to her after she'd drawn her into her mess of a life.

"What time is your flight?"

"Not until tomorrow morning," Jeanette informed her. The look of disappointment was etched on her face. Understandably,

18

Jeanette wanted to fly out much earlier than that. "I'm worried about you, Holly," she added.

"I'll be all right. Really," she declared. "Again, if there's anything I can do financially or otherwise, please let me know. You literally saved my life last night, Jeanette."

Jeanette answered with a smile. "Stay safe. That's payment enough."

Holly drew her into a warm hug. "Thank you so much. You've been an amazing friend."

"Now, go call your archaeologist friends!"

Chapter 2

Callie Hayden walked across the wooden deck, set her glass of ice water on the end table, and shrugged off her royal-blue swimsuit cover. She stretched out over the chase lounge, a bottle of suntan lotion in her hand and liberally rubbed it over her arms and legs. A slight breeze ruffled the strands of golden hair that had fallen loose from the confines of her one of a kind, emerald-studded barrette. The decorative comb was an early birthday gift from her husband, Decker, who had purchased it for her a few weeks prior to their return home from France.

The gentle lapping waves kissed the hull of the *Jade,* their 70-foot Hatteras yacht which Decker had named after the color of Callie's eyes. For the first time in several weeks, she could feel her muscles relaxing.

She rubbed a spot of lotion on her face, feeling the sun's rays beginning to burn her cheeks, then slid on her gold colored sunglasses. Once more, she settled back on the lounge, taking a sip of ice water with a slice of lemon to cool her parched throat. The edges of her lips turned up as she soaked in the warm, intoxicating sea breeze. *This is exactly what I needed*, she sighed aloud, her eyes slowly closing.

The rustle of clothes made her eyes flutter open. She pushed herself onto her elbow, slid her glasses to the tip of her nose and peered over the rim. It was Jeoffrey Stainton, their butler, a tray balanced on the palm of his hand.

"More ice water, Mrs. Hayden?" he asked, with his usual stiff, British accent.

"I'm fine, thank you, Mr. Stainton," Callie said.

"Very well," he replied. "Mr. Hayden called a moment ago. He'll be returning to the yacht shortly."

"Not soon enough," she answered. She and Decker had spent little time together without the distraction of work getting in the way. They had returned from an exhausting trip which had been a whirlwind of activity, consisting of lectures, tours, appointments, and briefings.

Callie flipped through a barrage of memories from when they'd gone to France two years earlier. They'd been invited to tour the Lascaux cave, discovered by four teenagers in 1979. The cave was located in the Vézère Valley, an incredibly beautiful vale surrounded by mountains and the Vézère River snaking through it. The landscape was an artist's canvas with its lush carpets of green grass and brilliant colored flowers that lined the embankments.

The cave was one of a chain of caves found in the Dordogne region of southwestern France. The complex of caves was placed on the World Heritage site by NESCE (National Educational Scientific and Cultural Establishment), in order to preserve the vulnerable sites by securing them from looters and treasure seekers.

The limestone-walled cave revealed a wonderful story to archaeologists and scientists, with its polychrome art paintings of various animals, along with geometric patterns throughout its interior. It also offered a wide reserve of impressive artifacts.

While there, Decker and Callie determined to take advantage of the outdoor playground. To whet their sense of adventure they rented two kayaks to paddle the pristine river. As they scudded along the lazy watercourse for more than an hour, Decker caught a glimpse of what appeared to be a cave, tucked behind thick underbrush, approximately twenty kilometers from Lascaux

Cave. Curiosity drove them to the river bank, and, pulling the kayaks out to explore, they began to scale a rather steep embankment.

Once they had cleared the brush aside, they were ecstatic to discover a large Paleolithic cave similar to that of Lascaux. It was nearly fifty feet in width and had a ceiling height of approximately eighteen-feet. An archaeologist's dream for sure.

Several of the artifacts they uncovered were handed over to the Musée d' Archéologie Nationale, France's National Archaeological Museum, located in Saint-Germain-en-Laye. The museum was a restored medieval castle and displayed Stone Age to eleventh-century artifacts throughout its many rooms.

Thirteen months later, Jason Aldrich, editor of *Archeology Today* Magazine, contracted them to write an article about their discovery and wondered if they would be willing to return to France to attend a worldwide symposium. He asked if they would include photographs of the cave as well as exhibit some of the artifacts. Jason assured them that he'd schedule all the meetings at the Lecture Hall. All they had to do was show up. How could they not?

The various lectures and magazine features brought them financial security, which allowed them the opportunity to pick up and go as they pleased. They had also acquired a small fortune from other archaeological discoveries along the way and had become well known in archaeological circles.

Significantly adding to their wealth was the unfortunate death of Callie's parents. They had died in a car accident soon after Decker and Callie had married. Her parents were independently wealthy from the purchase of several corporations, and high-yield stock investments. Callie, being the only child, had inherited over seventy million dollars. Because her parents had financed a myriad of archaeological institutions, she and Decker felt it would be a tribute to them if they continued to support those investments by continuing their work in the field.

22

Even though their home was in Malibu, California, Miami had become their get-away place—a place to reconnect. The *Jade* stayed docked in Miami most of the year, though sometimes, Decker and Callie would take her out when they went on digs to Central and South America and leave her anchored off shore as a base for supplies and communications.

The sound of a motor drew her back from her thoughts. In the distance, she saw the yacht's dinghy slicing a path through the green water in her direction. Her heart fluttered. Even after their five years of marriage, Decker stirred her.

They had met at Yale University in New Haven, Connecticut. Both had gained their master's degree in archeology. They left that area to go on digs throughout the world. Because they worked so closely together, it eventually brought them into a relationship and then marriage. Their life had been an adventure from the beginning. She could not imagine a day when they would not be actively involved in archeology.

She slipped on her bathing suit cover and strolled across the deck. Her lithe body pressed against the railing and she waved. She was greeted with a wide smile from Decker. His white teeth looked striking, in contrast to his richly tanned face. Like a flag, his Hawaiian shirt popped from the force of the wind. Amusement crossed her face. Decker was known for wearing Hawaiian shirts on most occasions. Today was no different.

Once he'd tied off the dinghy at the stern, he climbed the ladder to greet her topside. "Good morning," he said cheerfully and strode up beside her. His strong arms encircled her slender waist. "You look gorgeous as ever."

"Thank you, Decker."

"I made a reservation for tonight at one of the dinner houses. I thought I might dance your pretty little feet off."

"That sounds like fun."

Taking his hand, she led him across the deck to sit at a small, table portside. The umbrella overhead was welcoming after an hour of intense sun.

Callie's cell phone chimed. There was a fleeting moment when she considered not answering it. All she wanted was to shut the world off for the next week. However, when she realized it was her father-in-law, she reconsidered.

"Good morning, Garrett," she greeted.

"I've tried Decker's phone all morning and was unable to get hold of him. I thought I'd check in with you and make sure you're both all right." His deep voice was infused with both concern and relief that she had answered.

Callie winked at Decker and then put Garrett on speaker phone. She saw the corners of Decker's mouth curl upward, and his indigo colored eyes flash with amusement.

"Hi Dad, we're good. You needn't worry about us."

"Hard not to, Son. Seems like you get yourself into rather…" he grappled for the right words, "life-challenging situations. Actually, I was calling because there's a woman trying to locate you named Holly Romero."

"Um…Holly Romero?" repeated Decker. He flipped through the acquaintance list in his mind. It only took a minute to recall who she was. "Oh yes, her husband Leonard was on a dig with us several years ago in Egypt. I got to know him a little, though I've not seen him for a couple of years, nor have I spoken with him recently."

"According to his wife, Leonard was killed three weeks ago— murdered."

Decker sucked in his breath, taken aback by the news. "Where did this happen?"

"Honduras. He was on an expedition in the jungle," Garrett told him. "Holly was vague about it all and insists she wants to speak directly to you."

"I'll get in touch with her, Dad," he replied. "In the meantime, would you see what you can pull up on Leonard and his activities over the past couple of years?"

"Got it."

"What would we do without you, Dad?"

"The least I can do since you opened up your home to me these past years."

Decker jotted down Holly's phone number and said his goodbyes. Instinctively, he knew their short-lived vacation was over. He rubbed his chin, sighed, and fixed his gaze on Callie.

She reached over and touched his hand as if reading his mind. "It's all right," she reassured him. "Holly would not have called unless she was in dire need of help from someone she can trust."

"Let's not get ahead of ourselves, Callie. It might be she only needs some advice about what to do with some of Leonard's excavating equipment?"

"You're right. I'm jumping the gun," she agreed, intertwining her fingers with his. She laughed softly. "It's predictable. Seems whenever we get some time away, an adventure rears its irresistible head, and we can't seem to turn it down."

"You're an amazing woman, Callie Hayden. "Whatever would I do without you?" He pressed forward and kissed her brow.

Chapter 3

Decker leaned back in his chair, his black, horn-rimmed glasses settled on his nose. He looked deep in thought as he continued to read the *Archeology Today* magazine. There were several digs taking place that caught his interest. One that held his attention was the discovery of what appeared to be Ciudad Blanca in the La Mosquitia area in Honduras by a team of scientists in 2012.

When the phone rang, it broke him away from his reading. It was his father. No doubt he had scraped up some information on Leonard's expedition. Decker was itching to hear the details. Pressing forward, he grabbed his cell phone off the table.

"What did you find out?"

Callie sat across from Decker and extended a cup of steaming coffee to him. "Hi, Dad," she leaned over to speak into the cell phone.

Whenever there were questions to be answered, Decker always used the speaker phone so Callie could hear the details. It was a less painstaking way than to try and repeat everything back verbatim.

"Hey Callie, love," he said cheerfully. "I have a few facts for you two about Leonard's past pursuits. Ready?"

"Shoot!" Decker answered.

Garrett rifled through his research information, then said, "seems Leonard's greatest ambition was to find the City of the Monkey God, the White City or Ciudad Blanca, or

Hueitlapatlán…whatever they have determined to call it down in Honduras." He chuckled. "This last trip was his fifth and final one."

Decker rubbed his chin. "I was reading up on an archaeological team that went into the La Mosquitia area of Honduras. The team found dozens of artifacts dating back to the pre-Columbian era. They're going to go back to excavate. Do you think Leonard was involved with that particular group?"

"Apparently not. On his first expedition in, he took a ragtag group of four men, east of that location. At least that's the information I received."

"Could be Leonard had some doubts concerning their discovery and didn't believe it was the lost City of the Monkey God. Or I suppose it could be he was looking for something else altogether." His reply was more a statement than a question. Like a good game of chess, Decker's mind began to play out all the scenarios.

"I think that's safe to say," Garrett agreed wholeheartedly. "Two of the guides who went along with Leonard have shown up dead in Honduras as well, and another guide from his first expedition hasn't been located. Some of the natives believe that there's a curse on the ruins. They insist that the deaths of Leonard's team are because they had wandered onto ceremonial grounds."

Something to note, Decker thought. "A team of archaeologists brought in a plane to fly over the Mosquitia area using topographical LiDAR (light detecting and ranging) from what I was reading." He paused momentarily to take a drink of his coffee. "The team determined that it would be worthwhile to use infrared lasers in order to map out a small swath of land mass in that specific region from the air. I say small because it's a very costly operation. But by far, the most effective means to locate a site. It's a vast range of dense jungle. A good portion of it hasn't even been mapped out. On foot, it's a grueling endeavor,"

27

Decker informed Garrett, and with a short laugh, he added, "A new job for you, Pop. I'm sure they could put to use a good cartographer."

"That would interfere with my leisure time," Garrett chuckled, though Garrett was anything but idle. He preferred the hectic lifestyle and flying off to exotic places. He doubted he would ever retire, especially having Decker as his son. "Go on; I'm fascinated with this."

Decker continued. "By using LiDAR, they're able to collect data that generates three-dimensional pictures. From my understanding, that's how they discovered the ruins in the jungle."

"Much preferable than going on foot," Garrett remarked.

"They opted for this method because the Mosquitia region would take years to explore. The belt of land they imaged revealed that they were looking at a man-made structure and not a natural rock formation."

"No kidding."

"However, they've yet to determine if what they uncovered is actually Ciudad Blanca." Continuing, Decker added, "It's mere speculation presently, but the team of archaeologists are coming around to the conclusion that Ciudad Blanca is made up of several cities which expand outward over a large region and make up a vast metropolis."

"Interesting," Garrett said. "Now, if their conclusion is valid, and there's a real possibility it is, what does that mean for Holly?"

"I really don't know, but I'll give her a call."

"Holly has called a couple of times already this morning. Whatever the case may be, she made it sound quite urgent."

"Thanks for getting the information back to us so quickly, Garrett," Callie replied. "We'll keep you informed once we've spoken with Holly."

After their goodbyes, Decker punched in the number Garrett had given to him. The phone was picked up almost before it rang. Holly's shrill voice burst through the receiver. It was more than apparent she was frantic.

"Thank God! Thank God!" her voice cracked.

As usual, Decker put her on speaker phone so that Callie was able to listen in, and he settled back in the chair. "What's going on Holly? My dad informed me that Leonard was murdered, and said you've called several times asking for me. We're terribly sorry for your loss."

"Yes," she sputtered, on the verge of breaking into sobs. "I really need help, Decker. I don't mean to impose, but I'm desperate!"

"Okay. Start from the beginning."

Holly began unraveling the tapestry of events over the past two weeks, trying to give Decker as much information as she could, though she was limited in what she knew. "Leonard was going back to Honduras to continue his search for Ciudad Blanca. I'm not sure why, but he seemed obsessed to find it," she explained. "I hadn't heard anything from him after he'd left the last time. After weeks had gone by, I received a call from the authorities telling me that he had been shot, his body dumped in the river. Some of the local natives from villages surrounding the area discovered him and two of his guides."

"Sorry, Holly," Callie chimed in. Holly's grief was raw, and as if a dam burst, she broke down into a flood of tears. There was a span of silence while Holly gathered her emotions so she could continue. "Yesterday I came home from the store to find my house in shambles. There were items strewn everywhere. I realized that there was something going on beyond Leonard's death that apparently now included me." She swallowed the lump in her throat. "I packed a few belongings and prepared to leave and find a safe place to stay when the mailman showed up at my door with a package. It was a box wrapped in brown paper

29

from Leonard. When I opened it, I was shocked to find an artifact inside. I gathered that Leonard had sent it to me for safe keeping."

"What kind of artifact?" Decker inquired, a little puzzled.

"It's a stone statue—looks kind of like a monkey's face," she tried to describe it.

"Then what happened?"

"Like I said, I had my suitcase packed and ready to go and then I heard a car near my house. When I peeked out, I saw two rather gruff looking men coming up my walkway—there appeared to be another man sitting in the car." She paused, took a deep breath then continued her story. "I stuffed the artifact into my purse, thankful that I carry a large one, grabbed my phone, and ran out the back. To my horror, they chased after me. I tried to hide in a small dress shop but they saw me, so I fled from there. There was a small bakery down the street. I knew the waitress—she was a friend I'd worked with several years ago at the bank. I ran fast as I could to lose the men following me. Luck would have it, my friend was working, and when I explained my predicament to her, she hid me until they were gone—or so we thought."

"Can you describe the men?" Callie asked.

"One was a white Caucasian. Tall, very thin—He had a long scar running from his temple to his chin. The other man was much shorter with black hair. I believe he was Spanish—he could have been from Central or South America? He had a limp, but not so bad that he couldn't help chase me down."

"Go on," Decker prodded her.

"My friend, Jeanette, pulled her car to the front of the store. What we didn't know, was that the men were apparently waiting in their car and spotted us. The two men must have called the driver parked at my house to pick them up because they found us so quickly."

She took a moment to calm her nerves. Steadying herself, she continued to explain. "It was like a chase scene out of Miami Vice. They came after us with a vengeance. We tried to outrun them, but they pursued us across the city. They took several shots at us which shattered the rear window of Jeanette's car. It seemed like it was hours before they ended up slamming their car into another vehicle, allowing us time to get away."

"Are you all right?" asked Decker.

"Physically yes, but I'm a wreck. I don't know where to go, or what to do."

"Where are you now?"

"I'm at Jeanette's. She allowed me to stay a couple of nights at her place until I could figure out my next move. She's getting ready to leave and find somewhere safe," she explained. "I can't go back home, though. I was wondering if you and Callie might be able to help me out?"

"Of course we can," he assured her. There was no way they'd even consider leaving Holly alone to figure it out by herself. Obviously, her life was in danger. "Give me your address. We're still in Florida right now, but we'll purchase tickets to fly back to Malibu as soon as I hang up. I'll have my father pick you up and take you to our house. You'll be safe there." He sprawled out her address on a sticky note, and added, "It'll take him an hour from Malibu to get to where you are. Stay put and hold tight!"

He heard her release her breath as if she'd been holding it. "You don't know how much this means to me, Decker and Callie. Thank you!"

No sooner had Decker hung up than he was on the phone with Garrett to give him the details of what had transpired. He realized that they had much to tend to if they were to catch an early flight back to Malibu.

While Callie started packing their clothes, Decker made haste to the pilot house to see Carson Perry. Carson was the captain of the *Jade,* as well as his best friend and was invaluable to Decker.

31

He had been a part of his life for nearly fifteen years. It was Carson who did most of the groundwork, such as contacting different government agencies, making application for permits, getting a team pulled together, and making sure that they had the proper equipment for the terrain they would have to face, as well as stocking the yacht with adequate food and medical supplies. It was no small job, and Carson was the best at what he did. Decker never felt ill-equipped on any of the digs they had gone on thus far.

"Captain Perry," he said teasingly, stepping inside. He made a mock salute with two fingers to his forehead.

"Morning, Decker," Carson replied, his lips parting in a smile. He looked quite dashing with his captain's hat pressed over his brown, short-cropped hair, and dressed in his white starched shirt tucked into khaki shorts, white socks, and deck shoes. His face was richly tanned from long days in the sun. The wrinkles at the corners of his eyes and mouth revealed his forty plus years of age. "What can I do for you?"

"We're heading back to Malibu."

Carson burst out in a hearty laughter. "I could have predicted it!"

"Callie's exact response. You two know me too well. This has to do with Leonard Romero's murder."

"Leonard...murdered?" Surprise cracked in his voice. "When?"

"Couple weeks back. Long story, but to capsulize it, we believe he may have found Ciudad Blanca. His wife Holly, received a package from him which appears to be an artifact, though I need to confirm that. You know there are many man-made replicas. Hard to imagine Leonard being duped by a counterfeit, though. He must have believed it was the real deal, or else he'd not have sent it to Holly for safe-keeping."

"Unbelievable," Carson clipped, shaking his head in disbelief. "Did they catch whoever murdered him?"

"No. And worse, two men went after Holly, which is why she called Callie and me for help. Apparently, two of the guides on Leonard's trip were also found murdered and one is still missing."

"Hmm…Someone obviously believes that whatever Leonard found was valuable enough to warrant murder."

"Our main concern right now is Holly, and keeping her safe," Decker told him. "We may be calling on you in the next couple of days to prepare for a Honduran jungle expedition to get to the bottom of this."

"You know me. I'm happiest on water—always ready to go."

Decker slapped his arm. "Good for me that you feel that way. If you'd like to see if our usual team is available, it would take weight off my shoulders, and I'd be forever grateful."

"Done."

Chapter 4

The cords in Bruno Castillo's neck swelled with anger. His teeth grit with tension. "What! You let a woman dupe both of you?"

Bruno was beside himself. He thought this would be a simple matter. Now he was back at square one. Bruno was incensed and battled for composure. He couldn't understand how two of his men, Adrián Petit, a Caucasian from Los Angeles, and Honduran born Javier Almanzar, could not have apprehended Holly Romero. In his mind, it was a simple task. Find her and obtain the information they needed to location the artifact. He was sure Leonard must have told her or sent it since it was nowhere to be found.

He was puzzled as to how a five-foot, four-inch woman could best his men? "I should kill you blundering idiots for your incompetence," he growled menacingly.

The scar on Adrián's cheek looked more pronounced as his face reddened with embarrassment.

"Sorry, Bruno. How could we possibly know she'd find help?" he sputtered. He waited on bated breath to see if he would survive this ordeal. He was all too aware of Bruno's reputation. He had no qualms about putting a bullet through a person's head if it so pleased him.

"Imbeciles! Lamebrains, good-for-nothings!" Bruno bellowed. Disgust registered in his stone-cold eyes as he resolved what measures to take. Abruptly, he withdrew his Ruger LCP II revolver and aimed it squarely at Adrián's head, watching as beads of sweat gathered on his brow.

"Sorry? Sorry is for losers, you brainless, pile of dung. I don't know why I keep you around."

Adrián was riveted to the spot. His eyes bulged with fear. "Please, Bruno. I swear we will find her and get the information you need," he pleaded. "We'll do whatever it takes. Promise."

"Your promises are like dog vomit...they are smelly, and someone has to clean it up." He spat a wad of tobacco on the tip of Adrián's boot. Thinking he hadn't made them squirm enough, he slowly turned his gun to Javier and began laughing. A deep guttural laugh that had a demonic twist to it. Javier fell to his knees.

Bruno was accustomed to men fearing him. It was how he got what he wanted when he wanted, and how he wanted. It infuriated him when the men who worked for him did not fulfill their obligation. From past dealings with his hired hands, he knew it was not in his best interest to be understanding or kind. Those were the traits of a weak man. Weak he was not.

Bruno also had several high-ranking police commanders in his pocket. He'd paid a substantial amount of money for their silence over the past years. He even had one of the Chief of Police in Trujillo in his back pocket for a time, though now he was having to contend with his replacement. One who wasn't so willing to turn a blind eye to his dealings and who'd not been receptive to bribes. Down the road, Bruno would make sure the man saw things his way, or he'd find himself wearing cement shoes.

"Get up, you cowering fool," Bruno bellowed.

Slowly, Javier pushed himself to his feet, his throat constricting. What could he say that his partner had not already said? He tried to prepare himself for the bullet he was sure would slice through his brain—but how was one able to prepare for that? He stood breathless. Waiting. Nausea settled in his stomach like a rock.

Sick pleasure welled up in Bruno as he watched Javier shake with fear. A malicious smile twisted Bruno's thin lips. He was enjoying every moment of their squirming.

When he lowered his gun, Bruno saw both men slump with relief. Fortunately for them, this would not be their last day. Bruno needed them. At least for now.

"I pay you good money to get jobs done, don't I? Well, don't I?" Both men nodded. "You have one more chance. If you fail, you'd better pray I don't find you." His voice was cold as arctic ice as he spat out the warning.

"You won't regret it, Bruno," Javier said. His heart felt as though it would explode in his chest.

"We got the other lady's license number, so it wasn't all loss. I'm sure you can get some of your police contacts to locate a name and address. We can go to the woman's house who helped Holly get away. I'm sure she'll have information about where she's hiding." Javier saw a glint in Bruno's eyes that revealed he was pleased by the piece of knowledge.

Everything was falling into place, Bruno thought. Of course, the other woman would have useful tidbits to share with them. If Holly Romero was in possession of the stone relic, it made sense she'd hand it off to someone in the archeological field whom she could trust. Whoever that was, Bruno would find out and, unbeknownst to them, they'd lead Bruno to a storehouse of wealth.

"I'll call when I find out where the woman lives, and you'd better not let me down again!"

Bruno's eyes were venomous slits, threatening them even without words. He was not a man who made veiled threats. If he said it, he would do it. This was their last chance. If they didn't deliver, they would end up at the bottom of a river somewhere in the Honduran jungle like he'd done to Leonard Romero and his guides.

"Now, get your ugly faces out of here before I change my mind!"

Javier limped toward the door. It was lurking in his mind as he grabbed the door knob that a bullet could still have his name written on it. But, as he stepped out into the oppressive Los Angeles heat, he released his breath, knowing he'd live to see another day.

***

It didn't take long before Bruno found out whom the vehicle belonged to and where Jeanette lived. After contacting Javier and Adrián, he sputtered out the address to them and expected them to finish what they'd started. If nothing else, the woman Jeanette Adams would not be left to identify his men to the police. She knew too much. He hoped they weren't too late and that she hadn't already gone to the authorities.

Within an hour, Adrián and Javier had rounded the corner in a black, four-door sedan, one of Bruno's spares, since they had totaled his other vehicle. They spotted Jeanette's small, one-story, brick home and drove by slowly. To not draw attention to themselves, they parked a short distance away. They hurried back down the street and knocked a couple of times before they heard footsteps inside heading to the door. It cracked slightly. As it did, they blasted through the door, knocking Jeanette down onto the carpeted floor. The abrupt intrusion made her scream, and she tried desperately to get to her feet. A burning sensation traveled up her arm as the scarred man's fingers bit into her flesh and with a hard yank, he pulled her upright. His other hand clamped over her mouth to stop her screaming, then he dragged her into the living room. He forcefully flung her onto an overstuffed chair and pressed his face within an inch of her own, his eyes slit maliciously.

"You need to shut up!" When Jeanette stopped, his hand cupped her chin tightly.

"Where's Holly Romero?"

"She...she left," Jeanette managed to speak, her heart thundering in her chest.

"Where?"

"I d-don't...don't know," she stammered, feeling the pressure of his fingers dig deeper into her flesh.

Adrián lost his patience. He withdrew his hand and slapped her soundly across the face. "I said, where is she?" His voice pitched with excitement as he screamed in her face.

"I told you, I don't know!"

Jeanette struggled frantically trying to free herself from his grip. Her foot lashed out catching him in the groin, and she heard him yelp from pain. Briefly, he lost his hold. She pushed with both her hands on his chest and thrust him aside. Leaping to her feet, she darted toward the back door but was stopped by Javier whose fist caught the side of her head. She swayed dizzily.

Jeanette reached out to the wall to steady herself. Once more she made a run for the door, but Javier leapt forward and grabbed her waist with both arms. With intensified resistance, Jeanette managed to free herself. As she broke into a run, her feet tangled on the braided doormat, and she crashed to the tile floor. Pain shot through her in waves.

"Last time," Javier yelled. "Where did she go?"

"I don't know," her shrill cry pierced the air. "She said she was calling some archaeologist friend of Leonard's, that's all I know!"

He dragged her to her feet and pushed her toward the living room where Adrián had regained his composure.

"Did she call the police?"

"No," sobbed Jeanette.

Adrián hauled her back into the living room, hurled her into the chair, then walked over to pull the blinds closed. The room went dark except for a few threads of light streaming through the cracks forming eerie shadows on the walls. Adrián turned around, a sinister smile distorting his face and walked slowly toward her.

Chapter 5

Stepping out of the airplane from their morning flight from Miami, the drab weather was an unwelcome sight. Rain spattered on the cab's front window, the wipers slapping noisily as they swept aside the heavy spray flung onto the windshield from passing vehicles.

The cab pulled into the cobbled driveway and on through the eight-foot gates which led to Decker and Callie's home. The four-story, Spanish-style villa was lined with arched windows across the facade. The upper windows were decorated with wrought-iron balconies. Ivy twisted up the west side of the stucco villa, all the way to red-tiled roof. The villa would be a welcome change from the weeks of travel.

Even though they had gotten to indulge in a short stay on the yacht, Callie was already looking forward to sliding between the cool satin sheets on their king-sized bed. She was not fond of living out of suitcases, though she was always willing to do so for the sake of travel. All things considered, she was looking forward to a couple of days at their home in Malibu. Besides, she missed seeing Garrett and Riley.

Decker stepped out to grab their luggage, shielding his head with his lightweight briefcase. They both made a mad dash for the front door to escape the deluge. As Decker's hand reached out for the knob, the door flung wide open, and Garrett ushered them inside to the warmth of the great hall. Droplets of water rolled off their raincoats and onto the tiled floor as they shrugged them off and hung them on the rack to the right entry.

"Garrett," Callie smiled, raising on tiptoes to kiss his cheek. Standing next to his six-foot-five frame, Garrett made Callie feel tiny, being a measly five-foot-four inches tall. "It's a torrential downpour out there."

"It's been raining all week. El Niño," Garrett chuckled. "A bit of a letdown after all that Miami sun I'd reckon?"

"Good to be home," Decker said. His eyes swept the room then asked, "Where's Holly?"

Garrett motioned his head toward the spiral staircase. "Upstairs. Told her you were on your way, so she'll be down shortly. "I've been gathering information. When she gets here, we'll go to my study for a briefing."

Right then their golden retriever darted around the corner, his tail wagging happily when he saw his masters had returned home. He barked a couple of times to welcome them and spun in circles waiting for the warm hugs he knew would follow.

"Riley!" Callie said and stooped to take him in her arms. "Missed you, buddy." She reached into her pocket and produced a couple of dog treats she'd purchased before boarding the plane and handed them to him. Without hesitation, Riley devoured the biscuits.

Her eyes raked over the expansive living room. She'd forgotten how opulent it was with its fifteen foot, wooden-beamed ceilings. The white, adobe plastered walls and arched windows across the front made the room appear even larger than it was. It was comfortably laid out with two light gray-sofas, tossed with decorative gray and white pillows and two matching recliners. On the far wall was a limestone mantel. Two earthen colored vases were situated at each end, and at the center was a large white vase measuring three feet in height and was filled with dried lavender—Callie's favorite flowers. To the left was their wedding picture.

41

The floors were gray slate with a pearl tone woven into the stone. A white, plush throw rug was centered under the sofas— one of the few places Riley was not allowed to tread. Callie loved to curl up on the sofa before the fire and read on blustery days. Much as she loved the adventure and excitement in her life, there was a part of her that desired to camp out a few days at home.

"I'm going to go freshen up a bit and change my clothes," Callie said. "I'd also like to get my suitcase unpacked. I don't suppose there's some coffee brewing?" Her eyes widened, hinting that she'd love to have a cup.

"It's on," Garrett he replied. "I'll take a carafe to the study on my way."

"You're on top of the game, as usual Garrett. Thanks," she said. "Come on Riley." She patted her leg, inviting Riley to join them upstairs.

Callie and Decker plodded up the stairs, feeling tired from their flight. Opening the door to their spacious bedroom, Callie loosened her grip on her suitcase, sprang forward and dove onto their bed. Decker laughed and shook his blondish-brown mop of hair. He delighted in her childish exuberance. It made life full.

Even with the hammering rain, the hot temperature held. Decker strode over to the French doors and cracked them open. The spattering of raindrops was soothing, same as the fragrant scent of honeysuckle planted below their balcony. A welcome breeze swept through the stuffy room, lifting the edges of their gold, chiffon curtains.

Decker sucked in the refreshing air and sighed. He scanned the horizon and for a brief time simply watched the waves roll in. One could not help but drink in the beauty of it all. He thought of the cliché from the Wizard of Oz, "*There's no place like home*" and smiled.

"I'm going to jump into the shower and get changed," Callie told Decker, springing to her feet.

"A bit early."

She thumbed through the closet to grab a clean blouse and her capris. "It's the plane ride. I always feel like showering when I get off."

"I'll catch one later."

He dropped a kiss on top of her head. While she headed for the shower, he unpacked his suitcase and put his clothing back into the dresser drawers, then went downstairs.

When Garrett called his room a study, it was an understatement. He was a cartographer and topographer. His room took up the entire lower level of the home. Every wall was a bookshelf jammed full of maps, documents, and rare books. In one corner of the room was a massive dark wood table, strewn with navigational tools such as a Base Rover GPS survey system, handheld computer GPS, topographic levels, compasses, marking pens and computer graphics. Maps were spread out over the face of the desk, and strewn on the tapestried floor, along with stacks of books waiting to be re-shelved.

Without asking, Decker knew Garrett had already been researching the terrain in Honduras and had made calculations as to where Leonard might have skirted around the other excavation site.

The aroma of coffee filled Callie's nostrils as she made her way to the study. Because they had flown out extra early, she had not gotten her morning's cup. As promised, Garrett had a black carafe set out on the end table. It was like a magnet to her. She poured a cup for herself and Decker then walked over to the red leather sofa to seat herself across from Garrett, who settled down in a large matching recliner. Decker, not being able to resist, sauntered over to the table and began scanning some of the maps that were laid out, thinking to get the lay of the land in advance.

When Holly entered the room, Garrett was prompted to his feet. He pulled up a dark brown, tufted leather club chair to the side of the sofa and motioned for her to sit, but before she could,

Callie rose to her feet and stepped over to give her a hug. "I'm so sorry to hear about Leonard," she said. "It came as a total shock to Decker and me."

"Thank you," Holly replied. "I'm getting through it—taking it day by day. I can't tell you how much I appreciate the fact that you and Decker have extended such hospitality to me, and Garrett has been so kind."

Garrett moved to her side. "It's been my absolute honor, Holly. I can't even imagine what it must have been like out there alone with those evil men pursuing you. You must have been frightened beyond measure."

"Yes. It has been a terrifying experience."

Decker also moved from the table of maps and gave her shoulder a gentle squeeze. "Please, sit down and let's go over what you have and what we might be able to do to help you." They seated themselves. "Please, I know this is redundant, but we need all of the details."

Inhaling deeply, and with some reluctance to relive the past few days, Holly began to divulge what little she did know. Several times she had to stop to collect herself before moving on. Her hands twisted nervously in her lap, and there were moments when tears sprang to her eyes as she spoke about Leonard and his murder. Garrett got to his feet to retrieve a box of tissues for Holly to dry her eyes.

"Have you ever seen those men before?" asked Decker, after she had given them the details.

Holly shook her dark head of curls and shrugged her shoulders. "No. I know I was never introduced to them, nor did I ever see them when I went on digs with Leonard."

"You're sure?" Decker asked, knowing that heightened tensions often diminished a person's recall. He wanted to be sure she wasn't overlooking any important facts that might be useful down the road.

She took a moment to recollect the horrifying incidents in her mind. "I'm sure, Decker," she reiterated. "I realize everything happened fast. Much of it seems like a dream, but I'll never forget those faces. They were wicked and hateful. Leonard would never be found hanging out with that kind of trash. Even if he'd been desperate for someone to guide him through the jungle, I can assure you he'd never have hired them."

Holly opened up a large tote and pulled out a box that still had paper encasing it. She worked the lid off the box and pulled out the statue. She stretched it out to Decker who gazed at it for a long while, quite speechless. The limestone statue resembled a monkey. The question remained, was it a genuine artifact, or had someone carved it out much later than the pre-Columbian timeline, making it worthless? He wouldn't know until he had it examined.

"What do you think it means?" she asked.

"Since we're not sure where he discovered the artifact it's impossible for me to say right now," Decker said, pressing forward in his chair.

She sighed, her dark eyes swimming with both pain and confusion. "All I know is that he wanted to find some lost city in Honduras. He'd gone on several expeditions but always returned empty-handed. It didn't seem to discourage him. It only seemed to make him all the more determined to find it. It became an addiction to him. A cancer that was eating him alive, but he refused to give up." She took a deep breath, her fingers digging into the soft leather arms of the chair. "He did mention limestone mountains if that helps any."

"The limestone mountain does lend some credence to the story. Charles Lindburg flew over Honduras in 1927. He claimed to have seen what appeared to be a sprawling, white city from the air, and there was also an ethnographer from Luxemburg who claimed Ciudad Blanca had been found some twenty-five years earlier than Lindburg's account. He said it was situated between the Paulaya River and Plantain River." Decker indulged in another sip of his coffee before continuing. "He alleged there was a native in Honduras who had been out searching for rubber when he stumbled across the ruins. He purported that it was an expansive community, surrounded by walls built with white stones."

"Do you think it's still reasonable to believe there's a lost city called Ciudad Blanca?" inquired Holly curiosity flanking her words.

Decker shrugged. "There are many adventurers out there who still cling to that view. And, I can't fully reject Theodore Morde's version. He went on three expeditions through the jungles of Honduras to study the indigenous people who lived there. At the same time, he searched for archaeological sites and claimed he found an agricultural civilization behind a walled city, which he named the "City of the Monkey God.""

Holly looked at the statue still in Decker's hand, and her eyes widened. "Do you think Leonard may have stumbled onto it?' she replied.

Decker smiled. "Again, I can't say for sure. We've not dated the statue yet. But that's our next step. Obviously, Leonard discovered something, and he thought there was a need to protect it. Why else would he have sent it to you?"

"I'm curious, why did Morde call it the City of the Monkey God?" she quizzed, anxious to hear more.

"There was an article printed several years ago that claimed Morde had been told by his Paya guides, there were impressive ruins tucked back in the Honduran jungle. The published account said the city had been inhabited by the Chorotegas; they were a tribe associated with the Maya peoples who existed during the time of the Spanish conquest led by Cortéz. Seems their culture and language were lost during the colonial period. That's why archaeologists get pretty revved-up when they discover pre-Columbian artifacts and why there's a black market that deals in

46

artifacts from that era. The relics have substantial cash pay-offs if you have the right connections."

"Are they valuable enough that someone would kill in order to get his or her hands on them?" Holly asked.

"Enough that someone would kill for it," confirmed Decker. "What makes this situation with Leonard all the more believable is the Chorotegas worshiped a pantheon of gods. They built temples designed specifically to carry out sacrifices in order to appease their gods.

In the article, Morde described a long staircase that led up to an expansive temple where there was a sizable statue of a monkey god, and on either side of the stairs, were representations of monkey idols. At the entrance of the stairs were also rock-hewn representations of a variety of animals that lived in the jungle. Crocodiles, jaguars, etcetera."

Decker paused briefly to make sure he still had a captive audience. He did. "Morde regrettably committed suicide before going back on a scheduled expedition, and strangely enough, never revealed the location of this temple. Stands to reason, that if he let on to the whereabouts of the ruins, it would arouse every treasure hunter within miles to go searching for it and loot the place.

My understanding is that he did return home with several impressive artifacts that gave credibility to his story. Time will tell, I guess."

Garrett offered some more coffee to them and signaled for them to follow him over to the mammoth table. "I've detailed where a number of artifacts and ruins have been discovered over the past several years. See right here," he pointed, "these little red flags I've inserted identifies how many ruins have been found to date. Pretty impressive. I've also marked out the area between the Plátano River and the Paulaya River in the Mosquitia area to give us an idea of the how large of an area it is.

And over here, I placed a yellow flag, to indicate where there is a team of archaeologists excavating right now."

"Good work, Garrett," Callie said.

"That's a vast area to explore. If we go, we'll have to narrow this down," Decker replied.

Holly looked expectantly at him. "Does that mean you're considering going to investigate?"

"Once we determine the age of this statue, we'll make our minds up." He left the door open but made no promises.

Garrett placed his hand on Holly's shoulder. "We'll get to the bottom of this," he assured her. "We won't send you back out to face those men alone. Why don't you go upstairs and freshen up while we talk business? Meet us down here in, let's say, an hour for dinner."

Thankful for their hospitality, she nodded and turned to leave when the package in her hand slipped free from her fingers and fell onto to the wooden floor. The paper on the outside of the box tore several inches and curled back away from the box. She stooped to retrieve the package, startled when she noticed there was writing on the underside of the paper. Some of the ink was smeared, but with close inspection, it was obviously a map.

All eyes were on her hands as she carefully removed the outer paper. She turned it over, and her mouth dropped with surprise. It was a detailed map of the eastern area of Honduras in the La Mosquitia area. There was a deep red line that clearly revealed the route Leonard had taken along with the coordinates which he had scrawled out along the outside of the area.

Decker came alongside of her and took the paper from her trembling fingers. "Leonard, you were an amazing man," he said, "Seems he marked out the route he took. Dad, take a look at this map." Decker handed it over to Garrett. "Leonard had more than an artifact he wanted to protect. If anyone found out, he'd made this map of the area, and where he'd located the artifact, it would

48

be reasonable to assume someone might kill to get their hands on it."

Garrett bent his slender frame over the crude details, his mouth agape. "Good for him. Leonard knew how important it was to document every foot fall. He knew if something happened to him, the city would be lost again. This is outstanding. Outstanding!" he reiterated, with a short whoop exposing his delight.

"Looks like we're going to Honduras." Decker grinned.

With map in hand and coordinates, they'd be able to retrace Leonard's steps. How could they not go when he had placed the city right into their hands?

Chapter 6

Callie was stretched out on the bed, a book in hand when Riley cuddled up beside her. Her black-rimmed glasses were pulled down slightly on her nose so she could peer over the top, her golden hair stacked up on top of her head and secured with a wide clip. Her jade colored eyes were filled with mischief as she gazed at her husband.

Decker was relaxing on their chase lounge near the French doors in their bedroom trying to let down a bit after their flight home. There was a serious expression carved into his face as he read up on the excavations happening in Honduras, and he appeared oblivious to the fact his wife was studying him.

"Your father is interested in Holly," she remarked simply.

There was a moment of silence as if Decker had not heard her. When he looked up, surprise was written over his face, and he burst into laughter. "What?"

Callie grinned. "Yes. I was watching him. He definitely likes her."

He shook his head and set the book aside on the wooden end table. "Are you playing matchmaker, Callie? Her husband just died."

"I know," she agreed, "But that doesn't mean your father doesn't find her attractive. She is, you know."

"Callie, life would be dull and uneventful without you in it!"

"Have you called Carson yet? There's a lot to do," she said, changing the subject. "He needs to get permits, equipment, and our team together." Her organizational mind was already putting together the details of the trip. "I'll secure our tickets, but first I need to know what city we'll fly in to? Probably Trujillo? We can hire a couple of guides to take us up the river."

"Hold up. My head is spinning."

She grinned. "So, what are your thoughts?"

Decker chuckled at her exuberance. "You've been doing some research yourself, haven't you?"

She looked rather pleased with herself. "I don't lay around stuffing my face with dark chocolate truffles."

"No. I don't believe you do." Amusement was written across his face. And you were reading my mind. Trujillo was my first inclination."

The following morning, Decker was up early and put in a call to Carson who was already prepared for the trip.

"I've contacted the team. They're in. I'm stocking the yacht and speaking to authorities about packing into the interior. It's going a bit slow, but that's nothing unusual. Especially when you're dealing with government officials in other countries," Carson chuckled.

"Would you hire us some guides in Trujillo to take us through the jungle? We're going to need at least two. Three would be better. I'll leave that up to you since you can better judge how many guides we need by how much gear we have."

"Will Garrett be going?' Carson asked.

Decker gave an amused snort. "Garrett would disown me if I left him behind. And I'm sure we'll need Garrett's expertise."

Chapter 7

Soon as Carson hung up the phone, he saw Shane Pierce and Pete Polly come on board. They were the first two of a six-man team that would put out to sea and meet up with Decker and Callie in Trujillo. When available, they were always willing to join up with the team. Each of them possessed skills that worked like a marriage on board. They trusted one another implicitly, and all of them had become lifelong friends.

"Hey! Look what just crawled in," laughed Carson, who already had equipment strewn across the deck and was beginning to take stock of what they would need.

"How's it going, Captain?" asked Pete, better known as Polly to the crew.

"Going good, now that I have some of the team showing up," Carson said, his hazel eyes snapping with excitement. "I'm ready to head out. How about you?"

"Ready as ever."

Pete Polly was a jovial, well-rounded man in his thirties. Since youth, he had gone by the name of Polly. His hair was dark copper, a bit straggly, and raked the tip of his broad shoulders. He sported a bushy, wiry beard that matched his hair, and wore his usual trademark, a small braid running down the center. With his boisterous laugh and bulky frame, all the team concurred, Polly looked like a Viking.

Polly had been a part of the team for nearly five years and had shown himself to be invaluable to the rest of the crew. He was no stranger to the sea—a fisherman's son. Working alongside his father since he was a young man, he knew pretty much all there was to know in regards to repairing and navigating boats. No question, he had saved their hides on more than one occasion.

Shane was an oceanographer. He had worked several years in Baja aboard an ocean research vessel collecting data on declining fisheries, as well as doing research on coastal regions where erosion was occurring at rapid rates and was endangering some of the marine life in those areas. He'd since signed on with the *Jade,* whenever the Haydens opted to go on a dig, as their first mate.

Carson had already seen to filling the four-hundred-gallon water tank and the two-thousand-gallon diesel fuel tanks, which would see them to Trujillo staying steady at ten knots.

"It's going to take most of the next few days to pull this together," said Polly, picking up the list of items.

"If not more," said Shane, "But it beats sitting home doing nothing but watching reruns on television."

"Yup. I'm with you, buddy."

The list had most everything one could possibly need, such as mosquito repellent, hand-crank lights, buckets of sealed meals, backup batteries for the sat phones, water purification tablets, tarps, waterproof tents, sleeping bags, anti-snake venom, not to mention, handguns, bullets, and holsters. Those were only a few of the necessities they would need on the trip; the list went on and on.

They packed many of the items in waterproof bags. Taking very expensive equipment near water sources without proper protection could be a disastrous endeavor. Ziploc bags came in quite handy for some of the smaller items, and even for clothing. It wasn't long before the remaining crew began to meander on board.

Phil Simms was their chef. His arms were loaded down with foods for the pantry. "'Mornin', y'all," he sang out cordially.

53

"Ho!" Carson welcomed. "You made it in time to cook our breakfast?" he teased. Phil grinned.

"You need more hands to bring up the boxes?" offered Polly.

Phil motioned his head in the direction of the stairs where Sam Carter and Ted Bingham were close on his heels. Their arms loaded down as well. "Think we have it covered, guys, but thanks for the offer."

Sam was their electrical engineer. He worked on wireless telecommunications, radar system integration, the GNSS (Global Navigation Satellite System), and tracked their location and weather conditions via GPS. He was irreplaceable. Sam was the more reserved one on board, but he loved strapping on his guitar to serenade the men in the evenings.

Lastly, there was fun-loving Ted. He was their deckhand and maintenance man. There wasn't anything he couldn't tackle given time.

Chapter 8

The dinner table was spread with roast beef, boiled baby reds, steamed carrots, and salad. Decker and Callie would not be afforded such scrumptious meals in the days to come. However, over the years they had become used to packaged foods and not so good tasting water. It all came with the job.

"I'm going with you," Holly informed them quite forcibly as if perceiving she'd be met with resistance.

"You most certainly won't!" came Garrett's immediate response, and all heads turned to stare at him. "Sorry, I have overstepped my boundary. It's up to you, of course, Decker."

Decker pressed forward, the concern on his face was like a well-read map. His eyes looked at Holly with an emotional intensity that made her shrink back. "Why would you even consider going?" he asked, fighting to keep the harshness out of his voice. "This is going to be a dangerous venture, and you are ill prepared to tackle it."

"Leonard felt that what he'd discovered was worth his life," she insisted. "And I want to see the men responsible pay for what they did. I didn't ask to be drawn into this mess, but I intend seeing it to the end," she said, thrusting her chin out in defiance.

"It's not a place for an inexperienced person," he said.

Callie reached over to squeeze Decker's arm gently. "What if she were to come with us, but stay on the *Jade*?" She interceded for Holly. "Garrett and a couple of the guys will be manning the boat while we're in the jungle. At least she'd be relatively safe.

And with our communication system, she'd be informed about what we're doing out in the field."

Decker shrugged. He didn't like the idea, but it appeared Holly was not going to settle for staying put in LA. Adamant as she was, if he refused to give in, there was a possibility she might jump on a plane and follow them to Honduras anyhow.

"All right," he conceded, although it was clear he wasn't happy about the final resolution. "However, you'll need to remain on the yacht."

Nodding her head, Holly agreed to the terms. "Thank you," she said, relief taking the place of anger. Holly felt a bit ashamed of her willful behavior. "Believe me. I understand your concerns, and I'll stay out of the way. Promise."

"Trust you will," he said. "I'll secure a ticket for you. We leave here in three days."

Moments later Garrett entered the living room, his face crumpled with sorrow. Difficult as it was, he informed them that he'd been watching the news and saw that Jeanette Adams had been murdered.

Holly's face went white. She grabbed the back of the sofa to steady her trembling limbs. Unable to refrain, she broke down into sobs.

"It's not your fault, Holly." Callie tried her best to comfort her. "There's no way you could have known this would happen."

"She didn't do anything! She didn't know anything," stammered Holly, her shoulders shaking with emotion.

"I know," agreed Callie. "She's a hero. She gave her life helping you. Honor her by letting us find these men and put them behind bars where they belong."

"And what if you die trying to help me as well?" Her voice quivered. She didn't want to be the reason for their deaths too.

"We're offering," replied Callie. "I know how difficult this is for you. But you're not alone. We'll find these men." Callie gave her a hug. "Tell you what, go on upstairs, and I'll bring you some hot tea, okay?"

Holly nodded, turned, and plodded upstairs, her shoulders slumped with the weight of loss.

Callie stared after her and bit into her lip. Her whole body shook with anger. "We have to bring them down, Decker, no matter what it takes, or how long it takes."

Decker draped his arms around Callie. "I agree. Whoever they are, they're appalling and have to be stopped," he replied with narrowed, glacier-blue eyes.

The following morning around nine, Callie and Decker snapped Riley onto a leash, put on their running shoes and took to the beach. It had been too long since they had taken the opportunity to run. The day was already warm. Rods of light sparkled like glittering jewels over the waves, and a light breeze kissed their faces as they stretched out their muscles to ensure a safe run.

"I'm going to take Holly out to shop tomorrow," Callie told him, her leg propped on a bench off the jogging trail. "My clothes aren't fitting her quite the way they should. She has to roll up the pant legs, and my tops are too tight for her."

"Nice of you to do that for her," Decker said, appreciating Callie's sensitivity to others.

"I tried to put myself in her shoes—I can't imagine."

"She's had a difficult time, for sure," he concurred.

"It's possible that going to Honduras with us might actually be healing for her."

Decker was beginning to see Callie's logic, whereas he'd been adamantly opposed to the idea of Holly going at first. He was grateful Callie was his counterbalance. She was deeply compassionate and had the ability to observe situations from every angle to arrive at a fair verdict. Decker, on the other hand, was black and white. Sometimes that was a good trait. Other times it was a hindrance.

They jogged for nearly an hour, both glistening with sweat, as they dropped onto the sandy shore to catch their breath.

"I know this sort of erases our morning workout, but would you like a gelato?" Decker winked and smiled. Ice cream was Decker's one indulgence. He'd never been able to pass up a parlor. However, Decker was very self-controlled and took good care of his body.

"Sure." She leapt to her feet, stretching out her hand to him, "A perfect day for ice cream."

"Hey, you two," came the cheerful voice of the store owner when they entered. He had come to know them well over the past few years. "Strawberry and vanilla gelato, right?"

"You got it, Palmer."

Palmer glanced outside to see Riley tied at the entrance. He grinned and put a bit of ice cream in a small paper dish and handed it to Callie. "You know I have a soft heart for Riley," he said.

"Doesn't everyone," laughed Callie. "I know if he could talk, he'd tell you how much he appreciates your generosity, especially on these hot days."

"Glad you're back," he noted. "You here for long?"

Decker shook his head. "No, unfortunately. Another trip has cropped up. We'll be gone for several weeks. With any luck, when we get back, we'll be able to stick around for a while."

"If that happens, I'll give you free ice cream for a week!"

"Is that a promise?" Decker said.

"Well, for Riley at least." Palmer laughed heartily. "You two take care. I'd sorely miss you if anything happened to you."

"Appreciate that Palmer," Decker answered sincerely.

They found a bench, and sat down, placing the paper cup of ice cream on the ground for Riley to lap up, which he did without protesting. When he finished, he stared at theirs.

"Oh, no you don't, Riley," Callie scolded, with a wide smile. "You had yours." Briefly, Riley looked a little dejected, but as Callie patted his head, he was quite content.

Locking their fingers together, Decker and Callie strolled lazily back toward the beach house. The edges of the cones were beginning to overflow because of the heat. With his finger, Decker swiped a wandering dribble of strawberry off her chin, at the same time, he gave her a peck on her lips, unable to resist the temptation

Chapter 9

Decker managed to get them a direct flight into Trujillo. As they made their descent, they viewed the layout of the city. Trujillo was built on a bluff overlooking the Bay of Trujillo. As they peered out of the plane's window, they delighted in the beautiful image below, marveling at the swells of turquoise water capped with white froth, and the long golden beaches. Two prominent mountains jutted upward behind Trujillo. One was Mount Capiro, the other, Mount Celentura. Blanketing the mountains were a barrage of trees, the uppermost tips lost in a fine canopy of mist.

As they continued their descent, they could see several fishing villages dotting the coastline as well as a few hotels and restaurants. There was an air of excitement as they heard the screech of rubber burning against the asphalt runway.

When the plane came to a stop, and the door was opened, they stepped outside onto the metal stairs, a blast of hot, damp air assaulting them. Once on the tarmac, they were greeted with salty sea breezes and Calypso style music which seemed to be coming from the airport's interior.

They headed for the airport entrance to grab their luggage. Snatching their luggage from the baggage claim area, they were told their hotel was a short walk from the airport.

The Christopher Columbus Beach Resort where they would be staying was a bright yellow, three-story building that looked both comfortable and welcoming.

The *Jade* wouldn't anchor for a couple more days so they would simply bide their time and take in some of the sites until it arrived. Even so, they were champing at the bit to get on their expedition.

Decker had studied up a bit on what tourist sites were available to see. In the city center overlooking the bay, there was an old Spanish Fort, Fortaleza de Santa which served to hold back pirates from entering the bay. There were cantinas, lots of small shops, and baskets piled with fresh fruit and vegetables. On the whole, Trujillo was a place to relax and embrace the beauty of its surroundings. A diver's paradise.

Once they were checked in, Holly went to her room to unpack, as did Garrett. Decker and Callie decided they would settle on the veranda over coffee to unwind and rest up a bit. The view was spectacular. Rows of swaying palm trees hedged the beach for miles, and the vista was accentuated with a display of brilliantly colored flowers. Lastly, there were multiple swimming pools to cool off in.

"I think I've died and gone to heaven," Callie said, settling back in the patio chair. "I could stay here forever."

"That's not reasonable," Decker pointed out with an amused smile. "You know the next opportunity that comes, you'd be on the first flight out like your britches were on fire."

She laughed heartily. "So you say."

"So I know."

"You know me too well, Decker," she replied, taking a sip of her coffee. "But that's not a bad thing. Oh, have you heard anything from Carson?" Callie asked, changing the topic abruptly, something she did quite often.

"I spoke with him before we boarded the plane. They've already drawn anchor and are on their way," he told her. "Should be here in a couple of days. Carson located three men here in Trujillo who will help interpret and guide us through the jungle."

"Great," she said. "I'm so thankful for Carson."

"Our good fortune to have found him for sure," he agreed wholeheartedly. "And that applies to the rest of the crew as well."

Since it was early in the day, they all decided snorkeling would be a great diversion since they were forced to wait it out for two days until the *Jade* arrived. They found a local scuba and snorkel outfit near the docks and made the proper arrangements. The long, white, wooden boat was dressed in a yellow canopy to help shield them from the sun. The owner of the boat was a pleasant fellow in his early forties. He had sun-bleached hair and a rich dark tan which made his blue eyes even more intense.

"Where you from?" he asked, as he prepared the boat.

"Malibu," Decker told him.

"Name's Logan Mitchell." He stretched out his hand to greet all of them. It was a firm, confident shake. "I'm originally from California," he replied cheerfully, making small talk as they set out. The whirr of the motor filled the air as they scudded over the tips of the waves.

They continued out for a stretch of time, riding high on the swells of the Meso-American Reef, a popular diving place with a rich and diverse marine life tucked beneath them in the turquoise water. Logan began sorting out the equipment, making sure they each had their snorkel tubes, goggles, and flippers.

As they tumbled over the side of the boat, the warm Caribbean waters enfolded them. They bobbed over the waves, peering down into crystal clear water. The species reflected in the depths were diverse and abundant. A vivid infinity of colors decorated the bay and was more than a little appealing to the naked eye.

They dove below the surface and found themselves swimming alongside sea turtles, a couple of reef sharks, some as much as eight feet long, and down along the sandy bottom was a group of Black Tip reef sharks, identified by the black tips on their pelvic, dorsal, pectoral and caudal fins.

Holly touched Callie's arm and pointed to a long, brown eel, slithering through the water nearby. Off to their left, Decker and Garrett were examining a convolution of coral spires, teeming with small fish that darted in and out of pastel pink caves to take refuge from the larger predators. In every direction, they witnessed an explosion of color that contrasted with the turquoise waters.

Forced back to the surface, they realized it was time to go because their boat navigator, Logan, made a gesture for them to return. When they kicked their way to the side, Logan extended his hand and helped them back inside the boat. A part of them wanted to remain and continue their exploration, but they had to admit they were experiencing jet-lag, and aching muscles were cramping, which was their cue it was time to rest up.

Nearing dinner time, Decker, Callie, Garrett, and Holly all met in the lobby and took a cab to Ricardo's, a small restaurant inland a short distance from where they were staying. They were seated out on the covered patio by a cheerful young Spanish man. Since there was no air-conditioning, they welcomed the slight breeze the evening afforded them.

A variety of colored flowers curled up wooden supports along the façade of the deck, their fragrance sweet and welcoming and the floor was made up of orange square tiles, embedded with blue decorative patterns. Brightly painted murals were on the end walls, lending a festive atmosphere. To the back side of the patio was a six-piece band playing music that sounded similar to the Calypso music they had heard earlier in the airport. The lively beat of drums, guitars, and xylophone added to the ambiance.

The restaurant had been recommended to them by their hotel maître d´. He gave them a two-thumbs up and told them it had the best seafood in Trujillo.

For dinner, Decker and Callie ordered baked fish with a mango salsa served over the top. Garrett ordered a large goblet of shrimp topped with avocado and cilantro sprigs, Holly ordered fish tacos and a round of Margaritas for all of them to enjoy.

Decker shifted uncomfortably in his chair. He had been looking around several times sensing they were being watched but had not seen anyone suspicious, but the feeling remained.

His fidgeting caught Callie's attention. She looked at him curiously, wondering what was going on. As for Garrett, he was nose-to-nose with Holly, and after a short time, he clasped her hand and took her to the dance floor.

"Okay, buster," Callie said. "What's up?"

His eyebrows creased. "I feel as though we're being watched."

"I don't see anyone."

"I don't either. Still—" his voice trailed off.

Callie nudged him. "Didn't I tell you," she giggled. "Look at him and Holly!"

Decker smiled. It had been a long while since he'd seen his father look at a woman that way. Not since his mother had died to be sure.

When the next song struck up, Decker drew Callie to her feet and walked her to the dance floor. He pulled her into his arms and held her close. He breathed in her soft-scented perfume that smelled like gardenias. She looked picture perfect with her golden hair piled on top of her head and secured with combs and dangling silver earrings.

The music picked up a beat. Bent on having fun, he guided Callie through a rumba. Decker spun her around, then gently lowered her into a dip. Spectators began withdrawing from the floor and formed a circled around them to enjoy their enthusiastic and quite energetic dance.

When done, they were both out of breath. The onlookers clapped loudly. With a wide smile, Decker nodded his head. They hadn't danced the rumba in three years. He was surprised they even remembered the moves. However, they had not missed a step.

After dinner, the four of them decided to walk back to the hotel. A quarter of a mile later, they were back along the shoreline and strolled along the beach to watch the sunset. It was a pleasant evening. Even though it was warm, a pleasant breeze embraced them. The sky was a canvas of beautiful pastel colors—blend of purples, yellows, and reds. They remained quiet, taking the time to contemplate on what lay ahead of them.

They returned to the hotel after the sun had set and stood in shocked silence when they discovered their rooms had been trashed. Clothes were strewn everywhere. Dresser drawers pulled out and left topsy-turvy. Items were knocked over, papers thrown randomly from one end of the place to the other.

From the waistband of his jeans, Decker pulled out his handgun. At the same time, he brushed Callie behind him as a protective instinct.

Decker went through both rooms, opening closets, looking under beds, and peeked out the far window to see if anyone was hanging around on the hotel grounds. He saw no one, and when he felt comfortable they were safe, he motioned for them to come inside.

"Make sure you bolt the door tonight and lock any windows in your room," Decker said, tucking his gun back into his waistband. "Looks like your pursuers from Los Angeles decided to pay us a visit. Not much of a surprise. Guess it wasn't my imagination someone was watching us at the restaurant. Whoever's behind this must have ordered his cronies to watch us and while we were preoccupied they could get access to our rooms and ransack them."

Decker picked up the phone from its saddle and dialed the hotel office. "I was wondering if there was anyone loitering around the hotel earlier this evening?" he asked.

The office woman replied, "I'm not sure, Sir. I can check with security. Is there a problem?"

"You could say that," he said. "Our rooms were gone through. Can't tell if anything is missing right off, but I'd like to find out who might have seen fit to turn everything upside down. And not only our room. Holly Romero's as well."

"I'll speak with security and send them right up. I do apologize, Mr. Hayden."

It was only a matter of minutes before a man knocked at their door. He was dressed in security clothing and had a rifle in his hand. His eyes scanned the room, and his brows hiked when he saw the clutter. He looked at Decker with surprise. "What happened?"

"Someone decided to break into our rooms," Decker informed him, "and go through our belongings. Fortunately, we didn't have much with us other than clothing and toiletries. What I want to know is if you saw anyone suspicious hanging around here this evening?"

The security guard was silent for a time, obviously rifling back over the events of the evening to see if he remembered anyone. "There was one gentleman loitering here for some time near the entrance. He was leaning up against the brick wall near the gardens smoking a cigarette. I told him he needed to head out, that loitering was not allowed. He spat something out. I really couldn't hear what he said, but it didn't sound like a polite answer."

"Can you describe the man?" asked Decker, cocking his head curiously.

"Rather tall, slender Caucasian. He had a long scar on his cheek and brown hair to his shoulders. He was pretty scruffy looking," the security guard recalled.

"Anyone else?" Decker questioned.

The security guard shook his head. "Didn't notice anyone else. Would you like to change rooms? I can have housekeeping come and move you if you would feel safer?"

"I believe we'll be all right but thank you. Appears we have nothing they wanted," said Decker, not detailing the whole scenario. No need for him to know what they were up to or why the man was rummaging through their rooms.

When the security guard turned to leave, Decker said, "looks like we're going to have a couple of shadows here on out. We'll have to be on guard at all times. And we can't afford to be careless or distracted."

Chapter 10

Bruno and his men had flown immediately to Trujillo, Honduras, soon as Adrián and Javier had taken care of the woman who had helped Holly. They knew it would only be a matter of time before the Haydens started their search for the lost city. All Bruno had to do was wait it out. Bruno settled back in his high-backed leather chair, a cigar propped in the corner of his mouth. Delight danced in his eyes.

"I'm flabbergasted. You actually did what I told you," he remarked. Bruno sported a thick black mustache that curled up on either side of his mouth. He had a peculiar habit of wrinkling his nose and every time he did, it gave the appearance his mustache was flapping up and down like a crow in flight. His men often snickered and made jest of him behind his back because of the comical spasm, though they dared not ever let him hear, knowing there'd be harsh consequences.

Adrián grinned, showing a couple decaying teeth in the front. He did his best not to snigger as he watched Bruno's take-to-flight mustache. He knew better.

"Yeah," Adrián agreed, seeming quite pleased with himself. "We stayed close to the airport for days, waiting and watching for them to show up. You were right, boss. Holly found herself a couple of people willing to come here and finish the job her husband began."

Bruno blew out a cloud of heavy gray smoke from his lips. It spiraled around his head, making a thick canopy over the room.

"Greed is dependable. I knew they'd show up here. A matter of time." He propped his black boots on the mahogany desk and crossed his feet.

Adrián chuckled, looking quite pleased with himself. "It was unfortunate they didn't have the statue with them or the map, but we'll keep our eyes on their every move. Sooner or later, they'll lead us exactly where we want to go, and we'll be rich."

"I have several men to follow them and keep me informed as to what they are doing," Bruno said looking confident. His dark face was deeply wrinkled, his black eyes cut with a glowering intensity. His cheeks were shadowed with stubble from neglecting to shave the past few days.

When Bruno's men lost sight of Holly, he knew she would set out to find someone to help her. It made sense she'd locate like-minded people with an intimate knowledge of archeology to assist her. Doing some background checks on her husband Leonard, Bruno noted a few people she would undoubtedly seek out. The Haydens, with their knowledge and expertise, were at the top of his list. All the better for him. He figured he would simply let them do the hard work, confirm the existence of the lost city, and overtake them in the end.

It could not have worked out better, he concluded. He had stationed Adrián outside the airport and told him to monitor every flight coming in from the states. It was several days of waiting. Several days without much sleep, but Adrián spotted Holly stepping onto the tarmac with three other people and assumed they were the Haydens.

Adrián and Javier dogged them to their hotel then reported back to Bruno. Bruno threatened Adrián and Javier that if they lost sight of the Haydens this time, it would be the last thing they ever saw. Needless to say, they stuck like glue to the Haydens, slinking like reptiles in the shadows.

While the Haydens and Holly went out for dinner, Adrián had taken the opportunity to rifle through their rooms. He'd pulled drawers out to inspect the undersides, looked under cushions, behind mirrors and wall hangings. Wherever he thought they might conceal something of value. Unfortunately, he'd come up short of finding anything to crow about.

While Adrián rummaged through the rooms, Javier trailed Decker and the others. Fortunate for him, he knew one of the chefs and was able to worm his way into the kitchen where he had ample opportunity to watch their every move.

Bruno was quite pleased with how everything was turning out, despite the bungled mess in Los Angeles. He had also been informed that the Haydens yacht, the *Jade*, had set course from Miami, bearing westward and had rounded Cuba. They were now in a southerly route heading directly toward Trujillo. Little did the crew realize that the *Jade* would not lay anchor in the Bay of Trujillo. Bruno would see to that. The fewer men to assist the Haydens, the better.

"Now that they're onto us, what do you want us to do?" Adrián asked.

Bruno took another puff on his cigar, snuffed it out in the ashtray, and replied, "We'll stay quietly behind the scenes for a short time, but I want to know what they're up to. Don't let them out of your sight. I'll contact you and Javier when it's time to make a move. My guess is they're waiting for their boat to lay anchor."

Chapter 11

Decker grabbed the sat phone, thankful Carson had returned his call. "Carson," he said. "How's everything?"

"We're making good timing. Should dock in two days," he briefed him. "You? "

"Aside from our rooms being ransacked, we're great."

"No kidding!" he blurted out. "Did you find the culprit?"

"Not yet. Security guard told us there was a man hanging around the hotel with a long scar on his cheek. Sounds like the same hooligan who was after Holly in Los Angeles."

"It's heating up," Carson said. "Better watch your backs."

"Were you able to locate a guide for us?" Decker could hear the shuffling of papers in the background.

"Yup," Carson said, getting his information in order. "I have three men lined up. Manuel Rodriguez; Damion Asposis and Webu Broca. They live in the fishing village there along the coast. Manuel has been taking groups into the jungle since he was a young man. He's a reputable guide according to my research. Not as sure about Webu Broca. His name was passed along a little later, but I believe he may have gone with Manuel on a couple jungle excursions."

"Do you have a contact number for Manuel?"

Carson laughed. "I was told to ask anyone in the village, and they would know him." Changing the subject, he added, "Did you have the artifact with you? Whoever broke into your rooms didn't find it or the map, did they?"

"No, I didn't want to risk bringing it back. Eventually, I'll turn it over to the museum here in Honduras, but for now, it's in a safe place, and the map stays on my body. I'm not going to let it out of my sight," Decker assured him. "I think today Callie and I will go see if we can find Manuel. I'd like to set out as soon as possible once you drop anchor."

"I'll keep in touch with you," Carson said. "And let me know how it turns out with the guides. Without them, we're like a ship without a rudder."

Decker knew that was true. They needed someone capable of speaking several different languages, as well as someone familiar with the many tributaries and lay of the land. The jungle could swallow a person whole if they didn't know what they were doing. Dangers lurked in every direction. A good guide would steer them away from many of the hazards they could otherwise find themselves in.

While Decker and Callie prepared to find Manuel Rodriguez, Decker asked Garrett to stay at the beach during the day or take Holly to see the sights. Decker told Garrett how important it was not to let her out of his sight. The persons responsible for ransacking their rooms could possibly grab Holly and hold her hostage until they got what they wanted.

Setting out on foot, Decker and Callie walked along the beach toward a couple of the local villages. They wanted to find Manuel quickly and set their plans in motion. Even while they walked, he was certain someone was watching their every move. He had no doubt that sooner or later these people, whoever they were, would confront them. There was a chance Decker was reading the situation wrong. But he realized the men following them would stay off in the shadows and simply wait it out until he and Callie cleared a path for them.

Callie looked up at her husband with a wide smile. "You always look like a tourist, Decker." She couldn't help but be amused by his bright Hawaiian shirts. Today, like so many, he wore a silky, bright yellow shirt with large orange flowers printed on it. That, in combination with his khaki shorts, flip flops and golden-brown hair whipping back from his darkly tanned face, anyone would think he was a surfer right off the boat from Honolulu.

He smiled.

Callie was dressed in a white tank top, tucked into tan slacks. She had since slipped off her leather sandals, so her toes could sink into the warm sand. They walked hand in hand along the shore. Occasionally, she would dart out into the warm Caribbean waters and allow it to wash over her feet, then rush back onto the sand as a wave rolled in.

They strolled into one of the fishing villages lined with quaint, thatched-roof shacks, many of which served up a variety of seafood and cold drinks for the tourists. A few of the smaller markets along the way had a variety of seafood—mahi-mahi, swordfish, tuna, and snapper; as fresh as it gets. As well as conch, a delicacy served in the coastal towns.

Interspersed were specialty shops painted in brilliant colors of reds, bright yellows, and different shades of blue. Roofs were either made up of clay tile, thatched, or corrugated tin. Some sturdy; others dilapidated and in great need of repair.

A few young boys scuttled up to them, trying to pawn off carved rocks, claiming they were artifacts. Their enterprising creativity brought smiles to Decker and Callie's faces. But Callie was always gracious. She'd squat down to examine the stones and talk with them for a time before moving on.

She loved children. Though she and Decker had tried for years to have a child, it didn't seem to be in the plan for them. It was a long and painful journey, but they had come to terms with it and began giving some of their time to children's organizations to help fill the void.

They continued along the beach. Twenty-five-foot, fiberglass fishing boats bobbed over the curling waves. Most of the smaller boats were not equipped with motors and used long wooden oars instead. The fishing villages were typically poor areas, though able to subsist because of the bay's abundant sea life.

In the fishing villages lived the Afro-Caribbean Garifuna culture, which some believed had come to Honduras as early as the thirteen-hundreds. Others said the Garifuna came from western Africa on slave boats that were shipwrecked in the Caribbean in the sixteen-hundreds and made their way inland to St. Vincent Island, where they mixed with the native people and became the Garifuna.

The language in Honduras varied throughout the different regions. In Trujillo, it was mostly Spanish, Garifuna, Miskito, and English. Decker wondered if Manuel spoke enough English to adequately understand what their intentions were for the next few weeks and make sure their transportation was secured. It was always best to know the guides you hired before entering an unfamiliar area.

Decker slid his fingers around Callie's and pulled her along behind him to a souvenir shop. Lining the shelves were a variety of items displayed, such as conch shells, homemade dolls dressed in bright costumes, a stock of woven purses, and brightly colored skirts amongst a wide variety of handcrafted baubles made from nuts and seeds.

"Good morning," Decker greeted the shopkeeper with a wide smile.

"Good morning," was her cheerful reply. "Can I show you some of my shells or a coin purse for the little lady?" Her round face was flushed and full of vitality.

"Not today, thank you. I'm looking for a man who lives somewhere here in the village. Manuel Rodriguez."

"And what business do you have with Manuel?" she questioned with arched brows, her dark eyes surveying him suspiciously.

"I'm told he's a river guide, and we're in need of one."

74

Decker noted her protective carriage. It was obvious she knew Manuel and wanted to make sure their intentions were honorable.

She nodded with a wide smile and pointed her finger still farther westward. "Yes, yes," she responded, quite willing to assist Decker now that she knew his business. "He lives on down the road across from the butchers in a small home. It is painted a tangerine color."

"Thank you. Appreciate your help," Decker said cordially, amazed at how quickly it all happened. Carson was right. Everyone knew everyone here in the village. He guessed that was the way it was in small towns around the world. One person did a good act, and everyone knew about it before the following day. Likewise, if anyone did something horrific, that too would be widely broadcast throughout their quaint community.

"Well, that was like falling off a log as they say," Callie clipped jovially.

"And who are they?"

She shrugged. "I'm not sure, but I think they were pretty darned smart."

Decker laughed. "If everything on this trip was going to be this easy, we'd be in great shape."

"I wouldn't hold my breath, Decker."

"Believe me; I won't!"

To their right, they observed a few ladies sitting outside a small shack grating cassava root over sharp stones affixed to wooden boards. They transported the pulp to woven, cylindrical bags that hung from nearby trees known as 'ruguma.' Once they dumped the pulp inside the bags, they used heavy rocks as weights to squeeze out the liquid. Once the pulp was drained off, it was set out to dry, and later made into flour.

The women sang songs as they worked and seemed to have a rhythm that had been passed down over the years. They used the flour to make pancakes called Ereba, which was usually eaten with fresh fish and was a common staple among the Garifuna.

The ladies waved as they passed by.

They reached the butcher shop and as the woman had said, straight across from it was a small orangish building. It was rather ramshackle, but sufficient. Some of the boards were loose; some hanging free on the side threatening to fall with any amount of wind, but it was not unlike the other small structures surrounding it. It was a poor community, but the people were welcoming and hospitable.

When they stepped up to the house, they saw the door was wide open. Decker poked his head inside the door and called out, "Hello."

A slight framed Spanish man came to the entrance. He was wearing blue jeans and a white T-shirt. His face was weathered, and he sported a pencil-thin mustache. His hair was cropped short, and his dark eyes reflected warmth and kindness. He looked a bit puzzled to see someone at his door but motioned for them to come inside.

Decker and Callie followed Manuel into the small but comfortable room. There were a couple of chairs, and he motioned for them to take a seat. As they did, a short, heavier set woman entered the room from what appeared to be the kitchen, a long wooden spoon in one hand and a tin coffee pot in the other.

"Can I give you some coffee?" she asked politely.

Decker shook his head. "No, thank you. Callie?"

"Thank you, but I believe I've had my fill for the day."

"My name is Decker Hayden. This is my wife, Callie," Decker introduced, then directed his gaze on Manuel. "We were told you're a jungle guide?"

Manuel nodded in agreement. "I am."

Decker was happy to discover Manuel spoke perfect English and had only a slight accent. "The captain of our boat, the *Jade*, said he'd been given your name by someone here in Trujillo and that you'd be willing to take our team into the jungle. His name's Carson Perry."

"Yes, yes," Manuel said, understanding why they had come. "I've taken people through the jungle for many years. I'm well acquainted with the land and have gone for weeks on end with no fatalities," he smiled.

Decker laughed softly. "We'd like to go as soon as possible, and we'll also need a couple of vehicles."

"I can find a couple, or if you prefer, we could go on the chicken bus that leaves every few days bound for Tocoa. However, the route to Tocoa and Batalla is known for its frequent robberies," he informed them. "Plus, it's a much longer way to tap into the Rio Plátano."

"The chicken bus, huh?" chuckled Decker.

"The roads are not always the best, but I'll rent a couple of vehicles. I have a few trusted men that go with me, and I also have connections in Barra Plátano where we'll put the boats in. We'll make our way along the coast which will be much safer."

"Perfect," said Decker. "I'm waiting for my boat to dock within the next two days. It's carrying all of our necessities for the trip. There'll be five of us going with you. We're adequately supplied, but we'll take stock when the *Jade* anchors. If we find we're in need of anything, we'll take care of it. We use the *Jade* as a base for emergencies. When Carson arrives, he'll settle up with you on the terms of payment."

He nodded appreciatively.

"Then we'll be in contact in a couple of days," Decker informed him, and reached into his pocket. "Here's my card. If you need me for anything, I'm staying at the Christopher Columbus Beach Resort. As soon as the boat docks, I'll send someone for you. I'd like us to go over some of the fine points and have you available for answering any questions the team may have."

Manuel had a gentle spirit. Instinctively, Decker knew he could trust him. It wasn't anything Manuel said; it was years of working alongside guides and team members that helped him read the makeup of a person. After only a short time with Manuel, he knew he would serve them honorably. Decker was looking forward to knowing him better. He was also curious who else would be working alongside of them. Trustworthy guides were not always easily come by. Decker did not take his guides for granted. He always made sure they were paid well for their service.

Chapter 12

The crew was thankful for clear weather and sun washed skies, though it was blistering hot and little breeze to cool them. The *Jade* scudded across the Gulf of Mexico, bearing down at ten knots, her slender prow splitting the navy-blue swells.

Below deck, there was the faint humming of the motor. Other than the squall of seabirds overhead, and the slapping waves on the hull, there was little other sound. They were on a set course to Trujillo, Honduras and there was a sense of excitement hanging over the deck.

Carson and Shane were at their stations in the pilothouse stooped over tide charts. They kept a keen watch on the GPS, water currents, and depths. Unlike the others, they were afforded air conditioning. They could see the men were a bit sluggish.

"Poor guys," Carson said.

"Yup. I feel almost guilty," Shane agreed. "Not enough to trade places though."

Carson laughed. "I won't tell them you said that."

"Good or they'd probably toss me to the sharks."

Carson patted him on the back. "I think they're too smart to toss you over, Shane. We'd probably have run aground years ago, had it not been for your expertise."

"Is that a compliment?" Shane feigned surprise.

Carson grinned. "Don't know if I'd go so far as to say that."

They both laughed heartily.

On days like these, when the heat was unbearable, the crew would pull out the chess set or checker game. Today, being one of those days, Sam was hunched over his guitar, his curly, brown hair fluttering from the slight breeze. He serenaded the crew with humorous licks from the seventies. There were loud guffaws, foot tapping, ear splitting tones from those who couldn't carry a tune, but nobody cared. It was all in fun.

Standing to Sam's right was Ted Bingham, harmonica to his lips. Together, the two of them made quite a duo. They sang one song after another until, one by one, the crew returned to their assigned places aboard the boat.

It was not long thereafter that Ted and Polly were back to swabbing the deck, still humming a lively tune. Carson and his first mate Shane remained in the pilothouse keeping check on the navigational instruments. Storms at sea had a way of coming on quickly. The last thing they wanted was to be caught off guard.

Having a three hundred and sixty-degree viewpoint came in handy this day. As Carson scanned the horizon, he spotted a motor boat bearing down on them fast. The bow bounced up in the waves and water erupted from it. He could make out the figures of four men. They didn't appear to be military.

"Shane, what do you think?" Carson asked, his brows woven together with concern.

Shane grabbed the radio mic. He made several tries to contact the oncoming boat, but there was no response.

Shane watched the procession, trying to determine what their intentions might be. He didn't see fishing equipment aboard, but he did see a firearm in one of the men's hands. "I don't like it," he said. "I'm going to sound the alarm."

It was not uncommon in the Caribbean to run across pirates. These waters were notorious for thieves coming on board to brutalize people and taking whatever valuables they could find. Sometimes even kidnapping those on board for ransom. Assistance from authorities was not always forthcoming. That was why they always made sure they were well stocked with weapons, as well as the proper permits to carry them.

The boat was driving hard toward them. The men scurried across deck to find out what the warning was. Carson leapt down the flight of stairs, motioning for the men to gather together for a quick briefing.

"Boat approaching fast," he yelled. "Get your guns and meet back here as quickly as possible. Looks like we may have pirates after us!"

The men scurried to their quarters to grab their weapons and ammunition. Without hesitation, they loaded their guns and sprinted back onto the deck where Carson awaited them. The boat's prow sliced through the swells, closing the gap between them.

"Okay guys, find cover, I don't want to see anyone shot," Carson told them.

No sooner had Carson spoken than a gunshot sang out over the deck, splintering a side rail. The men lay low, taking cover behind whatever protection they could find. Another shot resonated, and then another. Chips of wood shattered, becoming sharp projectiles as they exploded from the impact.

Carson saw the boat drawing up port side and veering toward the *Jade* with intentions of boarding. The navigator of the boat cranked the wheel, barely missing the side of *Jade*. That gave Polly a moment of opportunity. Hand extended, he opened fire with his Smith and Wesson handgun. As their boat changed its course and turned sharply, Polly landed his shot on the side of their craft, a burst of wood shot outward, and one of the men flew backward out of the boat into the sea.

For a short time, the boat was waylaid trying to fish the man back inside, which bought the *Jade* extra time to place distance between them. It appeared the man was dead because when they had drawn him up out of the icy waves, they let him drop back into the water and let the sea devour him. The drama did not seem to squelch their thirst for pursuit, and once more their craft swung wide, cutting through the waves like a sharp-edged knife aggressively chasing after them.

Carson radioed for help but knew it would not come quickly, if at all. "Mayday, Mayday," he shouted over the hand mic. He was met only with static.

Unfortunately, they were on their own. Once more, the men scrambled for cover and raised their guns to site in their target. This time, the small craft swung around starboard side, the men on deck shifted their positions, waiting on edge for the blasts of gunfire they knew would come.

Another round of ammunition sprayed over the deck, but this time a yell resounded and heads turned to see Ted grasping his forearm, blood oozing out from between his fingers. Sam scrambled across the deck dodging bullets that whizzed over his head and slid over by Ted. He dragged him behind some barrels that served as a shelter for the moment. Taking a blue handkerchief from his jean pocket, he tied off his arm in a tourniquet to stop the flow of blood.

"It's more a flesh wound," Sam said, "but we need to stop the blood. If you can you make it to the medical room, there's a supply of bandages and disinfectants?"

"I can make it. Cover me."

As Ted got to his feet and began to run across the deck, Sam began firing an onslaught of bullets from his Ruger .380 pistol until he saw that Ted had gotten to the stairs and had ducked under the archway to safety. Sam slid back behind the barrels for cover and reloaded quickly. He saw the men had slouched down in the boat and had swung wide out of range to prevent being shot. While Sam reloaded, Polly opened up a round of fire to keep the aggressors distracted.

As they veered toward them, Sam and Polly took to firing once more. Wood on the small craft splintered and the plastic windshield exploded, spraying into the face of the navigator. He

82

tottered backward, then regained his composure and caught the wheel once more. Explosions of ammunition reverberated violently in the air.

Phil scrambled onto the deck with a rifle in hand. Lying himself out flat on the deck, he began shooting a succession of bullets at the aggressors. Another man on board slumped over one of the boat's seats. Blood gushed from a head wound. They eased back.

It appeared the antagonists were going to come at them again but then dropped off suddenly. Apparently, they hadn't expected the *Jade* to have such an arsenal on board. The attackers were now the targets and found themselves vulnerable to the bullets singing over their heads. Rather than lose more men, they turned back and sped off. Sam pushed himself to his feet hurriedly and headed to the galley to find Ted and make sure he was doing all right, Polly at his heels.

By the time Sam and Polly arrived, Ted had already cleaned up the blood and doused the wound with antiseptics. The stained red gauze pads were laid out on a stainless-steel tray, along with scissors and adhesive tape. Settled back on the lounge chair, he tipped a beer to his lips, a wide smile on his face. If he was shaken, it was not evident on his face. His green eyes, flecked with gold, held a hint of amusement.

"Well, I guess I needn't have worried," Sam chuckled.

"Like you said, it's merely a flesh wound." He shrugged it off. "Besides, we all need a little excitement sometimes, right? How many maintenance men do you know who has the opportunity to enjoy so many spontaneous adventures? It's a life worth living."

The door burst open, and Carson pushed his way through, his face pale. "Thank God!" he groaned. "I saw you running across the deck with blood dripping down your arm. Scared the hell out of me."

Ted grinned. "As you can see, I'm fine. A little queasy from the loss of blood, but I'll make it." Diverting their attention, he asked, "Everyone else all right?"

Carson nodded. "Yup. We're all good. Their boat was demolished when we finished up. Don't expect to see them back. At least I'm hoping they won't be back. If they do, I'm sure they'll bring more weapons and occupy a larger rig for protection."

"Decker's going to have a shock when he sees his boat," Polly said. "Guess it could have been a lot worse."

"I'll give him a call and let him know the trouble we had.

"I'm going back to the pilot house and speak with Shane," Carson said, turning to leave.

"Why don't you go lie down and rest up Ted?" Sam said.

"I'm okay. Really. Been in more pain than this."

"Suit yourself. I'm going to go assess some of the damage."

***

Carson dialed Decker's number and waited for him to answer. When he heard the familiar voice greet him, Carson sighed with relief. "Decker, how are you?"

As if Decker sensed the stress in Carson's voice, he asked, "It sounds like I should be asking you that question."

"Had a little mishap a while ago," he began to explain. "We spied a motor boat pressing in on us with four men on board. Nearly rammed us, but we swung around narrowly escaping impact."

"What!" Decker replied with a start.

"Assume they're pirates. As you know, that's not uncommon in these waters, and a yacht would probably make an easy target," he continued. "They opened fire on us thinking to cripple and board us. However, they were surprised by our swift counter attack. My guess is they were totally unprepared for a showdown." he chuckled.

"Everyone all right?" he inquired, concern skirting his voice.

"Ted was grazed," he informed him, "but it was nothing more than a flesh wound, and no real damage done. He's feeling his usual chipper self."

There was a sigh of relief from the other end. "Thankfully. Everyone else good?"

"No worries. We're fine. We'll be docking by tomorrow morning, and I'll send the dinghy for you and the others. "By the way, have you had any more incidents?"

"No. Whoever is after us is lying low," Decker said.

"I was somewhat flipping around the idea that the attackers might not have been pirates, but those guys who are trailing after you."

"Crossed my mind also as you were talking," Decker replied. "That's a possibility. Seems like a coincidence."

"Do hate to mention it, but the *Jade* is a bit torn up," Carson said a bit nervously.

Decker snorted, "Just a boat. I'm only happy all of you are okay. We'll deal with the boat later. So long as it can still maneuver, that's what matters."

"She's still treading water," chuckled Carson.

Changing the subject, he said, "Met up with Manuel Rodriguez. Nice man. I trust him. Once we go over the maps together and find the best route, we'll pack the long boats with our gear and head out."

When they cut the connection, Decker turned to Callie his brows woven in a deep frown. "Do you think you and Holly would be better flying back to Malibu?"

"Not on your life, Hayden," she was quick to say. "Where you go, I go. No discussion."

"You're one headstrong lady, Callie."

85

She grinned and cocked her head slightly, a playful glint in her eye. "That's why you married me. I'm not some high maintenance woman holding you back from gallivanting across the country. Had I been, Mr. Hayden, you'd have left me somewhere back in New Haven, Connecticut."

"Chances are," he laughed, humor reflecting in the depths of his eyes.

Changing the subject, Callie asked, "Do you think if we explain to Holly what happened aboard the *Jade* she'll reconsider and fly back to Malibu?"

Shaking his head, he replied, "I think Holly may be as stubborn as my wife. She seems intent on being here and seeing justice is served for the death of Leonard and the other two team members that were with him. When someone makes up their mind, it's difficult to sway them. Of course, that would be my preference, but she's an adult, and we cannot make those decisions for her."

"You're right," she replied. "I don't want her in over her head, which might already be the case."

"That's the case for all of us right now. These men, whoever they are, are persistent. They're not going to give up easily. Afraid we're going to be looking over our shoulders every minute of the day. And if we don't, I'm not sure we'll make it out of this."

She circled his waist with her arms and pressed her head against his chest. "We'll make it, Decker. I have total confidence in our team."

Sleep did not come easily that night while awaiting the *Jade's* arrival. Both of them tossed and turned. Callie heard Garrett walking around the room outside their door and smelled the aroma of fresh perked coffee. She and Decker were not the only ones battling their emotions about the trip and their safety. Knowing Garrett as she did, she knew his first concerns would be for them and Holly, not himself.

She grinned when she woke to find Garrett wrapped in a blanket on the sofa. At least he'd managed a couple hours of sleep, and with the stress of the next few days, he'd need it. No sooner had she stepped past him, that his eyes fluttered open. He pushed himself into a sitting position, wiped his eyes, and yawned. A smile touched his thin lips.

"Morning, precious jewel," he greeted her.

Callie strode over, bent down and kissed his cheek, scratchy with stubble. "Morning yourself," she replied. "Sorry, you didn't sleep much. To be truthful, I didn't either. I'm happy the *Jade* will be here this morning, I'm excited to see the crew. It's been a little nerve-wracking waiting around like this. I feel like it's past time we pack up and go."

"Decker still sleeping?"

She shook her head. "Shower. He'll be out shortly, and we can go for breakfast."

"I haven't been feeling very safe here in the hotel after our desperadoes broke in. I'm thinking the boat might be safer."

Callie smiled. "After hearing the crews' adventure at sea, I'm not so sure. Let's keep our fingers crossed, though."

Decker entered the room rubbing his hair dry with a fluffy towel. He looked up. "You look a bit serious this morning Garrett, what's up?"

"I was telling Callie I'm ready to check out of here and settle into the *Jade*."

"I think another couple of hours," Decker informed him. "But I'm ready to go too."

It was three hours later when the satellite phone rang, and Carson informed Decker they had dropped anchor in the bay.

Decker asked them to pull together their belongings and meet them at the docks. There was a sense of relief that the *Jade* had made it safely to its destination after their madcap adventure at sea.

The four of them made their way to the docks and waited patiently for the dinghy. All of them stood soberly, wondering what the days ahead of them would be like.

Callie noted Decker's brows were drawn into a frown and she nudged him with her shoulder. "This isn't your first rodeo, cowboy," she laughed softly.

A smile tilted his lips. Callie always seemed to know how to lighten him up. He draped his arm over her shoulder and pulled her close. They'd gone on many dangerous treks together and had come through them. But in the back of his mind, he knew a person could only flirt with danger so long before it caught up to you.

The bow of the dinghy sliced through the crystal-clear waters, swiftly approaching the docks. It was then Manuel stepped up beside them. Decker had sent word to him through a young lad they had come to know at the hotel. He would go aboard with them and be a part of the planning.

"Good morning, Manuel," Decker greeted him and slapped him on the back.

"Good morning, Mr. Hayden."

"Decker's fine."

The dinghy brushed up against the wooden dock and Sam tossed a rope to Decker who held the line steady while the others piled into the boat and took their seats, at which point Decker stepped inside. "Glad to see you, Sam."

"Likewise, buddy," Sam said and slapped Decker's arm. "A short time ago, I was wondering if we'd ever see you again after our mishap at sea."

Decker gave a snort. "It certainly has been unpredictable. How's Ted doing by the way?"

"You know Ted," Sam grinned, his brown eyes snapping with humor. "You can't keep him down for long. He was right back at it within an hour. He's got more stamina than a charging bull."

Decker shoved off from the deck. The dinghy spread the waters as it headed for the *Jade* anchored a short distance away. The water was transparent even in the deeper areas. Multicolored tropical fish could be seen dodging in and out of coral spires and twists of seaweed. Manta rays glided gracefully along the white sandy bottom, their wing-like pectoral fins moving fluidly, giving them the appearance of flying gingerly through the warm water. Some were as much as four feet across.

The day was hot. Both Holly and Callie fanned themselves trying to generate a little breeze where there was none. Occasionally, Callie would sweep her hand through the water and bring it to her sweat-beaded brow, which gave her some relief. She had to admit she was having some reservations about tromping through the steaming jungle, knowing how miserably hot it would be because there would be no draft at all. She imagined it would be similar to stepping into a steam room, with no shut off valve or door to let her out when the heat overwhelmed her.

As the dinghy sidled up to the stern of the Jade, Carson was awaiting them. He stretched out his hand first to Holly, and then to Callie, and greeted Decker with a hug. The genuine affection of Carson towards Decker had been there for several years. They had gone through many trials and crossed many seemingly impossible circumstances together.

"Phil has whipped you up a hearty breakfast. Omelets, bacon, and pancakes. Glad you made it on board. The smells have been driving me mad." Carson laughed.

There were three round tables set with white linen, plates and silverware, goblets filled with ice water and lemon slices, and a breakfast serving tray arranged with an assortment of muffins— A breakfast set for a king.

Callie took notice, looking over all the wonderful dishes he had prepared for them. "Everything looks extraordinary, Phil, as usual."

Garrett pulled out a chair for Holly, and once she was seated, he sat down beside her. "Thank you," she said appreciatively. "Well. What are all of you waiting for? I'm ravenous," she chuckled. Holly picked up her fork and stared at them; anxiously waiting for them to take their places at the tables.

It did not take too much coaxing. The team was itching to dig in and wrap their lips around the scrumptious meal Phil had prepared. Laughter rang out over the deck as they ate and talked about little to nothing, knowing that within the hour everything would take on a very serious tone. It would be time for planning and strategizing. Right now, it was simply friends greeting new friends and old friends making up for lost time.

Chapter 13

Garrett entered the chart room, Leonard's crude map tucked under his arm. He spread it across the table, and another larger topographical map over it to confirm the coordinates Leonard had jotted down. Garrett needed to pinpoint Leonard's exact route so the team could follow the same course.

Decker would be taking a handheld Trimble Base Rover GPS, so if Leonard's calculations were correct, the team would have fairly good success in locating the ruins.

"So, here is the Rio Plátano Biosphere Reserve," Garrett pointed out, "And nearby is the Plátano River where I think would be the best place to put the long boats in. The river will lead you into the jungle. The terrain is pretty rugged through that particular tract, and there are many mountains—Steep mountains," he stressed, wanting them to know what they were up against.

The team made a semi-circle around the table to acquaint themselves to the area. "We'll have to rent a couple of vehicles to take us there," Decker threw in.

"Yes," agreed Garrett, "And this will be the quickest route. This is the way Leonard traveled, and you're going to want to stay as close to his calculations as possible."

"Agreed. Manuel, can you round us up a couple of vehicles?" Decker asked.

"I'll take care of it this morning."

"Sam, would you make ready the dinghy and take Manuel back to the docks so he can locate the vehicles and round up the extra guides?"

"Roger that," Sam said and motioned his head in the direction of the door for Manuel to follow.

"We'll meet on deck and set out the gear. Each of us will have a backpack filled with supplies. Please, take only the bare necessities," Decker insisted, aware of people's tendencies to over pack. The bags were burdensome enough, especially in the concentrated heat. Therefore, everything they took needed to have an essential purpose.

Stretched out in lines on the deck were lightweight tents and sleeping bags. A medical kit, complete with bandages, disinfectants, anti-venom snake bite kit, sunscreen, iodine drops for water sanitation, mosquito and tick sprays, hand-crank flashlights, four inch digging trowels, shovels, hats, raincoats, water bottles, and rope hammocks. There was another pile to the right of where they stood that included climbing gear such as harnesses, rubber-soled shoes, carabiners, ropes, and pulleys. They'd seen the map and the extreme conditions they would have to face. They knew they'd have to go on foot and they would have to face steep slopes and limestone cliffs.

"You did an incredible job, Carson," Decker said, looking over all of the gear.

"If something got overlooked I didn't want it to be on my watch," he laughed. His dependability was why he had remained captain of the *Jade* over the past years, and why Decker always insisted he come along on the digs with him.

Holly strode up beside Callie with an anxious look on her face. "You sure you don't want me to come? I think I'll go crazy waiting here for news."

Callie smiled warmly. "It's best for you to remain here Holly. You've never been on an expedition before. Besides, it's dangerous enough for those of us who have the experience. This one is especially treacherous because we have no idea who or what is waiting for us. I understand your dilemma. Really, I do. But Decker and I don't want your blood on our hands."

Holly sighed and shrugged. "Thought there was a chance you'd change your mind, but I don't want to be a burden to the team, and I most assuredly would be."

"Garrett will watch over you and keep you safe. Any luck, we'll locate the ruins without a hitch and be back within a couple of weeks."

Holly chuckled. "You're optimistic. However, I know Garrett will do everything in his power to keep me safe. I do feel a bit guilty, though. You wouldn't be putting your lives in danger had I not gotten hold of you."

Callie touched her arm sympathetically. "Don't, please. This is what we do. You're not responsible for our choices. If you like, we could fly you back to the states to a safe house until we are finished?"

"No!" she replied emphatically. "That would be far worse. I'll stay here."

Decker stepped out of the pilot room, the hot air consuming him. He was dressed in jean shorts, a navy-blue Hawaiian shirt decorated with white flowers, and leather flip flops. A brown canvas hat was patted down on his head to shield him from the sun's rays. He smiled as he spied Callie and Holly near the stern.

"Manuel called in and notified us he had located a Wrangler jeep and two trucks. That should be sufficient," Decker informed them, bending down to help stuff packs. Each rucksack would have identical equipment except what clothing each person opted to take. Wick away clothing was recommended for the trip as drying wet clothing would be difficult with the humidity. Whatever they decided upon would have to stay under a specified weight to make travel as light as possible.

"When do we leave?" Callie asked.

"First light," Decker answered. "You'll probably want a shower and a good night's sleep."

***

Decker looked over at Callie who was tossing and turning on the bed. "You never could sleep the night before one of our trips," he said.

"I have to say, I'm a little restless knowing there are some men out there who would like to see us dead," she admitted. "There are always ruthless treasure hunters that could be potentially dangerous, but this is a bit more than that. We're being stalked like prey. You can bet they're waiting for us to load up tomorrow and they will be at our heels." Knowing that speculating what might happen was not beneficial, Callie changed the subject. "What happens when or if we find Leonard's discovery?"

Decker ruffled her hair with his hand and smiled. "We have to take it one step at a time, Callie," he responded, though concern flashed in the depths of his eyes. "You don't have to go."

She touched his cheek. "I go where you go, Hayden. We're partners, remember?"

Decker drew her into his arms and held her. Her breath was warm against his cheek. He stroked her golden hair with his strong hand in an attempt to comfort her. He would never forgive himself if anything happened to her. But she was right. They had always gone together on expeditions, and it would not change now. They would merely have to be on guard and not forget they'd have unwelcome traveling companions. Even if they couldn't see them.

Glancing down at Callie, he realized she had drifted into a peaceful sleep. He knew there were many unknowns, but he was confident they were as well prepared as possible. He also knew, at least for the time, they were safe.

He was not sure how late it was before he fell to sleep, but when he woke he felt exhilarated, ready to confront the wilds and whatever else they might encounter. Still in bed, he yawned wide and stretched his arms over his head. The spot beside him was deserted, and twisting his head, he saw Callie was already dressed in her khaki shorts, brown tank top, and her hiking boots. She had drawn her hair up into a ponytail and fitted it through the back of her pink baseball cap to keep the sun off her head. Her face glowed with anticipation.

"Come on, lazy bum," she teased with a wide smile. "Up and at um!"

He laughed as he swung his legs over the side of the bed and slid free from the cool white sheets.

"You're quite a little songbird this morning," he said. "With the lack of sleep, I thought you might not roll out of bed before noon."

"You're kidding, right? Got to have my coffee," she said, flipping her head back teasingly and stepped outside the cabin door.

Breakfast was already prepared when Callie reached the galley. She poked her head through the door and greeted Phil as he was setting up, then strode over to the table and dropped down beside Garrett. Leaning over, she dropped a kiss on his cheek.

"Wow, this breakfast looks amazing," she said. Fresh fruit and Greek yogurt were at the center of the table. Scrambled eggs, bacon, toast, and if that was not enough, bagels with a side of blueberry cream cheese.

"You look ready to go," noted Garrett.

"I am," she admitted. "I think I had a moment's reluctance set in last night, but it's gone today. I'm looking forward to going. The adventurer in me has risen!"

"You never cease to amaze me, Callie."

The rest of the team began to meander through the doorway, some stepping lively and bright-eyed. Others, like Sam and Ted, looking as though they needed to go back to bed for a few hours. Hair ruffled, eyes sleepy—Callie would bet they'd stayed up late over cards and a couple of beers. Polly however, was quite upbeat, greeting each and every one of them. He was always chipper in the morning, and the others teased him for being so enthusiastic even before the sun came up and before his first cup of coffee.

Polly had wanted to go along with Decker, but he'd had surgery on his stomach a couple of months prior to the trip. After a lengthy discussion, Polly agreed with Decker that he should stay on board and not risk getting a parasite that could create further discomfort for him.

"Sam, how are you," Callie welcomed him warmly.

He snorted. "A few more hours of shut-eye would do me quite well."

"Nothing a few cups of strong coffee can't cure," she laughed.

What had been quiet a moment ago, was now a rumble of voices and laughter as the team came together for the last meal before they disembarked. The loose ends had been dealt with by Carson. Except for the trek across the land to the Rio Plátano River, they were all but underway.

Chapter 14

Ganigi Ibagari, a rather slight built man who was born and raised a Garifuna, strolled casually down the dusty, potholed street. He wore a wide-brimmed straw hat over his jet-black hair that was rumpled and straggly. As he walked, he chewed a slice of mango, the juices dripping between his fingers and down his chin. He wiped it away with his shirt sleeve, not seeming to care whether his clothes got soiled or not.

He could see Manuel's home off to his right, and he smiled. He had known Manuel for quite some time. Over the years, everyone in the village had come to know who Manuel Rodriguez was. He was one of Honduras's finest jungle guides and had an excellent reputation throughout. Whenever someone requested a guide, the first name dropped was Manuel's.

When Ganigi showed up at his door, Manuel had a welcoming smile on his face. He extended his browned hand, which had cracked nails and ground in dirt from years of hard work.

"I was told you needed an extra man to help guide a team into the jungle?"

"You heard correctly."

"I know the jungle in the La Mosquitia area like the back of my hand," Ganigi claimed. "If you still need someone, I'd be more than happy to help you out."

Manuel looked him up and down as if taking inventory. He nodded. "Are you able to leave this morning? I was going to wait until we got to the river to find someone, but if you're willing and free, I'd be grateful. The pay is good."

"I don't have a family or a job, so there's nothing holding me here," Ganigi told him. "I'll do whatever you ask and stay as long as you need."

Manuel shook his head. "We'll be at the docks in one hour. Grab your belongings and meet us there."

Chapter 15

Decker, Callie, and the rest of the team were at the docks with loads of gear and packs. Manuel showed up with two battered trucks, one missing the rear window, one missing a door handle. There was also an old Jeep Wrangler that looked as if the wheels might jar loose once they got on the road. Decker's brows rose with question upon seeing the thrashed vehicles but decided to say nothing and trust they would see them to their final destination.

All hands began loading the gear. It was then Ganigi and the other guide, Webu Broca, came alongside them. Webu had worked alongside Manuel for two years and had shown himself dependable and loyal. He was dressed in frayed, cut-off blue jeans, a brown t-shirt, and old tennis shoes which were caked with dried mud and no socks. He was not a lazy man, apparent by the strapping muscles on his arms and chest.

Holly stepped forward to give Callie a hug. With tears in her eyes, she said, "I'll miss you. "Please, take care of yourself."

Callie smiled. "Don't worry. We do this all the time."

"Not when you have men tailing you with the intent to hurt you," she reminded Callie.

"Okay, so it's not quite the same, but we're prepared." She was resolute and didn't want Holly to spend her time wringing her hands, fretting about what might happen to them.

Garrett stepped up beside them. He dropped his hand on Holly's shoulder tenderly. "They'll be fine, Holly," he reassured her. "They're aware of the dangers and have made all the adjustments to keep safe."

"If you say so," she conceded, though there was doubt hanging in her voice.

Decker walked up with lithe strides and hugged his father. "Take care of Holly, Dad," he said. "And yourself, of course."

"Same to you."

Carson waved his arm and shouted, "We're ready to roll, Decker."

Decker nodded and grasped Callie's hand. "We have to leave, but we'll keep in close contact as we go."

Decker and Callie climbed into the Wrangler Manuel would be driving. Their equipment was jam-packed to the ceiling. The cloth seat was torn in several places and taped together. The jockey box door was missing, as was one of the windshield wipers. There was an area on the driver's side that had rusted through, and the ground could be seen.

Callie glanced over at Decker with questioning eyes and mouthed silently, "Will we make it there in one piece?"

Humor was imprinted on Decker's face, and he squeezed her arm gently as if to reassure her. He didn't have an answer for her and found himself wondering the same thing.

Manuel turned the key, and the motor growled but did not turn over. He pumped the gas and tried one more time with the same outcome. Several locals who had been standing around watching them load the vehicle offered to push them. Putting the Wrangler in neutral, the men put their shoulders to the rear and pushed until he popped the clutch. The motor sputtered and coughed a couple of times, then with a choked rumbling sound, they headed off down the road, waving at the men who had come to their rescue.

"Woohoo!" Callie laughed, "On our way!"

Callie fanned herself as there was no air conditioning and the heat bore down on them. Even with the windows down, the air was hot and stagnant, worsening when droplets of rain started to fall from the layered nimbostratus clouds. In no time the small droplets became a deluge. Water spattered on the window with such intensity it was difficult for Manuel to see out, and with only one wiper it was near impossible for Decker and Callie to see.

What was moments ago a dusty, dirt road, started to transform into gullies of water bubbling across the road. And, adding to the rainstorm, the wind began to pick up. The trees swayed over the narrow lane, and periodically limbs slapped the sides of the vehicle, forcing Decker to duck out of the way. Decker tried desperately to roll up the window with no luck; it appeared the window was hung up and wouldn't budge. The wind blew the rain in on them, soaking Decker's shirt.

The ruts deepened as the rain continued. At times the jeep would hit the water filled holes so hard, they were flung forcefully around the cab. At one point, Decker struck his head on the roof. He moaned and rubbed his head trying to ease the pain.

He heard Manuel sputter a quick apology, but it didn't slow him down. His face was pressed forward, his eyes squinting as if trying to make out where the road was.

After two hours of travel, they saw no sign of the rain letting up. The Wrangler hit a rut, and the jeep's front wheels slid off into a deep ditch to their right. Callie let out a yelp, as the abrupt halt threw her forward.

Manuel still was in possession of a smile and shrugged. "Oh well. We'll have to pull it out."

When Decker stepped out of the vehicle, his flip flops sunk into the mucky sludge. He felt the mud oozing between his toes and with each step he expected to lose his sandals. Rain poured off his canvas hat and rolled onto his shirt and pants.

Manuel's team was already out of the trucks with ropes. They tied the ropes onto the bumper and motioned for the others to fall in behind the Wrangler to push. Callie was put behind the wheel waiting for the signal from Manuel to gun the engine until the wheels could gain traction and break free. Another hour slipped by as they propped wood and rock under the wheels in an effort to create friction. Callie continued to rev the motor in reverse, and then shift it into first gear to create a rocking motion. Mud erupted from the tires showering the men behind. At last, having exhausted every means to engage the wheels, the Wrangler made its way back onto the road.

Callie couldn't help but laugh at the comical scene when she saw Carson and Decker walking up to the car door. Their faces and clothes were smeared with mud. All she could make out were two white eyeballs staring back at her. There was not an inch of their bodies that was not covered, and she realized Decker had lost one of his sandals somewhere in the mud.

"Think that's funny?" Decker chuckled, threatening to rub his muddy fingers on her face.

"Sorry, guys," she fought to control her amusement. "But you should see your faces."

"This is not the way I imagined our trip would start," Decker admitted, his adventuresome spirit a bit dampened by it all. Sliding onto the leather seat, he slipped his muddy toes into his sneakers. "I'm trusting we'll make it there before the next full moon— which is a month in coming."

Decker emerged with his new footwear and joined the rest of them. The rain continued to pelt over them. It was actually welcomed by the men as they stood and talked because the rain was washing some of the mud off of them. They bantered back and forth as to whether they should wait out the downpour. However, without knowing how long it would take, they agreed to go ahead and move on slowly and try to avoid any more incidents.

They came to a place in the road where it had become a rushing torrent. It appeared somewhat deep, to the point it forced them to stop and survey the situation, wondering if they should dare cross.

"What do you think?" asked Decker. He looked for sound wisdom from Manuel who drove these roads on a regular basis and knew them well.

Manuel rubbed his stubbled chin. "If we gun the engines and push through quickly we should be all right. But, if one stalls out, it could be a problem. Sometimes mud fills the tailpipe and kills the engine. If it does, we'll have to pull it out," he said matter-of-factly. Manuel didn't ever seem perturbed or stressed about anything. He'd simply shrug and smile.

Gunning the motor, they sped off through the current. They could feel the water pressure pushing against the side of the Wrangler. With mud and water flying, they managed to cross without incident. The other two trucks followed close behind.

After they had crossed and started to journey forward, they were forced to stop again. This time, it was to remove a tree that had fallen across the road. A bit frustrated they would be detained yet again, Decker and Manuel started to get out of the vehicle, stopping when three men with rifles stepped out in front of them. Their eyes were filled with malice. It was clear their intentions were to rob them. Backroad robberies were not an uncommon occurrence, nor was kidnapping and murder. Taking your pick, none of them happened to be on the day's agenda, at least not on Decker's.

"You've got to be kidding," he muttered under his breath.

The three men went to each of the vehicles and ordered them out. Their rifles were directed at them threateningly, and Decker had no doubt they would use whatever means necessary to get what they wanted. Once they were out of their vehicles, the men motioned for them to step off to the side of the road. While two of the three men began to rummage through the Wrangler, the other man held them back with his rifle.

Decker glanced at Carson. Both of them knew they would take the men off guard and disable them. It needed to be at the right moment while they were distracted. One of the men who obviously had a broken nose, as it slanted unshapely to the right of his face, found Callie's Panasonic Lumix DMC-FTS camera and began whooping it up. He raised it into the air as if he had found a gold mine.

When the man holding them at gunpoint turned his head to see what all the excitement was, Decker took the open door to strike. In one fluid movement, he caught the thief around the neck and spun his body around. Decker's arm clutched the man tightly around his throat. The sudden movement startled the robber, and his finger accidently pushed back on the trigger. There was a sounding blast as the gun discharged. The bullet shattered the Wrangler's window, and at the same time, it struck the man inside the vehicle.

As Decker continued his skirmish, he grasped hold of the rifle and drew it upward around the man's throat and applied pressure. The robber's hand reached back grabbing a fistful of Decker's hair. With a forceful stomp, he drove his heel into Decker's instep. The pain was enough that Decker's hand slipped from the rifle. The man came back with an uppercut that staggered Decker.

Once Decker had regained his footing, he shifted his body and delivered a spinning back kick to the man's stomach. His army training was now paying dividends. The robber howled in pain and reeled backward. Decker rushed forward to take advantage. His fist doubled, he prepared to land a punch to the man's jaw when he crumpled to the ground. Decker was momentarily startled until he saw Callie standing behind the guy with a large tree branch in her hand.

Decker smiled and winked. He had to give the woman credit. She was not bashful about involving herself, especially when someone was after him.

When Carson had seen Decker spring into action, he rushed the other man whose attention had now turned to the scuffle going on and was caught off guard. Carson's elbow smashed violently into the robber's jaw. There was a snap of bone, and the man screamed in pain. The robber swung his rifle butt, catching Carson in the gut. Doubled over by the blow, he did not see the next strike coming. The man smashed the butt of the gun into his upper back, sending a searing pain down his spine, and dropping him to his knees.

Decker turned his head in time to see Carson in a precarious position as the robber was preparing to bring his rifle butt down on his head. Decker knew he'd have to act quickly to prevent Carson from getting his skull cracked open. He lunged at the attacker, his right fist catching the man's chin and sent him sprawling backward, his arms flailing like a back-stroking swimmer. The man struggled to stand, but Decker pounced on him, his fist driving hard into the man's face. A couple more swings landed home, and the man's shoulders slumped as he lost consciousness.

Decker offered his bleeding hand to Carson and helped him to his feet. They grinned as they looked at each other, mud and blood all over their faces. "Never a dull moment," Decker said, moving his shoulders around to work out the kinks.

When they thought it was over, they turned to see Broken Nose, who had been hit by the stray bullet in the Wrangler, had his rifle pointed at Sam and Ted's head. Blood dripped down his shirt sleeve, but it was evident he was not seriously injured.

"I'll kill them if you take another step," Broken Nose threatened.

Decker and Carson stood silent, observing their new predicament. Everyone had been so distracted by the altercation they didn't think about the other robber, especially since he'd been shot. Decker could see sweat beaded up on Broken Nose's brow. Clearly, he was trying to figure out how he would outmaneuver them when the odds were against him.

"You have the camera. It's worth a couple of hundred dollars," Decker said. "You need to count your losses and hightail it out of here while you still can."

Broken Nose looked at his two partners laid out cold in the mud. He knew if he left them there they would come looking for him. His dark eyes darted back and forth trying to think through his options.

"You can't take us all," Decker continued. At the same time, he spotted Manuel sneaking up from the rear. Decker knew he had to keep the robber focused on him so he wouldn't see Manuel. "You could shoot one of us, but we'll be on you quicker than you can blink. We won't be merciful either. You can count on that!"

Broken Nose was chewing on the side of his lip now, his eyes round as silver dollars. "Okay," he conceded. "Back off, and I'll be on my way."

Soundless as a cat, Manuel jumped him from behind knocking the rifle loose from the robber's hand. They tumbled to the ground. Manuel straddled him, striking him several times with his doubled fist. The man lurched to his side, throwing Manuel off, but in an instant, Manuel got the upper hand. Rushing the man, Manuel caught him in a choke hold and applied enough pressure that the man passed out. Feeling him go slack, Manuel released him. Taking a look around him, Manuel chuckled. They were all slathered in the mud again.

"And we haven't even gotten there yet," he laughed. "But I'm glad we come out of this with only a few scrapes and bruises."

Slapping Decker on the back, Carson said, "I've been through some harrowing times with you buddy, but this beats them all!" He rubbed his jaw and beneath his eye was a purple bruise. There were a couple of scrapes on his cheek crusted with dried blood. But considering, he'd come out of it pretty good.

106

When they walked back to the others, Decker gave Callie a high five. "You're one tough lady," he joked. "Glad you're on my side."

She grinned. "Thought you could use a little help."

"Sorry about the window, Manuel," he apologized. "I'll reimburse you."

Manuel laughed and shook his head. "Don't bother. I came out of this with my life. I'm not worried about it."

"Still, I'd like to compensate you for it. After all, you're the one seeing we make it there safely. You're not responsible for robbers," Decker replied.

They brushed the glass and blood from the seat, collected the guns from the robbers then slid back into their vehicles. They wanted to believe this would be the last calamity they'd encounter. It had been quite an experience so far, and it was putting them behind schedule.

The journey was slow because of the road conditions and took several hours longer than any of them expected. By the time they reached the town of Barra Plátano near the Rio Plátano River discharge, half the day was gone. While Manuel went for long boats, they unloaded their vehicles. Decker paid two men hired by Manuel who would return the pickup trucks back to Trujillo. The jeep belonged to Manuel, who opted to leave it with a friend until they returned.

"At least the rain has stopped," Carson noted, as he washed his hands and face off in the river. The coolness felt quite refreshing.

The others followed suit and began splashing water over themselves to wash away the mud from their hair and clothes. After they had finished up, Manuel returned with several villagers carrying pipantes, hollowed out tree trunks they'd use to take them up the river, over their heads. There were a couple of others hauling outboard motors and paddles as well. The outboard motors were designed for the shallows which they would encounter and going upstream would take extra days if they didn't have them because they would have to fight the currents the whole way.

Decker dug through one of the packs that had life vests and hard helmets. There would be dangerous places along the river and safety was at the forefront of his mind. He knew the guides were skilled at what they did, but even with professionals, accidents happened. The river was flanked with large boulders, and there were several areas they would have to maneuver through white water rapids. And places where they would be forced to pull the boats to shore and carry them over the harsh terrain. It would not be an easy expedition.

Everyone fitted themselves in the bright orange vests and yellow helmets, and when they were adequately prepared, they filled the boats with equipment. Carson, Sam, and Ganigi would be in one boat, Decker, Callie, and Manuel in another, and Ted and Webu Broca in the last. There was one inflatable that would carry the majority of their supplies.

Chapter 16

It was late afternoon by the time they shoved off and began their journey inland toward the Río Plátano Biosphere Reserve, and eventually, they would go on foot toward the Wampu River. As they scudded through the muddy water snaking through the sanctuary, Manuel began relating what the purpose of the reserve meant to the people of Honduras.

"In 1982, the U.N. declared the reserve a world heritage site. What that means to us, is that this beautiful swath of land which includes five thousand, two hundred and fifty square miles of rainforest, tropical lowlands and mountains, is now being protected. It's been difficult to stop violators, but it's better than it was," he said, helping them understand a bit better how important it was to respect the land as well as the small villages tucked away in the jungle.

"What's that mountain," Callie asked, pointing to the largest peak, a swirling mist hovering over its peak.

"That's, Punta Piedra. At four thousand three hundred and fifty feet, it's our highest peak." The black orbs of his eyes swelled with pride.

"Many different Indian communities are located along the riverbanks, once untouched by the world around them. However, more and more, the world has pressed in to take possession of the land. Big corporations are building roads to log the rainforests, fishermen come in using dynamite to rake in large hauls of fish. Then there are the poachers who trap reptiles and small animals to sell on the black market for pets to people who live outside the country."

Manuel sighed. "One more thing that disrupts the stability of the villages here along the river is the drug traffickers who use the waterways to transport narcotics. Little by little, the villagers have been squeezed out by these intruders—out of the land that has always been their home, even though this is a protected area."

As Manuel explained the decay, great sadness etched his face. His dark eyes filled with a pain none of them could fully understand because they didn't have to stand back helplessly and watch the deterioration of the land or watch helplessly while the small villages had diminished to a handful of people.

The team was overwhelmed by the beauty of the river. It was quite wide at the point of entry and gave way to broad expanses of swamplands that were carpeted with reeds. Beautiful savannas blanketed with golden grain spires that swayed in the breeze, and mangroves pushing upward from the muddy banks. The steep terrain on either side was thick with vegetation and clusters of pine trees, and there were lagoons and shimmering waterfalls spilling over high cliffs. They stared in awe at the stunning diversity it offered.

The whirr of the outboard motors somewhat drowned out the chorus of the hundreds of bird species surrounding them. Overhead was the loud chatter of monkeys as they leapt through the clusters of trees. There was an overwhelming sense they'd stepped back in time. To the naked eye, everything appeared unspoiled, untouched by human hands, but that was simply a façade as Manuel had told them moments before.

The journey up river was slow but well worth the panoramic view it afforded them. Ten miles farther along, they saw their first Indian village. Children began lining the banks, jumping up and down, and waving excitedly at them. Manuel waved back with a big grin. He knew most of the communities because of his travels along the river over the years, and he appreciated their hospitality. Even those who had very little to give gave generously and without reservation.

As they glided through the winding, muddy river, they closed the gap on a small Indian tribe on the eastern side of the river. Manuel and the team paddled the pipante to the sodden banks, and he hopped out to tie off the boat. They dragged the other pipante out of the murky water, along with the inflatable raft full of the gear they had towed behind. The children rushed down to meet them, grabbing at Manuel who apparently stocked his pockets full of treats for them.

The children were especially enthralled with Callie's blonde hair. They would touch it, and a trail of giggles would follow, their dark eyes round with wonder. Their hair was jet black and cut blunt across their foreheads. The boys had a slip of leather tied around their waste to cover them, and several of them had red and black streaks painted across their cheeks.

As the team walked toward the thatched huts built on pilings to protect them from frequent flooding, the skies split open, and a deluge of rain followed. Unfortunately, they were in the rainy season, and it was a relief once they'd taken shelter in one of the huts.

Inside they were greeted with a warm smile from a small framed, copper-skinned woman. Her coal-black hair was streaked with sprigs of gray and worn in one long braid down the length of her back. A red flowered wraparound dress tied at the neck and her brown feet were encased in a worn pair of leather sandals. She shook Manuel's hand firmly and motioned for them to sit on the mats covering the floor.

"These are the Miskitu Indians," Manuel informed them. "They speak Miskitu which is Misumalpan, Macro-Chibchan language," he chuckled. "That's a mix of African, European, and Indian, by the way. They're a generous people and always

111

welcome strangers. This here," he nodded to the woman who was busy making them tea, "is Marel."

"Thank you for having us Marel," Decker said, and Manuel interpreted.

Both Decker and Callie could speak Spanish quite well, Callie more so. However, it was clear they needed an interpreter like Manuel because of the different languages and cultural barriers they would encounter.

While they sipped their tea, Manuel told Marel why they were going up the river. It was obvious Marel was uncomfortable when he mentioned Ciudad Blanca. There was plenty of superstition attached to the that name, and most locals refused to go past a certain area out of fear they would be cursed and killed by the spirits of the city. Yet, despite her distress, she was kind enough to say nothing.

Marel's husband, Syrus, entered through the door. He was a small man, slight built, and had the same blunt haircut as the children who had greeted them. He was tattooed with a thin veil of black geometric designs running from the corners of his mouth to the bottom of his sternum and across his breast. The intricacy of it looked to have taken weeks to achieve.

Syrus greeted Manuel with open arms. It was evident by their display of affection and mutual respect that Manuel was not a stranger to these people.

While the two of them talked in Meskitu, Syrus's eyes would occasionally glance over to where Decker and the others were, and then he'd turn his attention back to Manuel. When their conversation ended, Syrus turned and extended his hand to Decker.

Syrus motioned for them to follow him back outdoors. The rain had stopped, though the flies were like a thick blanket wrapping around them. As much as they fought against them, it turned into an impossible feat. The best they could do was use the small nets attached to their canvas hats to try and prevent them from going into their mouths and ears.

Five Miskitu men stepped out from the tangle of trees with two tapirs tied to poles balanced on their shoulders. Another Miskitu man followed with an armful of banana leaves. They waved at Manuel, shrugged the poles from their shoulders and withdrew their knives to remove the internal organs from the tapirs.

"You stay for dinner," Syrus said to Manuel in broken English.

"We'll leave first thing in the morning. Set the tents up under the mango trees behind the huts. Tonight, we will enjoy a feast of friendship," said Manuel.

Once the fire was blazing, and the smoke curled around them, the flies dissipated. The team slathered themselves with DEET in an attempt to ward off the mosquitoes. Their flesh was already welted from the bites, and the constant itching made it all the more unpleasant, but this was the jungle, and they were prepared for it as much as anyone could be.

The meal was delicious. They had never eaten tapir before. A tapir was a three-toed ungulate that looked like cousins to the wild pigs, though a bit larger and sported a long snout. If Decker's mind served him well, he believed they were an endangered species, though he assumed the Miskitu had permission to kill them for food purposes. They were also served berries and fried plantains. It was a feast, and once they had finished eating, they were ready for a good night's sleep.

Callie for one was happy to zip the tent flaps to keep out the pests. "The mosquitoes are like buzz saws," she chuckled softly.

"And the flies are like Pterodactyls," Decker added playfully. They both laughed heartily.

She drew his hand to her cheek and gazed into his tranquil blue eyes. "It's been good so far," she told him, "Except for the

113

vehicles buried to the axles in mud and being accosted by road marauders, it went fairly smooth, don't you think?"

Decker chuckled good-humoredly and pressed forward to kiss her sweetly. "You always try and end the day on a positive note."

"We have to make the best of all situations, good and bad," she replied, lying back and tucking her arms behind her head. She realized they were merely scratching the surface of the crises they would encounter.

The following morning after coffee and breakfast, they gathered at the river bank to say their goodbyes and thank the Meskitu Indians for their hospitality. Syrus stepped forward and draped a necklace of crocodile teeth around Decker's neck.

"These bring you good luck," he said. "They keep evil spirits from harming you."

"Thank you, Syrus. I'm sure they'll keep me safe."

Marel handed Callie a necklace of garlic and gave her several pieces of cactus cuttings. Manuel informed Callie the garlic would shield against the mosquitoes and the juice from the cactus plant would ward off the flies. It also serves as an ointment for bites and to relieve itching.

"That's very kind of you," Callie smiled, leaning forward to give Marel a warm hug.

"*Aisabe,*" Manuel said, thanking his friends.

"*Aisabe,*" said Marel and Syrus, waving their hands goodbye. "*Dawan yamni maimumbia.*"

Manuel smiled. "God be with you too, my friends."

As they began to penetrate the jungle, the canopy of trees slowly closed in around them, blocking off the golden rays of sunlight. It wasn't long before they were forced to put on their head lamps so they would have better visibility.

Early evening brought them to a rocky beach where they drew the boats to shore for the night. Under Manuel's instructions, they hauled the boats farther inland off the main river so drug runners wouldn't spot them. He used his machete to slice a trail

114

through the underbrush and had the team help clear an area to set up tents.

Their shirts were soaked with perspiration. Worse, there were leeches that seemed to come from nowhere, dropping from the foliage they had cut down. Water was not the only place leeches thrived in. Because of the precipitation and extreme humidity, they were able to manage even on jungle vegetation.

For the span of an hour, the skies opened up, and rain pelted the camp site. Decker was thankful it passed quickly. It was difficult enough trying to set up camp without the rain, let alone battling a downpour. At least the equipment had remained dry under the tarps they had laid out.

Decker managed to make a small fire so they could have some coffee. He smiled when he spied Ted and Sam standing along the banks, fishing poles in hand, and their lines cast into the water.

There was a whoop from Sam which drew Decker's attention. He turned around and saw an eight-inch fish dangling from Sam's line and a wide smile on his face.

"Way to go," yelled Decker, "But we need more than one for dinner."

"You sure know how to burst a fellow's bubble," Sam yelled back.

Surprisingly, after a short time, Sam and Ted came sauntering back to camp with a string of fish and plenty for everyone.

"You didn't realize I'm a fishing whizz, did you?" Sam bellowed.

"I'll cook them so long as you clean them," Callie said.

"Done," Ted replied.

"Okay then, fried fish it is," she said while going for the frying pan.

When the fish was served up, they all enjoyed the catch. According to Manuel, the fish were called *Joturus Pichardi*, a type of mullet. It was a white meat, very moist as well as tasty.

The fish were an important food source for those living on the river. More than that, it was a much better dinner than what had been planned earlier.

Decker and Callie placed iodine drops into their water bottles for the following day to kill bad bacteria. The last thing they wanted on their expedition was to be infected with a parasite and be laid up for days.

Sam withdrew his ukulele from out of his knapsack and began to strum the small wooden instrument softly. After a few minutes, he began to sing. He was like a magnet—one by one the men and Callie came over to the fire and seated themselves on large stones to listen.

Only when he was done did Manuel take center stage. "It's my responsibility to let you know some of the dangers we might come across during this expedition. First, I have to warn you about the black flies; they come out in droves after a rainstorm, you may have noticed, and they carry diseases you don't want," he chuckled. "The little guys carry a wallop of a bite that can be extremely painful as well. Do yourself a favor and spray yourself good with insect repellent along with your tent. We have some crocodiles in the river, so be cautious when you go down to bathe or wash out your clothing. We have plenty of reptiles, a few deadly ones like the coral snake, the rattlesnake, yellow chin and the dreaded fer-de-lance that can grow as long as seven feet, and ants you will want to avoid at all costs."

Ted whistled through his teeth. "Well, that does it for me, I'm heading home."

"It's a long walk back," Manuel said, then continued. "There are wild hogs, jaguars, diseased mosquitoes, anacondas, and perhaps the worst of all, the drug runners who use this river, and gold miners who are violently protective over their claims. Unfortunately, they don't hesitate to shoot first and ask questions later."

"I think I'll rest well tonight," came Callie's glum reply.

Decker draped his arm over her shoulder and smiled. "I'll protect you."

Manuel smiled. "I would recommend snuffing the fire before it's too dark because it will draw insects quickly, more than you are going to want. Also, it's better not to draw attention to our camp, since there are some unsavory people who use this river. Those of you using hammocks rather than tents, I'd advise you to spray yourselves down well and use mosquito nets for protection. Oh, and keep your knives handy," he chuckled.

Carson used a small shovel to toss dirt on the fire. He respected Manuel's wisdom, knowing he had maneuvered these waters many times before and knew what to avoid along the way. Manuel was much like himself. He had captained boats most of his life. He knew what to do and what not to do. When he gave an order, he expected it to be followed, not because he needed to control people, but because he knew foolish rebellion could be devastating to everyone involved and could even be the cause of someone's death.

Chapter 17

After coffee in the morning, they ate a hearty breakfast knowing it would be a laborious and exhausting day, especially with the extreme heat. They packed their gear, ready to take on the challenges the jungle presented.

The team was thankful to have experienced boatmen as they dodged giant moss-covered boulders and slipped through narrow passages. When they neared the shallows, they used long poles to push off the embankment so they wouldn't get moored on the sandbank. The pipantes glided through the rock obstacle course, but not without much muscle behind it, because they were forced to withdraw the rotor blades from the water to keep them from damage. The men's arms ached as they pushed through the surging water.

Enormous boulders were lodged in the water. Some marked with lithographs of leaping deer, jaguars, monkeys, and, as Ted joked, *peculiar looking stick people*. The carvings were a reminder of what they were searching for and why they had come.

Several times during the day they were forced out of the boats and had to lift them over their heads until they were free of the shallows. Other times, they had to drag the boats out of the water and walk along the banks for long distances because of small waterfalls or rapids that they were unable to maneuver.

The farther they went, the more violent the rushing water became. The pipantes rocked precariously as the waters slapped viciously at the sides. Water jetted upward like a geyser as the boats narrow prows sliced through the turbulent swells, then plunged downward.

"We need to paddle the boats to the shore, and carry them upstream past the rapids," yelled Manuel, his voice scarcely audible above the roar.

The pipante heaved to the side nearly spilling over, but Manuel's skill at using the long pole kept them from overturning. The water buckled and pitched, and they were tossed unmercifully, somehow skirting around the jutting crowns of rocks in their path.

The river took a wide turn, and the nose of the pipante drove upward from the force. A wall of water crashed over them.

Callie felt the water rushing beneath her, causing her to lose her balance and she tumbled over the side as the boat leaned sharply. The water sucked her down with brute-force despite her efforts to remain afloat. Her hip drove into solid rock and pain tore through her like a shockwave. She was at the mercy of the raging rapids. Once more, the undercurrent sucked her to the bottom. Her arms flailed in desperation, fighting to get back to the surface. The river was unrelenting.

She struggled to hold her breath, her lungs burning. The surging water engulfed her, drawing her body downward and dragging her unmercifully over the protrusions of rocks. When she thought she couldn't hold her breath any longer, her head shot up through the surface. She wheezed and choked, gasping for her next breath. Up ahead of her she saw a fallen tree. If she could grasp hold of it as she was carried by, she might be able to pull herself from the violent undertow. Her fingers grazed the wood as she stretched out her arm but was unable to grasp it. Once again, she was carried back into the roiling waters that threatened to possess her.

It felt as if a hammer struck her full force in her ribs as she was thrown fiercely against the hard stones along the bottom. A deep, guttural moan tumbled from her lips. Vaguely, she heard Decker calling out to her in the distance, but his voice quickly faded until all she could hear was the rumbling turbulence driving her. Her heart quickened when she caught a glance at a few long branches extending over the water. In another frantic effort, she stretched her weak arms, her fingers curling around the wet bark. A renewed strength rose up inside of her, and she managed to hold fast even with the force of the river lashing at her. Hand over hand she worked her way toward the embankment. Her foot pushed off from the rocky bottom propelling her closer and closer. Relief washed over her when her arm wrapped around a large rock. With one last push, she managed to crawl out of the water. Exhausted, she collapsed in a heap across the pebbled shore.

The boats managed to pull up along the shore, and when stabilized, Decker leapt from the boat and rushed back downstream to where Callie lay. He pulled her into his arms, his heart thumping fearfully against his chest. "Callie, are you all right?" his panic-strained voice cracked.

"Not sure," she moaned. Pain rippled through her. She had been thrown mercilessly and brutally against the rocks. She was unable to tell what damage it had caused.

"We're going to pull the boats from the water for now until we know how she's doing," Decker told the others, picking her up into his arms and carrying her back to where they had tethered the boats and over to an area void of rocks.

Her shirt was torn at the shoulder and blood had seeped through the light material. Removing her life vest, Decker peeled back the material to inspect the damage. There was a large cut on her upper arm that was gaping, and blood spilled down her arm. He grabbed a handkerchief from his pocket and pressed it against the wound to arrest the bleeding.

"Carson, will you fetch the medical kit for me? I'm going to have to stitch this up. The wound is deep, and there's the

120

possibility of infection," Decker called out, though he needn't have because Carson was already rummaging through the waterproof bag to locate the kit. "Sorry team. We'll be staying here for the day so we might as well clear a spot for camp."

Decker never regretted the days when he'd worked with the medical corps in the United States Army. He had tended to every sort of wound imaginable, from severed limbs to holes as large as a man's fist. Over the years, his medical training had served him well.

Decker wiped down Callie's arm with antiseptic and heard her moan from the sting.

"Careful there, doctor," she winced.

"I'm going to give you antibiotics. Sorry to say, I'm going to have to stitch you up, Callie. Can't take any risks out here. The cut is fairly deep."

"Do what you have to do. I don't suppose you have a bottle of whiskey?"

Decker laughed, "You scarcely ever drink. It would be quite a circus act if you did."

He dug through the medical kit and withdrew a needle and a container of pills. Handing her a flask of water and two antibiotic pills to take. "Sorry. This is going to hurt, but I have to do it," he told her as he put the needle in her shoulder to numb her flesh."

"You have such a good bedside manner Decker. You should have been a doctor."

"And miss out on all this fun?" He raised his brows and smiled wide. He threaded the needle and with expertise, began stitching the open wound. Once he had closed it up, he dressed it in clean bandages.

"You're a trooper, Callie," Carson told her, noting she scarcely winced as Decker sewed her up.

"It helps when you trust your physician," she smiled weakly.

Decker looked over his shoulder to see Sam and Ted had already put his and Callie's tent up. They'd also pulled out their sleeping bags and rucksacks.

"You guys are amazing," he grinned, "Thanks."

"Nothing you would not have done for us," Ted tossed back. "How's she doing?"

"She'll be all right, but she's going to be sore, and this is going to be a hard trek for her. But she's one tough lady, and she'll finish the course."

Carrying her into the tent, Decker helped her out of her wet clothing. He grimaced when he saw her hip and ribs were swollen and black. Fortunately, her skin had not torn open but had only been scraped up. However, it would take time to heal, and she would experience pain for several days. He examined the rest of her body to make sure nothing else had been overlooked.

"I'll be fine. Don't worry."

"I was thinking how grueling this trip is going to be once we have to pack in."

"I'm not going back, Decker. I'll make it. This is a minor setback."

"Well, let's see how you are doing tomorrow." He dropped a kiss on her brow. "I want you to rest, and I'll bring you dinner."

Callie didn't protest. Every inch of her body felt battered and bruised. Knife-sharp pain ripped through her hip and her back. She realized only rest would help her in the healing process right now, so she simply nodded in agreement, and saw his face relax that she was willing to comply.

Decker motioned for Manuel and Carson to join him over by some boulders. They sat down on the rocks and waited to see what Decker was going to say. He pulled out Leonard's map and spread it out on one of the stones in front of them.

"We're right here," Decker said, pointing to the map while looking at his handheld GPS.

Manuel leaned over to look at the map so he could get a fix on their location and said, "we'll have to go by foot once we reach this point." He dragged his finger downward along the snaking river. "There's an area up ahead where there's a vertical stone wall which will prevent us from going any further up the river. Unfortunately, there's no other way than to climb it. The river flows through a funneled region that the boats are unable to pass through and comes out on the far side of the rock wall. This may be the best place to make base camp."

Decker nodded in agreement. "I trust your judgment."

Carson looked on. "How steep is the terrain around that zone?"

"We'll need to use the climbing equipment," Decker said. "It'll be steep and quite challenging in certain areas."

He unrolled the topographical map and studied it briefly. "You can see here, Manuel," Decker showed him, "The different colors designate a variety of natural resources, such as the color green, it represents vegetation, the blue signifies water sources, etcetera."

"Okay."

"The topographical contours are these brown lines made up of different widths. Index contours are wider, and they help to determine the elevation of any given area. Also," he dragged his finger across the map, "these lines help to define the configuration of a mountain. If you look, the lines grow closer together at the top of the mountain; the more compressed they are, the steeper the incline."

Confusion creased Manuel's face, and Decker laughed shortly. "I need my father here," he explained, "he's a cartographer and could much better explain all of this. But, what it comes down to is the rock wall we have to scale is sheer. I'd say around one hundred feet by the looks of it."

Decker's thoughts went to Callie. He tried to stay optimistic about her being able to make the grueling trek ahead of them.

Her hip looked battered and swollen, and he wasn't sure how she'd be able to handle the strappings on the leg supports used to pull herself up the steeper inclines. He questioned if she'd have enough strength in her arm to heave herself upward or even be able to cling to surface lips to keep from falling? It was a quandary for him, one he'd have to face tomorrow. He fought to shrug off the plaguing doubts.

There came a loud cracking noise from out of the bramble to their left. The branches snapped and shook. Startled, Decker reached for his PX4 Storm, compact Berretta from its holster and prepared to fire, but relaxed when he saw Ganigi slashing his way through the tangle of vines with a machete. As he broke through the thick brush, the color in his face drained. He shuddered when he saw the barrel of Decker's gun pointed squarely at his face, and his eyes rounded like half dollars.

"Whoa, whoa," Ganigi sputtered, holding out his palm.

Decker stuck the gun back into its holster, but his face was etched with anger. "It would be wise from now on to announce yourself," he shot off a word of wisdom to their guide. "There are jaguars amongst other prowling creatures out there. You're lucky I didn't take your head off."

"You're right, sorry," he apologized. "I was only using nature's bathroom."

Before going back to the campfire, Manuel caught Decker's sleeve. "I want to apologize for today."

"For what?"

"I should have gotten us out of the water several feet before Callie went in. I miscalculated where to pull out of the river and got us caught up in the current. I've been on this river most of my life. I don't know how I misjudged it. I want you to know; it won't happen again. I'm terribly sorry for my incompetence. It could have cost your wife her life."

Decker shook his head, admiring Manuel's humble spirit. "Accidents happen, Manuel. We're all flawed and imperfect. Please, don't beat yourself up over it, we'll get through."

Decker patted Manuel's arms to reassure him.

As daylight slipped away, and darkness took its place, Decker took a plate of food into Callie, He sat cross-legged beside her bedroll. "How are you doing?" he asked, concern knitting his brows together.

"Aching," she admitted, seeing his worrisome expression. "I'll be all right. You know me. I bounce right back." There was an insistence in her voice.

"We'll head out early in the morning. Manuel said there are still white-water rapids we have to go through." He took a bite of stroganoff, looking up through long, golden lashes to see her response.

"I know what you're thinking. I'm going to continue," she replied stiff-lipped. "I'll make it, rapids or no. And it might sting a bit, but I can endure it. Promise."

"Not another word. You're a big girl."

Callie reached over and touched his hand. "I love you, Decker Hayden."

The jungle was a clamor of noise from the several green macaws chattering in the tree above and the raucous echoing off the white-faced monkeys in the foreground. There were also spine-chilling noises they'd never heard before--noises Manuel insisted were jungle spirits who had lost their lives over the centuries. His superstitions were growing steadily the farther they pressed on making everyone a bit edgy.

They tore camp down and started loading the boats when Callie met up with them by the river. If she was in pain, she was doing a good job at putting up a stoic front, though Decker insisted on checking the stitches, and applied more antibiotic cream and new dressings before heading out. The stitches looked good, and only a small amount of swelling and redness was visible, much to his relief.

Chapter 18

Occasionally along the banks, they caught sight of a few crocodiles, some caiman and water snakes. Because of the boating mishap with Callie, the very thought of having to deal with crocs was not a pleasant thought. The worse thing they had dealt with so far were the mosquitoes, sand flies, and ticks. Every day they slathered themselves with lotions and sprays. Even with those, they still counted multiple bites on their bodies.

In the evenings, she and Decker would inspect each other's clothing to make sure there weren't ticks on them that would eventually burrow into their flesh and have to be dug out. And, even with mosquito nets on their hats and tents, their defenses were penetrable by minuscule insects that were apparently invisible since they never saw them, but they packed a wallop of a bite.

Callie heard the thunderous pounding of thousands of gallons of water rushing over felled trees and large boulders, some eight feet high. Decker had warned her in advance that they would be faced with more white-water rapids, thinking it best to forewarn her after her harrowing experience.

Callie sucked in her breath and held onto the side of the pipante with white-knuckled intensity. She wanted to make sure she'd maintain her balance and not go over the side again. The wooden boat shifted beneath them and veered to the right with the current. It leaned precariously to its side. She held onto the lip of the pipante with white-knuckled intensity. There was a moment when she thought the boat might flip over. Relief flooded her when it did not.

As the boat lurched, she felt a jabbing pain in her thigh. She gritted her teeth and purposed she'd not allow the pain to determine her course.

The sharp bow of the boat drove upward as a wall of water gushed underneath them. The awesome power of the water lifted them high in the air and then brought them plummeting back down with a slamming force. The jarring motion threw Carson over the side into the current, but his hand caught the side of the boat, and he clung tightly, riding out the raging waters. His legs slammed against the stone, and pain shot through his thighs and calves. However, he counted himself fortunate that he had not lost his grip.

They came to an area where there was a five-foot waterfall, and a cliff of rocks made their passage impossible. Manuel paddled his pipante to the river bank and jumped over the side. He motioned for everyone else to do the same. It was extremely shallow at this particular section of the river, and the rocks beneath were slippery as they maneuvered the long boats to the shore. Water spilled over into their boots and drenched their pants.

"We'll have to go on foot," Manuel informed them.

Decker looked around. The terrain was growing steep as was the thick underbrush, as the topographical map had revealed. Not only that, but they had a lot of gear to carry on their backs. The trek was not going to be a pleasant one, especially in the hot, sticky air, but he had been preparing mentally for this moment.

"This would be a good time to drink some water. It's easy to dehydrate in this heat," Manuel said. "You'll be sick if you don't."

The team took his wise counsel and opened their canteens. They settled back on some of the boulders around them, taking a moment to rest up before trudging through the thick undergrowth.

"Beyond the falls, there are straight up limestone cliffs. The water funnels beneath the rock, so we won't be able to continue," Manuel continued.

"We agreed we'd set up a base camp here. If there are any problems such as getting separated, or someone takes ill, you'll come back here and wait it out until we come back for you. Does everyone have a compass? It'll be your lifeline should our GPS fail us," Decker told them.

When they all nodded, he motioned for them to start unloading. They each grabbed a machete and began slicing out an area back from the river's edge to set up camp. Even Callie was able to maneuver the thick metal blade for a brief time. She was feeling pretty good and was amazed at how quickly she was recovering. Not that she didn't experience some occasional shooting pains, but most of the time it was a dull ache.

Decker and Callie changed into their water-resistant pants with zip-off legs. Though it would be hot, they opted for long-sleeved shirts to hold in perspiration for fear of dehydration. The shirts would also serve to protect them from the bug bites and stings which they knew would worsen as they ventured farther into the jungle. They slipped on their lightweight hiking boots with rubber soles and then helped each other with their backpacks. Lastly, they patted down their canvas hats, complete with netting.

Decker gazed intently into Callie's eyes to determine how much pain she was experiencing. If she was hurting, she wore it like a trooper because all he could detect was an earthy glow on her face, a warm smile, and eyes that twinkled with an adventuresome spirit. That was his girl! Always the gutsy, high-spirited woman he had come to know and love.

Manuel and Ganigi would be in the lead and Webu would follow up from behind to protect the team. There were no shortages of jaguars in Honduras. And a person would be foolish to disregard the wild hogs that ran in packs.

At this stage, Sam and Ted would remain at base camp and set up a station for satellite communications with the team and with the *Jade*. They had GNSS (Global Navigation Satellite System) at their fingertips and battery-operated equipment which would monitor the team's progress. The system was geared with the capacity to pinpoint the team's geographical location using a version of triangulation. It had the capability of locking onto a particular location and measuring both distance and direction of the signal from two or three different logistical points. Sam was also equipped with antennas that could pick up information from a number of satellites and transmit a coded signal at precise intervals so he could determine the team's exact position; their longitude, latitude and even their elevation.

Before the team left, Sam checked all of the equipment to make sure it was functioning properly. He handed out batteries packaged in Ziploc bags to keep moisture from penetrating the batteries that would render them useless. Without proper communication systems, the team would be left on their own, and that was something Sam was not willing to risk. Of course, they had Manuel's expertise, but best to prepare for the worst scenario.

"I think that does it," Sam gave them a thumbs up. "Check in regularly and keep us updated."

"Will do." Decker slapped him on the back fondly and then turned to say his goodbyes to Ted.

Ted made the perfect assistant to Sam with all of his maintenance skills. He had earned the name *MacGyver* after the television show. Ted had the uncanny ability to troubleshoot most any mechanical failure. He used unorthodox methods such as paperclips or gum wrappers to rectify whatever problem they faced, and would have them back in perfect working order in no time.

Decker came alongside Callie and grabbed hold of one of the machetes, a necessity because they'd have to slice their way through the thick walls of vegetation. Then they were off.

Fighting the tangled mass was like cutting the rind off of a watermelon before you could visibly see the fruit inside. There was no real visibility other than green fauna and flora.

The farther they walked, the denser the canopy became, obstructing even the light of the sun. There were a few dapples of golden spears piercing the small cracks in the thatched umbrella, but not enough to light their way. Before long, they were forced to put on their headlamps.

Snakes, especially the fer-de-lance, could shoot outward six feet and inject its venom. It was one of their constant worries as they stepped over rotting logs, heaped stones, and through knotted vines.

Callie experienced a burning sensation in her thigh as they trudged uphill through the spongy carpet of moss and leaves. She took a deep breath, waiting for the Ibuprofen to kick in and give her some relief. If it didn't, she'd be forced to take a higher strength pain pill.

The men fanned their faces to rid themselves of the pesky flies and mosquitoes, for all the good it did. Even with the layers of spray, the mosquitoes' aggressive attacks were not hampered. The last thing they wanted was a mass of bites—a formula for malaria and other serious illnesses.

The team swung their machetes relentlessly. For all the work, it seemed to do little more than exhaust them. Thick walls of vines, twisting trees and underbrush surrounded them on every side.

"You realize, as thick as this vegetation is, we could probably walk right past Ciudad Blanca no matter how vast it might be, and miss it altogether," Callie said, swinging the sharp bladed knife in front of her.

"I believe it," Decker replied.

131

"How about stopping a minute and get some water down? Don't know about the rest of you but I feel dehydrated already," Carson said, swiping sweat off his brow.

They stopped long enough to gulp down a large measure of water to keep hydrated, and within minutes, they were back at it.

When they broke through into a small clearing, they took some time to catch their breath. Decker thought it was a good time to recheck Callie's wound and redress it if he needed. Spots of blood had soaked through the gauze, and though she didn't verbalize it, he could see in her eyes she was dealing with intense pain.

Decker dug through the backpack and pulled out the medical kit. He reapplied triple antibiotic medical cream to Callie's wound and changed the bandages. "It looks pretty good," he said. "We need to keep on top of it."

"Thanks," she sputtered, "You did a great job, Decker."

"Welcome," he smiled. "How's your pain level?"

"A seven, I'd say."

He grimaced, sensitive to her pain. He rummaged through the kit and withdrew a sealed container of medication. "Here, take one of these, they should help for a few hours."

She gladly accepted the meds and was grateful they'd stopped briefly, giving her the opportunity to rest up a little. No matter how challenging the journey was, the hardships she encountered seemed to be the gas that fueled her. Once adventure edged its way into a person's soul, there was no satisfying the restless nature it bred.

Manuel motioned for them to move on. As they pushed a bit farther, they came to a surging stream. It was several feet wide, and three to four feet deep, but the steep banks were saturated and had created a sludge that would be difficult to maneuver through.

"Here we go again," Carson laughed, remembering their car incident when they'd been knee-deep in mud.

Manuel went first down the steep decline. His rubber boots sank into the mire creating a suction that nearly pulled the boots right off his feet. The others followed, sharing the same difficulties, though Ganigi lost his boot and spent several minutes trying to wrench it free. Frustrated, he removed his other boot, opting to go barefoot the rest of the way.

The stones in the stream were slippery, dangerously so, with the current pushing against their legs. Every step had to be carefully executed before taking another. Decker slipped on a rock and went down hard, water spraying everyone close by. Everyone waited while Carson thrust out his hand to help him to his feet, then they began to forge on. In the middle, the water became chest deep, more than what it had appeared before crossing. They lifted their packs high over the heads to keep the contents dry.

On the opposite side, they were forced to battle the muddy banks again, though this time they would have to scale a sharp incline. The problem was the mud sloped upward like an arched ramp and butted up against a solid rock wall. They looked up at the vertical façade. It was evident they would need to use their climbing gear to manage it.

"Better roll up the pant legs. You can bet we'll be spending some time plucking off the leeches," Decker said.

Callie wrinkled her nose. "I'll never get used to the blood suckers. Slimy little creatures."

Decker was right. The blackish-brown leeches with suction cupped mouths had attached themselves to their flesh. As they yanked them free, small streams of blood trickled down their skin. Confident they had removed all the them, they refocused their attention on the sheer rock.

Manuel was proficient at rock climbing. No doubt he had done the climb many times through his years of leading expeditions. He strapped on the harness and used the locking carabiners to secure the rope, then fastened his helmet. He made

133

sure he had his belay rappel device in case he slipped and pulled out rope to suspend for the others who would follow. His nimble fingers stretched out instinctively, seeking for a lip to clasp hold of to draw him upward.

"He's every bit as good as Spider Man, don't you think," chuckled Carson.

"Appears to know his stuff," said Decker, slipping on his harness and hard-shelled helmet, then turned to help Callie with hers. "How's your pain?"

"Not too bad."

"Your arm strength is what I'm concerned with," he added. "I think you should try to ease your way up next and test it out."

"And what if it isn't? Are you going to make me stay here by myself?"

"I should spank you," he teased. "Let's try it and see how it goes. I may have to devise a makeshift lift to draw you up."

"No worries," she tossed back. "I'm going to do fine."

Callie had done at least one hundred climbs over the years. She stayed in shape by going to the gym as often as she could, and by jogging with Decker. Being flexible and agile were two necessary components needed when trekking or rock climbing and she was both.

Her fingers searched for a projection, then stabilizing her feet, she pulled her body upward. She felt a twinge of pain in her upper arm where the stitches were, but she was confident she could do the climb. She glanced up and saw Manuel had already rolled over the crest. Again, she caught a small bulbous lip and hoisted herself up another arm's reach. Cautiously, she scaled her way slowly along the face of the rock, willing herself toward the top until she felt Manuel's strong arms reeling her in. She curled over the abrupt rock ledge and lay there briefly to catch her breath.

Next, Decker hooked onto the line. His fingers were not as agile as Callie's, making it more difficult when he swung out to grasp the smaller appendage made available by nature. Decker drew himself upward when a portion of the lip supporting his foot broke away from the face. His body dropped nearly four feet until he was able to belay his fall. He could feel the skin on his stomach being raked off as he slid but was thankful he'd managed to keep himself from falling to the bottom.

"You all right?" Callie yelled down at him.

"Yup." He began his ascent once again. When he made it over the edge of the wall, he sagged against the red earth for a short respite. Regaining his strength, he pushed himself to his feet and lifted his shirt to inspect the scraped off flesh. There were trails of blood droplets, but at least he wouldn't need stitches. Even though his wound was superficial, his main concern was protecting himself from infection. They were in an area teeming with bacteria, so he rubbed on some antibiotic cream, not wanting to take any chances.

They waited it out until Carson, Ganigi, and Webu all made it to the top, thankfully with no more mishaps. Once they had a few minutes to recover from the climb, they gathered their gear and reentered the thick, interwoven barricade. The day began to fade into velvety darkness. With what remaining strength they had left, they cleared out a space to set up camp. They were sore, exhausted and ready to stretch out on their bedrolls to rest their fatigued bodies.

After a couple of hours passed, they gathered around the small campfire for dinner. Beef stew from sealed packets was their meal for the evening and for dessert, freeze-dried ice cream. A great invention, Decker thought as he shoveled it in. It wasn't the same as going to the gelato shop in Malibu, but a nice treat after a long, hard day's work.

After eating, Decker pulled out the sat phone to touch base with his father. It was good to hear his cheerful voice on the other end.

"How are all of you doing?" Garrett asked.

"Making some headway, but we have some distance to go," Decker said. "Had one incident where I had to stitch up Callie's arm. Seems she wanted to test out white rapids and see if she could win. Well, it was a toss-up as to who won, but thankfully she only got banged up a bit and she's hurting some."

"Thank God," he gasped. "Glad she's all right."

Callie was eavesdropping. She leaned forward and replied, "How are you and Holly?"

"Holly's right here. She's doing good. A bit anxious though."

"According to the map, and according to how slow we are moving through the jungle, it'll still be a couple more days before we come across anything," Decker said.

"We're all cheering you on."

"And we appreciate it."

Callie pressed in again, "Give Holly our love."

"Will do," Garrett replied.

Once Decker shut down the phone conversation and refocused on their surroundings, he could not shake the feeling someone or something was watching them. Decker couldn't determine whether it might be a jaguar following them, or possibly the men from Trujillo who'd been dogging their every move. Maybe his overactive imagination, he reflected. Whatever it was, it was unnerving, to say the least.

The stitches Decker had put in Callie's arm were healing nicely. There was very little redness and no sign of infection. Even the swelling on her thigh had gone down, though the bruise was still black and deep purple.

Taking care of Decker, Callie smeared his scraped-up chest and side with some salve. "Glad you didn't fall to your death," she expressed lovingly. "Don't know what I'd do without you."

He smiled. "Fortunately, you don't have to find out. Could have been lots worse and I'd like to think this is the worst thing we'll have to deal with for the rest of this trek."

"You and me both. And you're right. It could have been much worse. We can live with a few bumps and scrapes."

That night, there was a tremendous thunderstorm. Even the ground shook under its fury. Rain poured buckets of water over their camp, creating streams throughout the site. Streaks of lightning zigzagged through the umbrella of trees, followed by loud cracks of thunder.

Callie unzipped the door flaps, drawing them back to watch the light show. It was ominous. Her heart thumped with excitement as she watched, a sliver of fear running along her spine. There were a couple of times she wondered if the lightning would actually strike their tent. She'd never experienced anything so spectacular.

Decker touched the small of her back and felt her jump with a start. "Come back to bed, Callie. You need to be rested for tomorrow. It's not going to get easier."

Zipping the front flaps back together, she snuggled down into his strong arms, feeling more at peace. Thunderstorms had always struck a certain amount of fear in her. She remembered running into her parent's room when she was a little girl, diving beneath the covers on their bed. She recalled her father's strong arms drawing her close and smoothing back her hair, assuring her everything would be all right. She believed him and would fall into a restful slumber.

"Thank you, Decker."

"For what?"

"For not thinking I'm silly for being afraid of a lightning storm."

"Can't say I'm thrilled either, Callie. This is right on top of us."

She pulled the covers up around her. Her eyelids closed and she surrendered to the darkness.

At the first break of light, they packed up their belongings and prepared to head out. Breakfast and coffee down, they were ready to go. The ground was soaked through from the inches of rain that had fallen in the night, and as they walked along, mud poured over the lip of their boots.

It was difficult at times to keep from sliding down even the smallest of slopes for all the sludge, though there were far more dangerous slopes they'd have to face according to the three-dimensional map.

They climbed over the bramble and came upon a trail. It was difficult to discern what animal made the trail, but they opted to take it to save time cutting through the vines. It looked to be the wisest choice so long as it didn't take them too far off their charted course.

Decker's job was to make sure he was reading the handheld GPS correctly and never let his phosphorescent, waterproof compass out of his sight.

Another two hours passed before they heard rumblings coming through the brush. Even as the sound increased, it was impossible to determine what was bearing down on them. All eyes were watching, their bodies stiff with anticipation. Everyone had their guns in ready-fire position. Like an explosion, a wild pig with enormous tusks broke through the massive tangle of vines behind Webu.

Webu's eyes bulged with fear. There was no way the others could get a clear shot without taking Webu down. With trembling hands, Webu started to raise his rifle, but not soon enough. The pig bore down on him, its tusk ripping through the flesh of his leg. His shrill scream pierced the air as he dropped to the ground.

Decker steadied his gun and let off a barrage of shells into the boar's skull. With a piercing squeal, the pig turned, saliva and blood dripping from the side of its mouth. Its crazed eyes zoned in on Decker and with a grunt, began a maniacal charge toward him. As quick as he could, he positioned his gun, and fighting back panic, he centered the barrel between the boar's eyes. With a loud discharge, the bullet struck its target. The pig staggered, took a few more steps toward Decker, and then dropped to the ground with a shudder and died.

Decker ran to Webu who lay rocking back and forth holding his thigh. Quickly, Decker made a tourniquet from some strips of white material he had brought for this type of wound. Webu's pant leg was soaked in blood, and he was in obvious pain. By the extent of the wound, they'd have to make a travois to drag him along, or make a camp, and leave him until they returned—the latter unthinkable. He would not last two days alone in the jungle, wounded as he was. And, he would be left vulnerable to wild animals.

The hole in Webu's leg was fist-sized. He was at high risk of contracting an infection. Decker wasn't professional enough to deal with this kind of wound out here in the jungle, and he knew Webu would need medical treatment as soon as possible. He wrapped it as well as he could under the current conditions and administered antibiotics, but Decker wondered if his efforts would be enough to hold Webu stable until they got him help.

Manuel stood over Webu, his eyes filled with concern for his friend. He juggled every possible solution but wasn't sure what to do. He would have to sit down with Decker, and they'd have to come to some determination as to where to go from here. There was no easy answer, and he wondered if they'd have to call off the expedition until a later date.

That evening, Carson had a fire roaring and had quartered the pig. He had learned to wrap pig in banana leaves and place it beneath the coals to cook for a few hours. The aroma curled into the air around them. They were watchful because the scent could entice wild animals, such as a jaguar, to their feast.

They sat around the fire, silent for a length of time. It would be a painstaking endeavor to haul someone out of the jungle, and it would take twice as long as it had when they'd hiked in. But no matter, Webu was their first consideration.

"I guess we'd better come up with a plan," Decker broke the silence.

"We don't have many choices, do we?" Carson spoke out, handing out a couple plates of steaming pork.

Manuel nodded. "Webu has been a faithful friend for a long time. I can't leave him here alone to fend for himself."

"Of course we can't," agreed Callie, seeing his quandary. "We'll simply have to return and reschedule."

Ganigi stood up, drawing attention to himself. "Call base camp and let them know I'll stay here and watch him until someone is able to see him out of here safely."

It sounded reasonable and would be a good solution. Decker looked around for input from the others, and especially Manuel since he was the leader of the team. He watched Manuel mull over the suggestion of Ganigi staying to look after Webu, wondering what call would be the most practical at this given time.

Manuel nodded. "Make the call. If we can't find help, we'll have to go back. I don't like the thought of the team being split up this way though."

Decker got the sat phone out and called Sam. He explained their situation and asked if he could contact the authorities. Sam would have accurate readings of where their camp was located. The main thing was to bring in enough able bodies to carry Webu out safely.

"How are you two doing?" Decker asked Sam.

"Doing good. Much better than your team, apparently," he said. "How much longer do you think it's going to take you to find the lost city?"

Having studied the map, Decker felt like they would be at least three or four more days before reaching the spot Leonard had indicated. That was only if they didn't run into any more difficulties. The jungle was fraught with dangerous obstacles, and Decker hoped there'd be no further injuries along the way. They could use a bit of luck at the present.

"I'll make sure he gets help, Decker, even if we have to leave base camp and come get him ourselves," Sam assured him. "You need to find the lost city or whatever it is Leonard found."

"Not at the expense of a man's life," Decker answered. When he'd finished his call, he looked over to Manuel to make sure he didn't want to change his mind.

Manuel nodded as if reading Decker's mind and wanted to reassure him that so long as there was help on the way, he'd not feel as if he was abandoning his friend. He would continue the expedition.

"Let's try and make a secure camp here," Decker urged them. "I want to make sure we leave enough ammo to keep Ganigi and Webu safe. Also, let's clear a wide enough area to spot any jungle prowlers."

In the morning, they treated Webu as best they could. They would leave enough pain pills, water, and food to hold them over until help could arrive. They asked Ganigi to return to base camp once help came and stay there until they returned. That settled, they packed up their equipment, said their goodbyes and started out once again.

Chapter 19

Ganigi waited an hour after the team had left. He knew they couldn't get too far ahead of him or he could easily lose track of them. He glanced at his watch several times and paced restlessly. He could hear low moans coming from the tent and knew Webu was in severe pain. He was instructed to give him pain pills, but presently it did not matter to him.

"Ganigi!" Webu cried out. "Ganigi, are you there?"

Webu could hear Ganigi walking outside his tent, and he could not understand why he wouldn't answer him. Pain tore through his leg. He felt feverish, and sweat trickled down his face. As he tried to pull himself toward the doorway, he felt like a hot iron seared his thigh. The pain came in waves. His stomach churned, and he thought he would vomit.

"Ganigi!" he called out again, unable to understand the silence. Had something happened to him as well, he wondered? Silence…

Panicked now, Webu pushed himself onto his elbows and with all of his strength dragged his body forward toward the doorway. Through the open flaps of the tent, he could see Ganigi standing at a distance, smoking a cigarette. He was bewildered. What could Ganigi possibly be thinking? There was no rational reason for what he was seeing.

He groaned as he continued to push himself forward, every movement was like having knives thrust into his flesh. He spied the medical kit a few feet in front of the tent if he could only make it that far. He dug his hands into the ground and pushed off with his toes. Another foot—but the medical kit may well have been a hundred feet away. His body collapsed in a heap.

"Ganigi, please," he begged.

Ganigi threw his cigarette at his feet and ground it out. There was a wicked smile on his lips as he turned around to see Webu half way out of the tent. Poor sucker, he thought. It was his misfortune the pig gored him. Sauntering over to where he lay, he stared down at him. With no emotion on his face, he pulled out his handgun and pointed it at Webu.

"What are you doing?" Webu yelled.

"Sorry, Webu. I can't sit here any longer to babysit you," he replied coldly. With the flick of his finger, the gun rang out as it discharged leaving Webu slumped on the ground in a pool of blood. "So long, buddy. You'll make a fine meal for the jungle animals." With that, Ganigi clutched his pack and began to follow the trail of Manuel's team.

***

Sam was doing his best to contact authorities, but there was some kind of atmospheric interference. He cursed under his breath. He knew time was of the essence if Webu's injury was as bad as Decker said. If he couldn't make contact within the hour, he and Ted would have to go in after Webu themselves. It would leave all of their equipment unattended, but they would have no other alternative. It was their responsibility to make sure Webu got back to the river where he could be transported out of the jungle.

"How's it going?" Ted asked as he walked up beside him.

"Not well right now, Teddy," he grumbled. "I'm unable to make contact. There's a lot of static presently, so unless something changes, we may be hauling our butts up those boulders ourselves."

143

The mere thought of bringing Webu back was nerve-wracking. The terrain was grueling without having to carry someone out. Putting Webu in a harness would be extremely dangerous for him if his thigh was mangled, but if that was the only alternative, they'd have to figure out how to accomplish it and give it their best effort.

"At least Ganigi is looking after Webu. He'll see to it he takes the pain pills and has adequate care," Sam said, still finagling the satellite antenna.

"They also left them with a sufficient supply of food, water, and ammo," Ted replied. "They'll be able to fend for themselves against predators."

As Sam continued trying to make contact, he asked Ted, "Do you know how to put together a travois?"

"You're asking *MacGyver*?" he chuckled, "give me a twig and a string, and I can make whatever you want."

Sam shook his head and smiled. He always appreciated Ted's good humor. "I'm going to keep trying to make contact, at least for the hour. If I can't, we'll have to head out of here. Why don't you see what you can put together to haul Webu back on?"

Ted turned and began searching out raw materials with which to build a travois. The jungle vines were strong, and he could use them as rope. He hesitated using the other ropes because they would need them to climb the sheer wall and whatever else they might encounter along the way.

Sam made another try on the radio when he felt something cold and hard against the back of his skull. Turning slowly, he came face to face with the steel barrel of a rifle. Without hesitation, he raised his arms high over his head, his heart picking up a beat.

"Get to your feet," growled the man behind the rifle.

Sam got to his feet. Out of the corner of his eye he saw another man walking behind Ted, a gun to his back. They were in a predicament, for sure. His mind reeled trying to figure out

144

what he could do to escape. Whatever they did, they'd have to be extremely careful if they were to outwit them.

Adrián and Javier had trailed the team from the start but had lagged a distance behind so they'd not be seen. At one point they had lost sight of them, though it didn't take too long to discover their whereabouts once they'd spotted smoke curling up off the river bank. Until now they hadn't realized the team had split up. But with all of the satellite equipment, the two men would know exactly where their friends were.

"Grab your packs and don't make any foolish moves, you hear," Javier said.

"What do you want?" asked Sam.

A cold smile tilted Adrián's lips. "Why we're going to take a little stroll through the jungle, and you're going to lead the way."

Sam noticed the man fit the description of the man who had ransacked Decker and Callie's suite in Trujillo. Sam was not sure what their plan was, but it was apparent they wanted to locate Decker and the team. So long as Sam and Ted didn't try any heroics, maybe they'd dodge getting shot. Their only salvation was that these two men needed Sam and Ted to guide them through the jungle.

Adrián dug through their belongings and withdrew their firearms and ammunition.

"You won't be needing these, will you?" A sinister laugh tumbled from Adrián's lips. He tucked one of the firearms into his waistband and tossed the other gun to Javier, who followed suit.

Adrián told them to take only what they needed because he knew the trek ahead of them was hard enough without added weight to drag along.

The day was sweltering. Sam wiped the sweat from his forehead as they slashed their way through the tangle of vines. In the distance, he could hear the rumbling of thunder. It seemed afternoon storms were commonplace during the rainy season.

145

Decker's team had taken the majority of the equipment, and though they had some, it was not the best scenario for venturing through a dense jungle. However, it was clear they'd have to make do with what they had.

As they reached the base of the vertical rock wall, it was clear they would have to use their harnesses, belay devices, and rope.

Analyzing the situation, Adrián insisted Sam be the first to go because he was the one who had the most adequate skills to accomplish their plans. Sam didn't argue and remained compliant. He knew if they could manage to keep themselves alive with some ingenuity, they might be able to help Decker and the team down the road.

Adrián held his gun to Ted's head and warned Sam not to do anything foolish, or he'd take pleasure in taking Ted out of the equation. Sam had no doubt he meant it. As it was, Ted didn't have as much value as Sam regarding experience. But they did need extra hands for the packs and equipment, and that seemed to be Ted's lot to bear for the time.

The second his foot met with the stone wall, the sky split open and surges of water cascaded over them. In an attempt to keep the equipment dry, they raced to cover everything with canvas tarps. Bursts of light flashed before them as lightning exploded, followed by ear shattering thunder. The whole ground shook beneath their feet. Water streamed down the vertical rock, forming pools at their feet. There was a loud explosion, followed by a tree toppling over, narrowly missing Sam. He dropped and rolled out of its way just in time. Another thunderous rumbling followed, and two more trees dislodged from the torrential rains smashing through the thicket feet away from where they stood.

They pressed their backs solidly against the rock trying to keep themselves out of the way of falling timbers. None of them had ever faced such fury as the storm continued to batter them. The wind was relentless, and they were forced to wait it out. After an hour of being ravaged by nature's fury, the rain stopped.

A dense vapor encircled them. The heat and humidity were like a sauna, and with it came swarms of flies, intent on invading their mouths, noses, and ears.

"I can see why people go mad in the jungle," Ted voiced, shaking his head to discourage the flies though it seemed a useless endeavor.

"We need to move on," Adrián insisted.

Sam looked down at his shoes that were pressed down into wet clay. The wall of rock would be difficult enough, but with mud packed on his shoes, it would be treacherous. "How do you expect me to climb?" Sam asked. "The rock is slick from the rain, and this curtain of mist is going to make it nearly impossible to see any rock protrusions to grab hold of."

"If you want your friend here to live," Adrián sneered, "then you'll find a way." Once more, he raised his gun threateningly to Ted's head.

"I'll do my best, but remember, you have to climb this cliff as well, and my guess is, you're not as apt to succeed as I am."

Adrián slapped the side of Sam's head with the barrel of his gun. Sam grunted as a sharp pain drove through his skull. A spatter of blood dribbled down his cheek. He gritted his teeth and rode out the pain, then turned to gather his climbing gear. He knew this would be a difficult climb under normal circumstances, but there was no other alternative. With little else he could do, he faced the wall, took a deep breath and began searching for his first rock lip to lift himself.

He found pockets for his fingers and pulled himself up a couple of feet. He made several attempts to gain a stable foothold, but the mud made it impossible. He dropped back down, removed his shoes and grabbed a pair of tennis shoes from his pack. They would not be the best to climb with, but certainly better than the other shoes. He stood on a tarp to prevent his tennis shoes from becoming packed with mud, then watched as the others changed into something different as well.

"Take your time buddy," Ted said.

It was a slow progression climbing the face, but Sam had overcome much more difficult obstacles and knew he would make it. How the others would fair he was not too sure, but he'd make every attempt to see them safely up for Ted's sake.

Once Sam pulled himself over the top, he had them send up the packs. He gave as much instruction as possible because the two men appeared to have never climbed before. Adrián made the first attempt at it. Several times his foot slipped on the surface and he'd drop a couple of feet. After several attempts, he caught on how to use the belay to keep from plummeting to his death. Once on top, he motioned for Javier. The process took nearly two hours.

Ted pulled himself up over the edge as the rain ruptured again. Streaks of lightning began to zigzag across the sky, and thunder shook the already saturated ground. They slogged through mud, exhausted. A lightning bolt slashed violently to the ground up ahead of them, a tree exploding into a ball of fire as if soaked with gasoline. The sound resonated like a sonic boom.

"We need to put up a canvas shelter," Sam told Adrián. "At least until the rain stops. We'll ruin all of the equipment and everything in the packs if we don't. Most of what we have is already wet."

Adrián was not one to listen to anyone, but in this matter, he accepted Sam's instruction, knowing Sam was experienced, whereas he was ignorant of the ins and outs of jungle expeditions. Shrugging with resignation, he motioned for Sam and Ted to assemble a shelter for them. Once they finished, the four of them sat beneath the confines of the tarp to wait out the storm. Gun barrels still fixed at Sam and Ted's head.

"What exactly do you want," Sam dared to ask.

"What's it your business?" Adrián snarled, his lip curled in a sneer.

"It's not my business. I was only wondering," Sam tried to make small talk, if for no other reason than to gain a little trust with the two men.

Adrián laughed shortly. "Wonder away, my friend," was his sarcastic response.

It was another hour of waiting before the storm passed. At this rate, it would take a week to catch up to Decker. As they took down the tarp, they shook it best they could to eliminate as much rainwater as possible, though it was fully soaked and it made the packs all the heavier to tote.

They moved in what seemed to be a snail's pace and had exhausted themselves from the physical challenges the jungle posed. Visibility was zero, and though Sam and Ted had their headlamps, Adrián and Javier did not. Therefore, they felt it would be too dangerous to continue. Adrián relented and told them to set up camp. The greatest concern for Sam and Ted was there were only rations for two people. At the rate they were traveling, there was the distinct possibility they'd run out of food before they caught up with the team.

"We need to ration the food and water," Sam told them and saw the look of dread on Ted's face. He understood all too well what Sam was implying.

"Then it will be you and your friend here who will start eating half rations." It was clear Adrián was not going to give up anything for them.

"That's right, if anyone is going to go hungry, it will be you first," Javier jumped in, trying to show some authority, lame as it was.

After dinner, Adrián said he would do the first watch. While bedding down, Ted and Sam's hands and feet were bound. Adrián did not want to take any chances of the two sneaking off in the night. He would keep his eye on them day and night. They were his ticket to a good life, and there was no way he would let them out of his sight.

149

The next morning, they skipped breakfast and began their trek once more. They came to a stream that was a raging torrent after the storm. Sam felt he should try to cross over first with a rope and affix it to one of the trees on the opposite side so the rest of them would have something to guide them across. He had them hold fast to the rope and ease it out as he struggled against the fast-moving water. He was swept downstream a short distance until the slack was taken and began working his way across hand over hand.

When he made it to the other side, he crawled up the muddy bank and attached the rope, then motioned for the others to tie off their end and cross over.

Clothes soiled, his brown hair matted with mud, Sam felt weighed down. His body ached beyond measure, but he knew he had to push forward.

"Hold tight, the current is very strong, and the rocks are slick!" Sam called out.

Javier went next, his feet sliding out from underneath him, though he managed to hold his grip. He battled across and was relieved when he managed to access the top of the slippery incline.

While the other two pulled themselves along the rope to the other side, Sam and Javier spent time pulling off leeches. If that wasn't bad enough, ticks were everywhere on their clothing. It took another twenty minutes to shake out their clothing and check their scalps for any that might be burrowing into their heads. The men were exhausted by the time they got to the top of the rise; their clothes packed in mud.

Each step felt hindered, lessening after some of the packed mud began to break up. It was near sundown when they spied one of the tents from their team. Cautiously entering the camp, Adrián and Javier had their guns drawn in case they were walking into a trap of some kind.

"Hello," Sam called out, but there came no answer. He called out a second time. Still, no answer.

Once in the camp, they all stood in startled silence at the remains of a man. It was apparent animals had been feasting on the body, and the humidity and heat had worked like acid on his flesh.

Sam closed his eyes and took a deep breath. By the clothes and the tent, he came to the gut-wrenching realization the body was probably Webu's. He was perplexed. Sam was told Ganigi had remained with Webu to watch over him. He had to wonder if Ganigi had been drug off by a wild animal. Nothing else made sense.

"I'm bewildered," Ted said.

"You and me, both," Sam replied.

Adrián turned the body over, wrinkling up his nose from the smell. "Phew, looks to me like someone shot him in the face."

"What!" Sam burst out.

"Must have become a burden," Adrián said without so much of a twinge of remorse.

"The team would never—" Sam started to reply, but his words were cut off mid-sentence.

Adrián laughed. "You're fools. You didn't even suspect one of your guides works with us."

Sam and Ted stood in stunned silence. They had spent days with Ganigi and had suspected nothing. It was reasonable to assume Ganigi had gone back in search of Decker and the team after killing Webu. Unfortunately, they had no way of warning Decker and the others.

"Nothing more to do here," said Javier. "Let's go." He pushed Ted forward toward the narrow trail Decker's team had cut out.

Sam began feeling a bit light headed and dropped down onto a stump. Sweat ran down his forehead, cheeks and off his chin. "I need more water," he groaned, beginning to see signs of dehydration.

Reluctantly, Adrián pulled out the water container and gave him a large drink. "You better not be pulling my leg," he grunted.

"If I don't make it, you won't either, you fool," Sam lashed back. Sam felt the sting of a rifle butt against his cheek from Javier's own hand. He tumbled backward, his head spinning.

Angrily, Adrián grabbed Javier's shirt and drew him an inch of his face. "You wait for my orders before you do anything," he warned him. "He's right. If you kill him, we'll never make it out here. He's the only one who knows the path Manuel is taking!"

There was venom in Javier's eyes. "S…sorry," he mumbled under his breath, feeling like a school child being scolded by his mother.

"Get up!" he yelled at Sam.

Pushing himself to his feet, Sam dusted himself off. A trickle of blood dripped down his cheek. His head was pounding from the blow, and he prayed under his breath he'd be able to continue in the suffocating heat. It had been hot, but with the thunderstorms, the humidity had become unbearable, as was the sickening horde of flies following them after the storm.

He gathered what strength he had left and began to trudge on behind Ted who was given the machete to clear more brambles and vines from their way. The two men seemed quite content to let them do all the work and did not seem to care whether it made them sick or not. They didn't even seem to understand the concept of dehydration.

Sam thought if he could make it until they made camp later on and could use some rest and more water in him, he'd be able to go on. He was staggering, his breath growing more labored. He could hear words of encouragement coming from Ted in an effort to help Sam ride the nightmare through. "You can do it, Sam," he said. "Keep walking, it won't be much longer."

Mercifully, Adrián stopped the forced march and had them set up camp. As they spread out their bedroll, Sam dropped on top of it, welcoming the rest that followed. Adrián apparently was growing concerned for him, not because he cared for Sam, but he didn't want to be abandoned in the jungle. He was not a fool. Adrián had heard all of the stories of people found dead in the rivers, men who went in but never came out. Sam was their only chance of surviving this godforsaken, wretched land. It was with that understanding, Adrián made sure Sam got a hearty meal and water to replenish him.

Several times the satellite phone chimed, but Sam and Ted weren't allowed to use it. Adrián didn't want any communication between them for fear Sam would say something to tip Decker off, and the expedition would be shut down. He was not going to let that happen after everything they had gone through so far.

"How are you doing Ted?" Sam inquired, trying to find a comfortable position to lie with his hands tied.

"Me?" You're the one that got slammed. How are you?"

"I'll live. And Ted, thank you for prompting me to continue. There was a fleeting moment when I thought it would be easier to give in to the elements. You kept me going, buddy."

"Glad you changed your mind, Sam. I wonder how Decker and the team are doing?"

"Better than we are, I imagine" Sam concluded. "I'd say Ganigi is probably still following hard after them. However, being alone will make it increasingly difficult for him to catch up. I'm not sure if Ganigi can make it on his own for very long."

"After watching him, I think he does have some experience leading people through the jungle. He appeared to be quite familiar with his surroundings, unlike these two buffoons."

"They might be buffoons," Sam agreed, "But they are dangerous buffoons. I'm taking them quite seriously."

In the morning when Sam woke, his one eye was swollen shut, and though he did not have a mirror, he wagered both eyes were black and blue. He still had a bit of a headache, but he wasn't sure whether it was due to dehydration or a rifle butt to

153

the face. Every muscle in his body rebelled. He had gone on many expeditions, but he had to admit, this one beat them all.

Once more, Sam and Ted were forced to watch the other two men eat breakfast, and they were denied. In the back of Sam and Ted's minds, they had to wonder if they'd make it through another day. Deprivation of food and water in combination with the oppressive heat was taking its toll on them. If only they could hold out until they met up with Decker's team...

Chapter 20

"I've been trying to contact Sam and Ted, and it's futile," Decker said.

"What about the *Jade*?" asked Callie.

Decker shrugged, "Not as yet. It sounded like someone had picked up on my last call, but for whatever reason, it wouldn't connect."

Callie could see lines of concern etched on her husband's face. "Any ideas about what might be wrong?"

"I suppose there could be some atmospheric change, but it's unlikely," Decker tried to explain. "Could be the canopy is so dense it's shielding us from satellite reception. That does occur on occasion, and there is the possibility of equipment failure since I can't connect with Sam or the *Jade*."

"How close are we to Leonard's find?"

He pulled out the maps and looked them over for a time. "Close. I can only assume Leonard's calculations are spot on."

"I'm thinking we should make a greater effort to push through," Callie said, laying her hand on his shoulder. "There's nothing we can do about bad reception right now."

"You're probably right. We need to find whatever Leonard stumbled onto and then head back and see what's going on with the rest of the crew."

They ate their breakfast, packed up their gear, and prepared to head out. They were all worn to the bone. The jungle had inflicted war on them for daring to enter, but they had shown themselves strong. They had confronted the extreme conditions it offered, and they were confident they would finish well.

Heading toward their final goal, they found the brush near impossible to penetrate. They rotated who would use the machete to hack out their trail. It was slow going forward, but they were determined.

After a couple of hours, they heard a low rumbling. When they broke through the wall of twisted bramble, they found themselves in a clearing, and beyond was a waterfall surrounded by large boulders. Overhead was the steady movement of monkeys that had been following them for quite some time, making a racket as they swung across the branches.

Callie looked at Decker with a look that said, "*Let's jump in.*" The water was too inviting to pass up. Callie was kicking off her shoes and removing her socks ready to dive in.

"There aren't piranhas in here, are there?" She raised an eyebrow in a questioning manner.

"No piranhas here," Manuel assured her. "However, do not urinate in the water. There's probably toothpick fish in this area, and unfortunately, if someone urinates, the fish will swim up their female or male parts and latch itself onto them. If that should happen, they must be surgically removed."

"Gads, really?" she replied with disgust.

"Better to warn you."

Callie looked at Decker a bit hesitantly, rethinking her idea. However, it was hot, and the water was so inviting, she could not help herself. Throwing caution aside, she dove into the water. When her head popped back up through the clear water, there was a wide smile on her lips.

"This is amazing, come on Decker and Carson. You, too Manuel." She flipped over onto her back and lazily began to backstroke. This was the best part of the whole jungle, she surmised. She wanted to relax there for hours; the water was so refreshing. She had spent too many days in the scorching heat and welcomed the cool liquid washing away the build-up of sweat and dirt.

Soon after discarding footwear, the others jumped in as well. Decker swam out to where Callie was and playfully dunked her head beneath the water. When he released her, she sliced at the water with the palm of her hand spraying him full in the face. They laughed and continued to play and simply enjoy their time.

Decker swam towards the waterfall and saw what appeared to be a large recess behind it. It was possible the water had eaten away at the rock over the centuries, but the longer he eyed it, the more curious he was to find out if it was a cave.

Many pre-Columbian cities had underground tunnels constructed as a means of escape. There was also evidence to support that some caves were connections to water sources, and he didn't rule out, that if it was a cave, it might be an ancient burial ground. The adventurer in him considered the prospects of exploring the cave to find out whether it led anywhere or not. He knew they were narrowing the gap to their final destination, and with luck, the cave might be a back door to the ruins.

Decker made his way to the backside of the falls when he saw ripples of water to his right. On closer inspection, he saw a brownish-gray figure moving rapidly in his direction. His heart sped up realizing it was an anaconda slithering through the water. "Snake!" he yelled, and the others started to scramble toward the bank.

Decker began to fiercely beat his arms against the water in an attempt to escape. Too far from the shore, he instinctively knew he couldn't out swim the lithe, deadly reptile. Though he couldn't see it, he sensed it was going to overtake him at any moment. He kicked his feet still harder, desperate to distance himself, but he was no match for the incredible power the snake possessed. In a heart-stopping moment, the anaconda began to overwhelm him.

He twisted backward to face his attacker, his heart hammering in his chest. He reached out with both hands to grab the snake's head. The brute force and agility of the anaconda made it impossible to repel its aggressive attack. They thrashed in the water, twisting, writhing, and battling. At the same time, Decker used his strength to hold back the triangular head, and found himself staring fearfully into black, evil-looking eyes.

The snake began to coil around him pulling him downward under the water. As it did, Decker felt the pressure restricting his breath. He slipped his right hand to his belt in a frenzied search for his tactical knife. The compression on his body was increasing, and he was having a hard time maneuvering. There was a flicker of hope as his fingers curled around the handle. He fumbled blindly, tempting to wrestle it from its sheath, but the snake's body coiling around him was diminishing his movement.

No matter how hard he resisted, he knew he was losing the battle. He felt his body being dragged to the bottom of the pool. His lungs burned from the lack of air, and he felt himself losing consciousness. A veil of darkness shrouded him. Frantic, he realized he'd have to catch a breath in short order, or he'd be feeding the anaconda his dinner for the day. With what little strength he had left, he sliced through the underbelly of the anaconda, though it was not enough to free him. Blood poured from its side, but it held fast. No longer able to fight, Decker surrendered to the blackness.

Callie could no longer remain passive on the sidelines. Adrenalin surged through her, and she dove in after him, Carson at her heels. Her heart was racing as her arms wildly slashed at the water. Her mind swirled with raw emotion.

Carson had his knife already out, holding it between his teeth and prepared for the battle. Both he and Callie simultaneously dove beneath the surface where the water was boiling with activity. Without thought to their own lives, they grabbed hold of the snake's head, wildly trying to free Decker. The anaconda held its prey in a stranglehold not willing to relent.

Carson came to the quick realization he was not going to free Decker with his bare hands. He grasped the knife from his mouth and thrust it deep into the throat of the anaconda, then again into the snake's belly. Blood began to seep out of the snake, and its body began to relax its hold on Decker. Decker's body slowly spiraled downward. Panic-stricken, Callie caught his arm, dragging him to the shore.

"Decker!" she cried out, feeling for a pulse, but felt none.

Callie had taken a course in CPR the year before. She listened for his breath; there was none. She locked her hands below his ribs and began pumping his chest. She repeated the procedure, but Decker was not responding. Callie screamed out his name in terror as she continued pumping on his chest frantically, then administered mouth to mouth. Callie began to sob uncontrollably. The terrifying thought of life without Decker began to invade her mind, when suddenly Decker's body jerked upward, water bubbling out of the corner of his mouth. She put her ear next to his lips and heard faint breathing.

"Looks like he might be going into shock," Carson sputtered, tossing a blanket over him.

They all sat in stunned silence. One moment they were splashing around laughing, the next Decker lay dying on the rocky shore. They couldn't believe how quickly circumstances could change. They continued to watch, waiting to see if Decker would regain consciousness. It seemed like hours even though it was mere minutes before they saw his eyelids flutter. He blinked several times before his eyes remained open.

"Thank God," she breathed and kissed his cheek several times. "Don't you do that again, you nearly scared me to death!"

"You're scolding me?" he said weakly but managed a short laugh. "Tell that to the snake."

"You mean this guy?" Manuel said, holding the ten-foot anaconda. "Dinner."

Callie wrinkled up her nose. "Have at it, Manuel. I've had my share of snakes for a lifetime."

Decker laid there for quite some time before he attempted to sit up. He shifted his body to stretch his muscles that were bruised and aching. His head swirled dizzily, so he opted to stay off of his feet until he could regain his strength. "I guess I should be grateful I didn't have to urinate as he was squeezing me!" He chuckled and winced at the same time, remembering the story of the toothpick fish. Though he made light of it, he still could not drive out the raw emotions churning inside.

Callie slapped his arm gently. "You're not funny, Decker."

"Sort of."

Callie simply shook her head, amusement flashing in her eyes.

Manuel was good to his word. He had built a small campfire near the pool of water and was roasting the snake over the coals. It was clear he did not have an issue eating snake meat. They watched as Manuel pulled off some chunks of meat and popped it into his mouth. He saw them staring at him.

"What?" he grinned. "Snake is delicious."

"Not me," Carson replied. He pulled some protein bars out of the pack for the rest of them so they could regain some energy before moving on.

They spent several hours relaxing by the water, mostly because they wanted to make sure Decker had recovered fully before they continued on. Except for some bruised ribs, he seemed to have bounced back.

***

Later that day they heard Carson suck in his air sharply. Their heads turned his direction and saw Carson looking at a band of

160

tribal Indians brandishing spears, their sharp blades pointed threateningly at them. Slowly, with hands raised in surrender, they moved to their feet. They could not help but see the intense, black eyes staring at them accusingly as if to say, "*Why are you trespassing on our land?*"

"Could this day get any worse?" Decker muttered under his breath. He glanced over at Manuel to see what his reaction was. After all, he lived in this environment and would surely know what their intentions were. Surprisingly, he couldn't read Manuel's facial expression. Worse, Manuel wasn't making any effort to talk to them. It was a bad omen to see his hands also in the air.

One of the Indians stepped forward, pointing his spear at Decker's gun. No need to say more; Decker understood that clearly. He slipped his gun from its holster and laid it on the ground before the native whose face had thin, blue and red lines painted on it.

Decker motioned for the others to lay down their weapons as well, his mind trying to outthink the situation. Decker looked once more to Manuel. "What now?"

He shrugged. "Do what they say."

"Can't you reason with them?"

"I don't know their language," he replied, his face scrunched up in a somewhat apologetic twist.

"Well, that's dandy."

The natives pushed them into single file and began wrapping their wrists with leather straps, then nudged them forward down a small trail west of where they were. After a short distance, they were led into a small village with thatched roof houses built on stilts. No doubt to protect them from the heavy rains that brought flooding with them. Little children ran along side of them with wide, curious eyes. The boys were dressed in only loincloths strapped around their hips. Several of the older girls wore what looked like woven grass halter tops and skirts to cover them.

The men bound them to trees. Decker thought Manuel might be able to read their body language even if he was unable to interpret what they were saying. But it was growing obvious the natives were extremely agitated that they were on their land.

One of the natives leaned down running his fingers through Callie's golden hair and said some words. Whatever he said, the rest of the natives let loose a bout of laughter, and all of them turned to stare at Callie.

Decker struggled with the cords trying to free himself. He would die trying to protect Callie. He saw her fear-ridden eyes widen. One of the natives saw Decker resisting the straps securing him, and with the club in his hand, struck him on the head. A stream of blood trickled down his forehead, dripping onto his tan, cotton shirt. Decker swayed unsteadily. He had only moments ago survived drowning, and now he had to deal with their barbarism. His head spun, and nausea overwhelmed him.

He fought to maintain consciousness but was unable to hold on. He tumbled into a black vortex.

"Decker!" Callie gasped.

Another native walked toward them with a staff in his hand. His face was painted black around his eyes, looking like a superhero character mask. He walked up and down looking at them as if trying to decide their fate. He mumbled some words to the other men, and they all turned and walked away.

"Decker," Callie said again, "Can you hear me?"

Decker moaned as he regained consciousness. Blood was dried on the side of his head and had caked in his ear. There was a large knot where his flesh had split open. "I hear you, Callie. Are you okay?"

She nodded. "Do you have a knife in your pocket, Decker?"

"I do," Carson said. "I'll see if I can snag it." Carson wriggled back and forth, trying to slip his fingers in his back pocket but couldn't quite seem to grasp the handle. He cursed under his breath.

"I have one in my boot," Manuel said. "Maybe if I try and scoot my body around this pole, I could get my feet near your hands Carson, and you can fish it out."

They looked to see if anyone was watching them. When they didn't see anyone, Manuel began to snake his body in a fashion that brought him to the back side of the pole. He pushed his feet forward trying to reach Carson's bound hands. He grunted and kept stretching as if he could will his legs to grow longer but was still short of reaching Carson.

"What do you think they are going to do with us?" Callie asked Manuel.

"Don't know. I'm not familiar with this tribe. "I thought I knew all the different natives that lived here, but I've not pushed this far back. Most of the people I know fear to venture this deep into the jungle. They believe it's an ancient burial ground and if anyone dares to trespass, he or she will not make it out alive."

"I'm beginning to believe it myself," grumbled Carson, shifting uncomfortably.

"Keep working the leather ties and pray they'll stretch. One of us needs to break free," Decker pointed out. "Or who knows what might happen to us."

"You don't think they will eat us, do you?" Callie asked with her face pinched up.

Decker rolled his head to look at her. "If that's the case, you won't have to worry about it; there's not enough meat on your bones to satisfy them."

"Ha! Really?" She rolled her eyes.

"What if we offer them something, like a compass or a lighter?" Carson picked through his mind trying to think of something that might save their hide.

"That would mean we'd have to get into our pockets," Decker reminded him, a bit of sarcasm in his voice.

They all grew quiet trying to figure something out, all the while twisting their hands in an attempt to loosen the ties. They spotted a woman coming near them with a jug. Her face was tattooed with tribal designs in black. She wore a grass skirt, grass halter, and around her neck was a necklace of what looked to be bone and teeth. She held a dried gourd and tipped it forward to Callie first. Callie was thankful the woman was going to give them water. At the moment Callie was parched from the heat and wanted nothing more than to quench her thirst. Even though she knew the water could make her extremely ill because of the high bacteria and parasites, dehydration was the greater concern, and so she opted to take a large swallow.

"Thank you," she muttered with a wry smile, even though they couldn't understand her.

After she'd gone, Callie said, "I can't imagine her caring for us if they plan on killing us. They can't keep us tied forever, so it's possible they're trying to figure out why we're here and if we intend any harm?"

"I'm sure that makes perfect sense, Callie," Decker agreed. "However, since they can't talk to us, I don't know how we can let them know we have no intentions of hurting them."

Things were looking rather bleak at the moment. They had lost all communication with Sam, Ted, and the *Jade*, and they were still a couple of days from locating their target. Now they were tied to a pole, forced to wait out their uncertain future.

Callie was still praying they wouldn't be on the dinner menu for the evening.

Chapter 21

The small round table was set with white linen. A single rose stood tall in a glass decanter at the center. Soft music drifted through the warm night air, flowing in from the *Jade's* intercom. Garrett looked dashing in his black slacks and white, starched, short-sleeved shirt. He sported a royal blue tie with diagonal white stripes.

He rose to his feet when Holly came out of the stairwell and walked gracefully toward him. She had a wide smile on her lips. Wearing a baby blue chiffon dress that met at her knees and a silk sash cinched at the waist, she made an elegant picture. Her dark hair was piled on top of her head except for two ringlets that brushed past her ears.

"Madame, you look stunning," Garrett exhaled and pulled her chair out for her.

"You look quite handsome yourself, Garrett Hayden."

He took a seat, and at the same time, Phil walked out with a bottle of Piper-Heidsieck 2006 Vintage Brut Champagne. There was a loud pop as he uncorked the bottle, bubbles oozing out of the small neck. He poured the honey colored Champagne into crystal wine goblets, the bubbles sizzling against the glass.

"Thank you, Phil, this is lovely," Garrett complimented.

"You have outdone yourself, Garrett," Holly said.

She had been taken aback when she was in her cabin, and Phil had brought in a gold embossed envelope. When she opened it, she found an invitation for dinner aboard the *Jade*. He held a box in his arms which he handed off to her. When she removed the lid, her jaw went slack. Her eyes lit on a beautiful gown tucked inside along with blue satin heels.

Garrett had wanted to see a sparkle in Holly's eyes. She had been through so much these past weeks. He had rifled through a couple of clothing items to find the appropriate sizes and then called a seamstress in Trujillo who was recommended to him on the phone. He asked the seamstress if she could design a dress that would suit Holly's height and approximate weight. The seamstress had done exceedingly more than anything he could have imagined. Holly looked beautiful.

"I don't know what to say. Thank you, of course. What's the occasion?" She inquired, a wide smile tipping her lips.

"No occasion," he said. "But we've been on this boat for days, and I thought it would be nice to relax and pretend everything is perfectly normal."

She smiled warmly and knew what he meant. She had been downhearted for a while. "This is a welcome change, I must admit. I was going a bit stir-crazy." She sipped gingerly on the edge of her glass, the subtle taste of dried apricots and blackberries lingered on her tongue. "This champagne is superb."

"So glad you like it," he admitted. He had looked over several bottles stowed in the galley for special occasions. This champagne particularly was one of his favorites, and he was happy she enjoyed it as much as he did.

A perfect evening with a perfect woman, Garrett summed up. His feelings had deepened for her over the weeks. Of course, having just lost Leonard, he would never impose his feelings on her, though he was optimistic her feelings for him would come naturally over time.

Once more, Phil strolled out with an oval platter heaped with a colorfully displayed salad. The salad was an assortment of blood orange slices, grapefruit slices, avocado and red onion with a fragrant orange-olive oil dressing. Phil pushed his

166

gourmet talents to near perfection. They both thanked him as he turned to leave.

Looking up with tears sparkling in her dark eyes, she said, "I so appreciate this, Garrett. I've not felt this good since before Leonard's death. So much has happened I scarce had time even to mourn his leaving me." She reached over to touch his hand. "The dress, the food, and champagne, all of this is so very special. You're an amazing man, and I wouldn't have made it without you, Decker and Callie."

"My pleasure," he returned, feeling emotions stir in him. "I'm thankful we were able to help you in such a tumultuous season in your life."

They had barely taken a bite of the salad before they heard the padding of feet again, and glancing over their shoulder they saw Phil approaching with the next course. Striped bass with baby red potatoes, sprinkled with parsley and parmesan cheese, and a side dish of string beans drizzled with a lemon dressing, all of which were Garrett's favorites.

They lingered over their food and talked about their lives and their heart for the future. How easy the words flowed as they sat beneath a full moon. It shimmered like thousands of lit candles over the gentle swells of the bay. The sky was brushed elegantly with a velvety canopy of stars, and it was difficult for both of them not to allow the romantic backdrop to play on their emotions.

"Dance?" Garrett asked, taking to his feet and holding his hand out to her.

Holly felt like a schoolgirl again at her first dance. She took his fingers in her small, fragile hand, and felt his arm slip around her slender waist. They moved fluidly across the deck to the soft music pulsing through the intercom and embraced the sweetness of the moment. For a brief time, they found solace in each other's arms. Somehow, with everything going on around them, they managed to shut out the world.

167

They walked hand in hand to the boat's railing and breathed in the salty bay air. "Do you think Decker and Callie will find Leonard's lost city?"

Garrett smiled. "If it's there, I believe they will." Garrett never underestimate his son's cunning and ability—that went for Callie as well.

"What do you think is wrong with the satellite communications?" she asked, knowing they had been shut down all day.

"Wish I knew," he answered. He had been concerned, but there was nothing they could do presently. If many more days passed without hearing from either Decker or Sam, Garrett wondered if he should put another team together and go in after them.

As if reading his mind, Holly shook her head. "Don't even think it. Trying to put another team together would be insanity. More than half the crew are already gone. If you don't hear something soon, then the authorities should be brought in."

"You're right. Better to wait it out a couple more days then call a meeting between the rest of the crew," Garrett told her.

"You know best," she reasoned. After all, Garrett had been on several of these expeditions with them and knew how they worked better than she did.

Chapter 22

They all realized being tied to stakes through the night would make them vulnerable to wild animals; prey to some of the most aggressive hunters, like the jaguar. Surely the natives were aware of that fact. The team wondered if the natives might show a little mercy and see fit to place a guard close by to ward off any danger.

Turning his head, Decker gazed at Callie whose head was dropped back and her eyes closed. "Praying?" he asked.

Her lips twisted into a smile and she rolled her head to the side. "That would be the most practical thing to do right now, wouldn't it? Wondering how we'll dodge the bullet this time?"

"We've made it this far, haven't we? Look at what we've overcome already. This dance can't be over yet."

"I love your positive outlook," she said. Her face pinched up.

"What's the matter?"

"My shoulder is aching terribly," she admitted. The stress on her arms from being drawn back behind her was pulling on her stitches.

"Sorry, Callie."

"How's your head?" she asked, seeing his hair was matted with dried blood.

"I'll live."

Callie sighed and closed her eyes again. She had battled with the bindings but had gotten nowhere. She wondered how long they would leave them tied up, unable to move or even go to the quaint, vine bathroom if they needed to. If only Manuel had been able to communicate with the natives, she pondered. But that was not the case, and here they were, helpless and exposed to the wilds.

The snapping of branches to their left drew their attention. Vaguely, they could make out the silhouette of four figures coming toward them. Now within feet of them, they were puzzled to see a young, blonde haired woman who wore a single braid down her back. At her side was a man in his early twenties with dark hair and a well-trimmed beard. Following behind were two natives.

They were laughing as they entered the small village, and then stopped short when they saw the four of them bound to posts. The girl rushed over to them, her mouth gaped. "What's going on here?"

Decker was stunned. "That is the question of the day, isn't it?" he replied dryly. "We were ambushed, bound, and brought here. Since none of us can translate their language, we're in a bit of a predicament. And who the devil are you?"

"My name's Alice Peterson, and this is my assistant, Joseph Baker," she introduced. She undoubtedly looked as perplexed by the situation as Decker did. Whatever the case, she was determined to figure out what was going on. She turned her attention to one of the native men standing beside her and began to speak to him in his dialect. The native nodded, then turned quickly and sped off.

She put her attention back on Decker and asked, "Who are you?"

"Name's Decker Hayden. My wife, Callie," he replied, "My assistant, Carson Perry, and our guide, Manuel Rodriguez."

"What on earth are you doing here?" she quizzed, still perplexed by the situation.

"We're archaeologists," he told her. "We're trying to locate a lost city that was discovered by a friend of ours who was murdered here in the jungle."

"I don't understand why people keep pushing their way into the jungle and disrupt the lives of those who live here." She sounded disgruntled.

So, the little tart was going to lecture them while they were helplessly tied to posts! Decker's mind reeled. He felt anger boiling beneath the surface and fought for calm.

"We have no intention of disrupting the natives here. We were minding our own business. For your information, we're not treasure hunters. Anything we discover will be turned over to the proper authorities so looters don't come. We respect and honor the lives of those who live here."

Alice noted the sharpness in his voice. "Sorry," she apologized, "I've seen so many villages affected by the drug lords prowling these areas, loggers who are decimating the land by burning thousands of acres of rainforest timber, and poachers who are stripping the land of food sources…it's…"

Decker cut her short. "I understand. However, that's not our objective. We believe in the preservation of cultural distinctions, and we have no intention of disrupting anything."

She believed him. Still, she wondered why they were taken prisoners if they hadn't done anything wrong. At that moment, a few of the native men walked back to where they were tied up. They began discussing the situation between themselves. Alice translated what Decker had told her.

One of the natives stepped forward and stooped low to touch the crocodile tooth necklace that had been given to Decker. He looked deeply into Decker's eyes and then sputtered something to Alice.

"He wants to know where you got the necklace," she said. "He says it has protective powers."

"I received it as a parting gift from one of the natives along the Rio Plátano. He said it would bring me good luck," explained Decker.

She smiled. "Well, he was right, because if I wasn't here to translate, you might all have been killed." She turned her attention back to the native who stood patiently to hear what Decker had communicated back to her.

Once Alice offered a plausible explanation as to why they were there, one of the natives walked behind them and one by one he began cutting the cords holding their hands. Whatever Alice told the natives seemed to satisfy them.

Decker and the others struggled to their feet and looked at Alice. They were wondering what would happen to them now. The whole ordeal was surreal.

"Come on," she motioned with her hand. "Let's go sit near the fire, and we'll talk."

There were some logs situated around the blazing fire pit where they all sat down. Everyone's eyes were still locked onto Alice. The day had been quite an ordeal for them, and they were anxious to hear what she had to say.

"The natives saw you carried guns and they didn't know what your intentions were. You can understand that," she told them. "Because you were unable to communicate with them, they decided to tie you up until we got back to find out if you were here to harm them. Guns don't usually convey that you're friendly."

"So, why are you here?" Callie inquired, rubbing her arm which was still quite sore.

"I'm from the World Health Organization," she told them. "We come in and vaccinate the children and see how the Indians are holding up. With people coming and going, they bring diseases. They can cause sicknesses that could wipe out an entire village. It's important we come and make sure the tribes don't become obsolete."

172

"That's wonderful," Callie said. "I'm also thankful you can speak their language. I was wondering if we were ever going to be freed, or if they intended on eating us for dinner."

"I guess this is a lucky day for you," Alice agreed with a chuckle.

Decker turned to Callie. "Let me look at your arm," he said, rolling up her sleeve. The stitches were intact, but there was some swelling and a touch of redness. He looked around to see if his medical bag was visible, and spying a heaped pile of their rucksacks off near one of the huts, he asked, "Is it all right if I go grab my bag for some medical supplies?"

"Are you a doctor?"

"Not of late, but I was in the army and have stitched up my share of people." He pushed himself to his feet and dusted off his pants.

"Here, I'll go with you just in case," she offered.

Callie looked over at Carson. "How are you?"

"Tired," he told her. "And hungry."

No sooner had he spoken than a couple of women walked over to them with large wooden bowls. They set the bowls down in front of them. One of the bowls had meat of some kind, possibly wild boar, wrapped in banana leaves. The other bowl was acai berries and chayote, a vegetable cultivated by the Mayans, heavily spiced with hot peppers. The food looked delicious, especially since they were ravenous.

Alice and Decker returned with the medical kit and Decker proceeded to swab antibiotic cream on Callie's wound. He pulled out fresh gauze, tape, and scissors and bandaged the stitched lesion. "I wonder if I should give you a shot of antibiotics?"

"You worry too much, Decker, but I think I'll be fine. Thank you for your concern."

Joseph fixed himself a plate of food and sat cross-legged beside them. "I was told one of you did the tango with an anaconda?"

173

"That would be Decker," Carson said, remembering the whole nightmarish scene.

"I imagine that was a bit overwhelming." Joseph inhaled sharply. "We've been lucky so far, though we did see a couple coral snakes, and a caiman. The worst we have encountered is the tornadoes of mosquitoes and those atrocious biting flies. I could go the rest of my life without those aggravating creatures."

"Can't argue that," Decker agreed with a chuckle. "The flies are vicious, especially after the rain. It was a skill to ward them off. We swatted at them with such vigor we started calling it the 'Honduras salute."

Joseph laughed boisterously and slapped his thigh. "Good one!"

Out of the corner of her eye, Callie saw Carson sweating profusely. He looked quite ill. She nudged Decker's arm and motioned to him. It was reasonable to assume Carson could have drunk contaminated water or ate spoiled food—maybe a mosquito carrying Malaria?

Decker scooted over beside him, his doctor instincts taking over. "What's going on, buddy?"

"Darned if I know. Feeling ill," Carson told him, his body trembling with chills. His face was ashen and had droplets of sweat dotting his brow.

"Stomach?"

He nodded. "Afraid so. And a bad headache."

Decker looked over at Alice. "Is there a place where he could sleep and where we can watch over him?"

Alice rose to her feet and left them for a time. When she returned, there was another woman at her side. The native woman motioned for them to follow her and took them to a split bamboo hut with a thatched roof. The shack was built on pilings, no doubt to keep it from being destroyed during the rainy seasons which usually brought intense flooding to the jungle area and it was also a safeguard against snakes.

Inside were a couple of woven floor mats made from reeds, most likely from the marshlands down river. Decker helped Carson onto one of the makeshift beds in the far corner and resolved that he and Callie would stay with him through the night to monitor his fever. If it was malaria, Carson would have a battle ahead of him. It was a serious disease that had taken many lives.

Through the night, Carson tossed and turned, his temperature at one hundred and three. His clothing was soaked through. He vomited several times and welcomed the cool rags Callie draped across his forehead. She also placed a wooden bowl beside the bed for him to use in case he threw up again.

Decker gave him Ciprofloxacin, a potent antibiotic, and Ibuprofen to hold the fever at bay. He checked Carson's heart to make sure it was not beating rapidly, and for mental confusion. Both were a sign of Malaria. He was thankful Carson didn't show signs of either. Most likely, it would be parasitical and would be more easily eradicated with medication.

However, if he didn't improve in the next two days, Decker would be forced to leave him in the care of the World Health Organization. Alice and Joseph would be able to reach help for him via helicopter. Alice had told Decker there was a clearing a quarter of a mile from where they were, where a helicopter could land safely. It was how Alice and Joseph had made their way into the jungle the week before.

When all was said and done, Decker wondered if he should have taken the path of least resistance and had them fly in as well, then go the rest of the way by foot. It certainly would have saved them several mishaps. Then again, he wanted to trace Leonard's exact footsteps and make any adjustments to the coordinates if there were any to make.

It would grieve Decker to leave Carson behind. They had gone on so many archaeological digs as a team, and it would not seem the same without him. He depended on his knowledge and cunning. Carson had many life experiences to draw from, much more than either he or Callie. Besides, he was his "right-hand man" and his dearest friend.

He did not know when, but at some point in the night, Decker could no longer keep his eyes open and fell asleep. When he woke, he found Callie snuggled in his arms. Slender fingers of golden light filtered through the bamboo walls and fanned out across the floor. To Decker's delight, Carson was sitting upright, his legs crossed, and a cup in his hand.

"Well, hello sunshine," Decker chuckled. It appeared Carson had conquered whatever ailment he had. His fever had broken, and there was a healthy flush to his cheeks again.

"One of the native women came this morning and gave me something to drink," Carson told Decker and held up his cup. "Tasted like dung. I have to admit, it took every ounce of my strength to swallow it and wondered if it was going to stay down."

"I dozed off sometime in the night," Decker said. "I didn't hear anyone come in."

"Well, whatever she gave me appeared to have healed me. Jungle medicine. Can't beat it."

"Couldn't be the antibiotics I gave you last night?" Decker reminded him with a raised brow.

"Feeling insecure, Dr. Hayden?" he laughed. "No really, I appreciate all you did for me. You too, Callie,"

Callie had stirred when she heard their voices. She yawned widely and stretched her arms over her head. "I'm glad you're feeling better. I know it would have killed Decker to leave you behind."

"There's no way I'd let you go without me," Carson said. "Even if I had to crawl like a baby."

Decker grinned, his turquoise eyes flashing with humor. "I'd drink up some more of that dung tea then. You were pretty sick."

It was unanimous. They'd stay another day to make sure Carson was feeling up to moving on. Decker tried several more times to make contact on his sat phone, but again, Sam and Ted didn't pick up. The longer communications were severed, the more concerned he became. This was an unusual predicament, one that had only happened once before.

No luck with Sam, Decker tried the *Jade* one more time and with great relief, Garrett picked up. "I was ready to send out an army," Garrett sighed with a great sense of relief. "We've had a streak of static here, and I haven't been able to connect. Still not able to reach Sam."

"Yeah, that's a worry for me too, Dad," Decker said. "We're all okay. Carson was sick overnight but is looking much better this morning. We were forced to leave Webu and Ganigi behind. Webu was attacked by a wild boar—put a cannon size hole in his leg. He was in pretty bad shape when we left. I'm trusting Sam and Ted got him the medical attention he needed."

"Sorry to hear that, son."

"I'd like to believe Ganigi did what we asked him to do, but seriously Dad, I'm beginning to have suspicions about him. I've always had an underlying unease—nothing specific, but I sensed something was not quite right. I wish I could shake the feeling."

"You have always had good instincts, son" Garrett agreed. "I hope you're wrong, for Webu's sake."

"Me too."

***

Later in the day two of the tribesmen walked back into camp with Ganigi. They poked him with their spears to encourage him forward. He looked quite pleased when he spied the rest of the team.

"Manuel!" he called out. "Thank God, I thought for sure they were going to kill me."

"Ganigi," Manuel said with surprise. "What are you doing here? Where is Webu?"

"So sorry," he mumbled nervously. "Webu didn't make it. His wound kept bleeding, and no one came. I made a grave for him though so the animals wouldn't get him," he lied.

"Thank you. Webu was an honorable man and a dear friend. I'm deeply saddened, but thankful you're all right."

Decker stood in silence, his body stiff with tension, and his turquoise eyes leveled on Ganigi. All of his suspicions began to surface. Even though he had nothing specific to attach to his lack of trust, he settled in himself he'd not let Ganigi out of his sight from this moment forward.

***

Callie offered to help Alice give vaccinations to the village children. A couple of the children let out a yelp as the needle pinched their flesh. Tears meandered down their dirty cheeks, and Callie did her best to distract them by making funny faces. Even though they fought against the impulse to smile, they could not resist her, and they found themselves smiling and making faces back.

When evening fell over the village, they all sat around the campfire. The natives prepared a feast for them, and several of the men took up playing drums. The women began to twirl in a circle around the fire and motioned for Callie and Alice to join them. With a wide smile, Callie leapt to her feet. She tried to mimic the other women, her hands motioning above her head and her long hair swirling outward looking like a shimmering waterfall in the firelight.

Decker laughed as he watched her play. She enjoyed life so much and having her along with him was a complete pleasure. He resisted when she first motioned with her hand, calling him to join her on the dirt dance floor. Running out of the circle, she grasped his hand and pulled him to his feet. Laughingly, they began a light-hearted dance which brought a bout of laughter from the team and the natives alike.

When they were done, Callie took her seat on the log near the fire, but Decker walked over to where Ganigi was standing alongside Manuel. "Ganigi, how did you find us?" he asked.

"I followed your trail," Ganigi explained.

"We were at least two days ahead of you. Why didn't you go back to base camp where Sam and Ted were? I believe those were my instructions."

Ganigi shifted uneasily. "I thought it would be easier than trying to climb down the rocky bluffs without any help. Sorry."

"So, you didn't see Ted or Sam?"

"I didn't see anyone. Webu only held out for one night. The poor guy couldn't fight any longer. His wound was bad, and he began bleeding again. I did what I could to stop it, but it wasn't enough."

"Next time, if there is a next time, and I leave instructions to follow, I expect you'll do it. Otherwise, I'll send you packing!" His stern voice bore a clear warning to Ganigi, and it was apparent by the look on his face Decker would follow through on any threat he made.

Sitting back down with Carson and Callie, Decker told them about the cave he had seen behind the waterfall and wondered if they should go back to inspect it or push on. He always valued others input, and this time was no different. If the cave was a dead end, it would be more wasted time. However, if Decker was right, and the cave did pan out to be a channel that would lead them to the lost city, it would be worth their investigation. They were very close.

179

"There could be a nest of anacondas," Callie broached the sensitive subject, still queasy because of what had happened to Decker.

"I'm not going to lie, Callie," Decker said. "There could be a den of them. We have no way of knowing. We need to be prepared."

"It would be a shame if we didn't at least make an attempt," Carson added. "It makes sense there'd be a backdoor into the city. With all of these rocks, it's possible there is a network of subterraneous passages."

"In years past, many of these limestone caves were used as burial grounds," Decker mentioned. "It could be it served as a conduit for fresh water."

Callie was weighing the situation in her mind. She had to admit she was entertaining some fear. It was not an irrational response by any means after what they had gone through, and those memories were cauterized into her mind.

"You're right," she replied. "It would be foolish not to take a look and see if it's a means to the lost city."

"You're sure?" Decker asked her.

"I'm sure. I never want fear to be the controlling factor in my life, Decker," she told him. "It was more than a little difficult watching the snake take you down that way, but our team is constantly facing dangerous situations, so if I let this dictate my decision, eventually, I'll start making all of my decisions out of fear."

"Wise woman," Decker said and winked.

Chapter 23

They began gathering their packs and tossing them in a heap, preparing for their departure. They thanked Alice and Joseph and asked them to express their gratitude to the natives for their generosity and hospitality. Although there were language barriers to overcome, the natives embraced them with love and kindness. They were now considered friends.

"You guys take care of yourself," Alice said, hugging Callie. "I enjoyed spending time with you and thank you for helping me with the children."

Callie smiled., recalling the day before when she had assisted Alice in giving vaccinations to the village children while the men went on a hunt. "Believe me, it was my pleasure. I adore children."

"When you're back in Los Angeles give me a call," Alice invited her. "We'll have some coffee."

"You're on Alice."

"We'll be here for another couple of days should your team need anything," Joseph called out.

Decker waved his hand. "Thank you. We appreciate it."

Putting on their packs, they began to retrace their steps back to the waterfalls. The rumbling water from the falls could be heard even at a distance. There was great anticipation as to what they might find once they scoped out the cave. The recessed area was probably rock erosion created by the plummeting water over the façade, but that possibility was not enough to keep them from checking it out. Something inside Decker beckoned to him to search it out. His body hummed with excitement.

When they arrived at the falls, Decker set down his rucksack and stood for a time observing the area. "If we go carefully, we can make it over the rocks along the side until we reach the waterfall. We can slide behind the water which will save our packs from being drenched. There's a foot's length bank there."

"Splendid idea," Carson agreed.

"Tell you what," Decker said, as they reached the rocky edge. "I'll be the first to go in and check it out."

"Are you sure you don't want me going in with you, Decker?" Carson offered, thinking there might be more wisdom having two people go in in case there were any more problems. He too had not forgotten the scene with the anaconda and his friend being drug to the bottom of the pool.

"Don't worry," Decker patted Carson's shoulder. "I'll be more than a little cautious, believe me!" Before heading off, Decker dug through his pack and withdrew his long-bladed knife. He raised it in front of his face and smiled. "I dare one of those slithery snakes to take me on!"

"Careful," Callie said tenderly touching his arm.

Decker winked, then began to skirt around the large body of water. The closer he got to the cave, the larger the rocks became, forcing him to heave his body up and over the tops. Sometimes even having to leap over the gaps between the larger boulders. There were a couple of times his foot slipped, and he went down with a thud, bruising his legs and lower back, but he pushed himself back up and continued.

The day was extremely hot, and Decker welcomed the light breeze that fluttered across the water and acted like air conditioning. As he closed the distance between the rocks and the falls, he could feel the refreshing mist dampening his face. His eyes were in constant look out for any snakes. When he made it to the bank of the falls, he sighed with relief.

The rocks had become slippery with algae the closer he'd gotten. It was like a well-oiled surface, making it difficult at times to keep traction. His fingers searched for areas to cling to where there wasn't slime until he could duck safely through the opening.

With one momentous thrust, he found himself inside the cavity. He pulled out his hand-crank flashlight and flipping it on, he shined the light along the walls. He saw it wasn't merely a recessed area but stretched out for quite a distance. As he walked slowly along the uneven rock floor, he could see there were two arteries in the cave so it would be a matter of choosing which one to follow. With any luck, there would be an opening at the other end.

He moved back to the entrance, poked his head out, and motioned for the others to join him. He waited them out, moving throughout the cave to see if there was any evidence to show mankind had used the cave. He was down on his knees shuffling through some of the rocks, biding his time until the others made it inside.

It was a slow progress as they made their way over the boulders leading to the entrance. There were a couple of slips, a few soaked pant legs, but nothing severe enough to hinder their joining Decker inside the cave.

He cautioned them as they entered. The floor was slick with water pockets and unstable because of large rocks which were scattered across their pathway making it hazardous. There was also the possibility of snakes which could easily hide out in the dark crevasses.

The team turned their headlamps on. The light flickered off the walls creating eerie shadows throughout the large cavity. Callie sat down on a large stone to slip into her heavier hiking boots which would have better traction. She also pulled out a long-sleeved flannel shirt because the air had cooled considerably.

"Now, this is a dilemma," Callie said, noting there was more than one main vein to follow—one to the right and one to the left. It looked like it would be a coin toss as to which way they should go. "What do you think Decker?"

"To the right might be right," he chuckled, making light of it.

"You are incorrigible Hayden!"

"It's only guess work at this stage. We'll head this way and see what's there and if we're able to make it through. If not, we'll head back and try the other passage." He shrugged his shoulders and started making his way to the right. He smiled thinking he was starting to sound like Manuel with his Que Sera, Sera approach to life.

It was difficult at first because a slide of rocks was stacked precariously along the narrow walkway. Manuel slipped, and his ankle turned. They stopped and wrapped his ankle, thankful it wasn't broken. Manuel insisted he was fine and he'd be able to continue. It was a warning for all of them to pay close attention to their footing.

Water dripped from the ceiling and echoed through the corridor. There were stalactites hanging downward like layered cones dripping a milky white substance made up of calcium carbonate and other minerals known to occur in limestone caves. The stalagmites rose in colorful spirals toward the mineral covered ceiling. It was breathtakingly beautiful.

They pushed along single file as the walls began to narrow. The air around them continued to cool and had become cold. At one point, they had to turn sideways to squeeze through. Callie and Decker, who were in the front, turned when they heard laughter and saw Carson trying to shove Ganigi through. With humor imprinted on their faces, they stood and waited for the two of them to make it over to the other side.

"I needed one less bite of sandwich," grunted Ganigi, as he stumbled forward.

"A few curl ups might be in the future?" Decker tossed in playfully and then stopped. "Hmm…" he surveyed the passage before him. "This area is even more narrow than the last. I'm not sure if we can make it through there."

Callie stepped forward and stuck her head into the constricted channel. It tapered as it made a gradual incline. There was no way to determine if it was passable or not. "Let me slide in there and see if it goes anywhere. We could always use the pick and chip out a section if it widens out eventually."

It took a few minutes for Decker to contemplate what she was offering to do. He didn't like the thought of her going on ahead in case there were complications. On the other hand, she was rather stubborn, and when she made up her mind to do something, it was near impossible to dissuade her.

"Okay," he said. "However, I'm going to tie a rope around your waist in case you come to a place where you get pinned. That'll give us some leverage anyhow."

Decker dug through his pack until he found one of their ropes for climbing. He fitted it snugly around her waist and pulled on it several times to make sure the rope would not come undone. When satisfied, he withdrew his knife and handed it over to her. She looked at him with a bemused grin.

"Always thinking ahead, aren't you?"

"Since we can't see very far up the shaft, I think it's better to go prepared," his worry was not unwarranted as he remembered his tango with the snake.

"If I come face to face with Mister anaconda, Manuel will have himself dinner tonight." She made a joke of it, but she could feel her stomach quiver.

Once inside the cavity, she felt like a rabbit scurrying up a hole, slightly wider than her shoulders. She spied a few spiders running from her as she eased forward through the hemmed in passage. She felt the wet rock penetrating through her clothing. At one point, as she thrust herself forward, she heard the material

185

on her blouse rip and felt the sting of the jagged surface raking her stomach.

"See anything?" Decker yelled.

"Not yet. I can't see any daylight," she hollered back, her voice echoing in the small chamber. "I don't think this is going to go through; it appears to be narrowing. If I'm having difficulty maneuvering, I know you won't make it."

"Okay. Come on back." Decker said after it had grown apparent they wouldn't be able to push through it.

Callie began shifting from side to side, trying to propel herself backward. The exertion was taking its toll on her arms, and her muscles began to cramp. She stopped several times battling the cramped quarters she'd managed to wriggle through. Going backward was much more difficult. There was a slight bend in the rock where Callie found herself stuck. She squirmed back and forth, pushed with all of her strength, but couldn't seem to move.

Okay, Callie, you got in, so you have to be able to get out, she reasoned in her mind. She struggled, fighting to move to her side in order to give her more room. After an enormous amount of wrenching, she managed to twist her body sideways, but then she needed to have a way to push herself backward.

"I could use a little help," she called out, starting to feel a bit of panic well up in her. She had never been claustrophobic but being pinched into a narrow gap without being able to dislodge herself, she was beginning to experience it. She felt the tugging on the rope. At the same time, she writhed like a fish out of water, and after a violent struggle, she felt her hips give way, and her body slipped backward enough to free herself.

By the time she made it out, she was desperate for water. Sweat was running down her forehead and into her eyes. She had never been so thankful to see Decker in her life, and welcomed his strong arms around her, giving her comfort after her ordeal.

"I shouldn't have let you go in," Decker sighed feeling a touch of guilt for giving in to her.

"It was my choice," Callie assured him. "It wasn't my most favorite exploration, but someone had to do it, and better me than one of you guys; you wouldn't have made it even half the way I did." She tipped the canteen to her lips and took a few healthy swallows to wet her dry throat. She coughed a few times from inhaling particles of sediment that had dislodged in the passage.

"Are you up to going back to take our chances on the other passage?" Decker inquired, seeing it had taken its toll on her.

"I'm good," she assured him. "A bit shaky, but that won't stop me."

Turning back, they headed toward the other rock channel. They fought back disappointment, but maybe next time they would have better luck. Once more they had to battle the stacks of loose rocks making their way more complicated and dangerous.

The sound of rushing water began to fill the interior, and they knew they were closing in on the main cavity behind the falls. Back where they started.

"It's all right, Decker," Callie consoled, seeing his frustration. "We all agreed to explore the cave. If it doesn't pan out, we'll set up camp near the falls, and start out tomorrow the way we had originally planned."

"I agree," Carson said. "It'll put us behind one day, that's all."

"Thanks," Decker replied. "I know this was a flip of the coin type of scenario. I had my hopes too high. But if it doesn't work out, it doesn't."

They rounded the corner and could now see the falls. "Here we are. Anyone up for lunch before taking on the next tunnel?" Carson asked.

"I could sure use something," admitted Callie. "I worked up an appetite."

They dug through their pack and retrieved some of the sealed food pouches. "Mmm… I have macaroni and cheese," Carson said.

"I'll trade you," Callie offered. "I have beef stew."

"You're on," he agreed, tossing his pouch over into her hands, and then Callie tossing hers.

Decker chuckled. "I pulled out powdered ice cream. Suits me fine." Laughter followed.

The steady drip of water from the cave's ceiling resonated through the cave. It seemed strangely unoccupied by animals. They had at least expected a few bats or even snakes for all the rocks, but so far, the perimeters appeared mostly untouched.

Decker wondered if he'd made a wrong decision about their overland trek as it was taking several days longer than what they'd anticipated. And now, as he looked around the cold rock walls, there was no sign of humanity except themselves. He had thought there would be lithographs, man-made spear heads, or at the very least ground stone tools for grinding grains. As yet, there was no evidence the cave had been used. It was disappointing, but they still had one more passage to explore.

Chapter 24

The rifle butt slammed between Sam's shoulder blades. Pain knifed through him, and a guttural moan slipped out of his lips. He had not wanted to give in to the pain and give the two men the satisfaction of knowing they had defeated him physically, yet they had. His lips were cracked and dry. He knew the symptoms of dehydration were beginning to take effect. He felt his body pitching forward from the blow and with his hands bound, he could not break the fall.

Seeing Sam writhing on the ground, Javier took the opportunity to remind Adrián, "If you kill him, we'll never set foot outside of this jungle alive, isn't that what you told me?"

Adrián turned his wicked glare on Javier, droplets of sweat running down his brow. "They're slowing us down," he growled through clenched teeth.

"You need to be reasonable, Adrián," he argued the matter, feeling his emotions bubbling to the surface. "You have no idea where we are or where we're going. I don't want to die here! We're running low on supplies, running out of time and if we don't look at our situation carefully, none of us are going to walk out of here alive."

Adrián looked as though he was mulling over Javier's words. It was true, their supplies were dwindling, and if they didn't catch up with Decker and the team soon, they might possibly be rodent food. What was most annoying, was Javier's whining about it. The pressure was building up around them, and there were times when Adrián had the impulse to thrash Javier within an inch of his life. He had always thought Javier was weak and spineless.

In the end, Adrián relented, even though it galled him. At the same time, he realized there was truth in what Javier was saying.

"Fine!" he snapped. "Give them some water."

Ted and Sam were desperate for water. They took down several large gulps, soothing their parched throats and also helped to rejuvenate them.

They were both experiencing exhaustion, and even though they knew their captors were struggling from the same extreme environmental conditions, they weren't restricting their intake of water, which made the hike in a bit easier on them.

The day was growing darker by the minute. Sam could only guess that clouds had moved in, threatening another thunder shower. It was difficult to determine what the day would be like because the canopy was so dense and generated only scanty rays of light.

When they took a short reprieve, Sam sat next to Ted on a rotting log. There was a limestone embankment behind them. Intent on finding some means of escape, Sam fumbled around with his hands behind his back looking for a sharp stone to slice through the ropes. The two men were talking and not paying attention to Sam and Ted, so Sam took the interval to use to his advantage.

Ted caught on to what Sam was doing, and he too began thumbing through the rocks behind him. They were careful not to become obvious, so their movements remained subtle. If they could only break the cords on their hands, they could use their fighting skills to overcome them.

Sam nearly laughed aloud as his fingers curled around a stone with a jagged, sharp edge. He slipped the rock between his palms and began to manipulate the stone with his fingers up and down in a sawing fashion. He felt a couple strands of the twisted hemp unraveling.

"It's time to go," grunted Adrián, walking in their direction.

Sam had not managed to break through the rope. He tucked the rock into his palm. He'd have to wait until they stopped again or until their two captors were distracted so he could continue. As far as he could tell, Ted had not found anything to use on his ropes, so Sam would have to pass him off the stone once he'd managed to sever his.

There was a bright flash of light followed by a loud crack of thunder. The ground beneath them shook from the violence. Instantaneously, the skies opened up, and sheets of rain poured over them. It only took a short time before water was streaming around their feet. The ground turned to mush, and mud oozing into their shoes. It felt like a sauna, but there was no thermostat to turn down. Their feet were starting to peel and blister from the moisture, making it more and more uncomfortable to walk.

"I'm beginning to hate the jungle," Ted sputtered.

"You and me both, Ted," answered Sam, wishing they were all back on board the *Jade* and sailing off to Miami. He envisioned them chugging down an ice-cold beer and jumping into a nice cool shower. He could only dream.

They found large leaves four-foot-wide to duck under to be out of the torrential downpour. It was not a tent to be sure, but it did serve to keep them a bit drier. With his back turned away from Adrián and Javier, Sam once more took to sawing the rope until he felt another one of the strands snap. He glanced over at Ted with a smile, then continued.

It wasn't long before the rains began to subside. "We can probably push on," Javier said, his hand grabbing Ted's arm and pushing him forward.

As they pressed deeper into the vine-wrapped jungle, Sam could see that Adrián and Javier were starting to lose their momentum. They, too, were overwhelmed by the heat, and from the non-stop foot travel. They were all, to varying degrees, being punished by their harsh surroundings. The jungle did not play favorites, and it was sinking its talons into their minds and their flesh.

"I need to drink," moaned Javier. He dropped down on a fallen tree and nestled his head between his legs gasping for breath.

"Shut up, you baby," snarled Adrián. "We're never going to catch up to the others with all your lollygagging." He took the canteen from his shoulder and tossed it to Javier.

Javier mentally began an assault on Adrián, imagining for a moment that he took his knife from his belt and thrust it deep into Adrián's stomach. There was a morbid joy he experienced as he watched him die slowly. Painfully. "Thanks," he sputtered with disdain.

Once more Sam took the opportunity to work the rock against the strands of rope around his wrists. One more thread snapped. The cords were weakening, and he felt the tension on his wrists diminishing. He worked his wrists as well as the stone, pulling…tugging…twisting; then it gave way. He released his breath. Relief consumed him.

Moving alongside Ted, Sam dropped the stone off into his hands. Ted would need to work quickly to free himself before they discovered what they were up to.

Sam clasped the unraveled rope in his palm to conceal the fact he was no longer secured, and for the first time since they'd been abducted, he could see a flicker of expectation flashing in Ted's eyes. The thought of being free gave both of them a renewed vigor they had lost over the past few days.

As Ted prevailed in his battle with the hemp rope, he winked at Sam. It only took a second for Sam to act out. He lunged forward, his arm wrapping around Adrián's neck in a choke hold. Adrián reared back trying to shake Sam, and they tumbled to the ground. Sam held fast even as Adrián began to roll back and

192

forth. His hand went up to clutch Sam's thumb, and with a jerk, there was a snap of bone. Sam howled. With his free hand, he gripped a chunk of Adrián's hair.

Sam and Adrián had made it to their feet, and Sam having been trained in combat fighting, did a spinning back kick catching Adrián square in the stomach. The kick's momentum sent him sprawling backward his arms flailing. Unable to keep his balance, he tumbled into a somersault.

Leaping to his feet, he rushed Sam like a raging bull taking him to the ground. Sam threw his elbow into Adrián's jaw, and there was a sickening cracking sound and a loud howl. Rolling to the side, Sam scrambled to his feet, blood dripping from the corner of his mouth. Both hands were doubled up waiting for Adrián to make his move, and when he did, Sam lit into him with iron fists. Adrián, exhausted, and no fight left in him, buckled to the ground.

When Ted saw Sam take into Adrián, he took advantage of Javier's stunned composure. His fist doubled up, he caught Javier under his jaw. The jarring blow forced the rifle out of his hand, and it dropped to the ground. Ted rushed him, striking him square in the solar plexus, fully winding Javier. His fists pummeled Javier as he straddled him.

Javier bucked like a bronco, throwing Ted aside, his hand searching madly for the rifle, but Ted overpowered him, knocking the rifle out of reach.

Javier clawed at the ground and fought to stand back up, but once again he was met with Ted's punishing blows. The past few days had nearly taken the life force from him, and those pent-up emotions surfaced like a sweeping fire, vengeance mounting with every swing. Reaching behind him, Ted caught the barrel of the rifle. He swung it around striking Javier in the head, and his body went slack.

It was that moment they realized they were free. Wasting no time, Sam and Ted grabbed their packs, the rifles and took off on foot fast as they could go.

The two of them hurried as best they could. With what little strength they could muster, they hacked through the tangled wall of debris with the machetes. Sam was aware they were low on supplies, mostly water, and water was what their bodies demanded in the suffocating heat. They were also faced with the fact they didn't have a compass, GPS, or map to direct them. They would have to pay close attention to any evidence of broken branches left behind by Decker's team. Fortunately, they had come across a few signs that helped point the way.

"How are you holding up, Ted?"

"Now that we're rid of those two lunatics, I'll be fine."

"They won't be far behind you can be sure, so we're going to have to keep pressing on no matter what," Sam hated to say, but knew it was true. Their very lives depended on finding Decker and the rest of the team, otherwise, the elements would soon overtake them.

"So long as you're with me, I know we can make it, Sam."

"Blind faith could get you killed," he said but knew what Ted meant.

As Sam continued swinging the machete, his hand cramped with excruciating pain. In his scuffle with Adrián, his thumb had been broken. It had swollen double the size, and his face was twisted in torment. He would have to find something to use as a splint and wrap it. Presently, he was not going to stop.

With inward determination, they continued to hack their way through the bamboo barricade. Their shirts were soaked through with sweat, their mouths pasty from the lack of water. Every muscle in their body was twisted in knots, making every step a torturous endeavor.

Above in the canopy, they spotted several monkeys swinging from branch to branch, their howls echoing around them—

sometimes so ear-piercing, it made them shudder with apprehension.

"Do you think they'll attack us?" Ted asked, feeling nervous because all of the chatter.

"Let's hope not. We have enough to contend with."

Ted stopped short, bent down, and picked up a piece of material. A grin spread on his face. "We seem to be on the right track. Look here." He dangled a small swath of material in front of his face.

"Looks like a piece from Decker's shirt."

"This is as good as a compass," Ted declared.

"Keep your eye peeled. It's the only way we'll find them."

They pressed on with renewed vigor.

Sam lifted his foot to step over one of the rotting logs, then froze. Beneath him, in a hollowed-out area, he spied a gray, scaled body and then heard a loud rattle. His breath stuck in his throat. Cautiously he moved his leg backward, all the while keeping his eyes focused on the snake. It had glided forward and was now coiled, preparing to strike.

As its body hurled forward, Ted thrust out a chunk of wood that had been lying at his feet. The snake's venomous fangs sank into the wood, short of Sam's shin bone. Sam stumbled backward landing on his backside and sighed with relief as the snake slithered off.

"Ted, I owe you one!"

"Think you've saved my hide a couple of times already."

If that wasn't enough drama for one day, twenty minutes farther along, Sam and Ted were mortified to come face to face with natives, their faces painted with blue and red stripes. For a time, they all stared at each other in stunned silence and then the natives pointed their spears at them, motioning for them to drop their rifles. Doing as they were told, they laid the rifles down on the hard rock ground and raised their hands up to take a non-combative stance.

"Somehow this doesn't seem real. Are we dreaming?" Sam snorted, shaking his head. "What did we ever do to deserve this, Ted?"

"All I know is it must be you, Sam. My slates clean," he said with a chuckle even though circumstances looked dire at the moment.

At a distance, they could see forceful waterfalls and heard deep rumbling as it flowed over the giant boulders down into a wide pool. They had no idea where the natives would take them. And all they could see was another obstacle they'd have to overcome.

"What I wouldn't do to jump into that water," sighed Ted, imagining for a moment what it would feel like on his sweat-caked body.

"You and me both, Teddy."

Sam talked to the natives a lot on their way to the small village, even though it was apparent they didn't speak English. The gesture would give the natives the impression they were harmless with no intention of hurting them.

"I could ask you what you are doing?" Ted questioned Sam's sanity. "However, maybe I don't want to know."

"Better to do something rather than nothing," was his glum reply, but had a smile on his parched, cracked lips. "I'm battling the temptation to surrender to depression."

"Know what you mean. This is surreal."

The village was not large. There were twelve huts altogether and standing outside looking on with curiosity were several women and a few elderly men. Some of the children ran up alongside them with wide smiles.

They were taken to one of the huts and were pushed roughly inside. They could hear the men talking among themselves, though they had no idea of what they were saying, or what they intended to do with them. Of all the quests they had gone on, this was the worst they could recall. Whatever direction they went, they were met with opposition. Surely, luck had to be in their favor at some junction, thought Sam.

His thoughts threatened to overtake him, a young woman with golden hair tied back in a ponytail entered the shack. She had two bottles of water in her hand and extended them out to Sam and Ted. Their mouths gaped. Was this a hallucination? Had the sun fried their brains? Questions whirled in their heads, and all Sam could do was laugh.

The woman stared at him as if he had lost his mind. "Are you all right?" she questioned.

"Are you for real?" he choked. "Or have I died and gone to heaven?"

"I'm real. My name is Alice Peterson. Who are you, and why are you here?"

"Are you kidding," his voice shrill. "Did you see those spears the natives have? They were at our backs all the way here thinking to make shish kabobs of us…that's why we're here!" His voice sounded a bit brittle.

"But for what purpose?" she asked, wanting Sam to give her a better explanation.

"We're looking for the rest of our team," he explained. "We were kidnapped and held by two deranged men with guns. It took some doing, but we managed to get away. You can only imagine how horrific this all seems—break free from some crazy goons only to be captured once more—it's a little more than mind boggling."

She smiled kindly. "I'm sorry for your circumstances, but the natives can't speak English, so they had no idea why you trespassed onto their land."

"We want to find our friends," sighed Sam, feeling light-headed and he swayed unsteadily.

She knelt down and grabbed the bottle of water. "You look dehydrated; you need to drink as much as you can right now and splash some of the water on your head to cool down."

"Who are you?" Sam questioned again, confused by her presence.

"Like I said, my name is Alice. I work for the World Health Organization. I was sent here to administer vaccinations to the children for whooping cough, measles, and polio. They're very susceptible to these diseases, especially since white people keep insisting on coming into the jungle and bringing disease with them." Suddenly, she felt like this was déjà vu! She laughed aloud. What were the chances?

What could he say to that? It was true. On their way, they saw areas that had been ravaged by mankind. It was a cycle that was ever growing, and the evidence was all around them.

"Look, we travel alongside archaeologists who believe in the preservation of antiquities. We have no desire to plunder and take away from the rainforest, or from the natives," Sam continued to explain, feeling as if he might pass out. His head was whirling, and he was starting to see double.

She looked as if she believed him, though there was still some skepticism lurking in her penetrating blue eyes. Tension began to drain from her stiff shoulders.

"So, where are these other two men who held you captive?" she continued her investigation, wanting all of the details before fully trusting them.

He gave a short snort. The last thing he wanted to do was to relive the last two days of his life, but it looked like she was not going to give up until she heard the whole wretched affair.

"I managed to free my hands by using a sharp stone on the ropes they tied me up with," he explained. "Once I was free, I gave the rock to Ted. When they least expected it, we overcame the two men, grabbed the packs, the rifles, and headed off into the jungle. All we wanted was to find our leader." His shoulders sagged, and he felt nauseous. "This sounds like a bunch of hogwash, doesn't it?" It sounded even ridiculous to his ears.

"I guess it depends on who your leader is?"

"Decker Hayden," he revealed, his head swirling. Rolling his head to the side, he vomited. "Sorry," he sputtered.

Alice could see how pale his face was and his eyes looked glazed with fever. "I'm going for some medicine, you two lay down on the mats and rest up. You don't look like you can go anywhere right now."

She did not need to coerce either of them. They were at the end of their strength and had already stretched out over the mats and were fast asleep within minutes. Alice took a moment to round up her medical bag. She had pretty well concluded they were ravished by the jungle.

Returning, she took their temperatures. They were running at one hundred and two degrees; both were shaking like a leaf. It was difficult to know if they'd picked up some bacterial infection but that would probably be the case. However, it was clear dehydration was their biggest problem. Her first impulse was to have them drink as much water as possible. She had packets of electrolytes she'd stirred into the water to rehydrate them. And she'd wrapped them in wet rags in expectation of bringing their body temperatures back down.

A red flag had shot up in her mind after Sam had told her about the other two men who had held them captive. If they were still out there, they could pose a real threat to the villagers or even to her and Joseph. They would be leaving the next day to fly back to Trujillo and then on to California. In the meantime, she wanted to be of service to these two men and nurse them back to health.

Alice let them sleep and checked in several times to see if they were doing better. Sam's temperature had dropped one degree, which was a relief. She was hesitant to leave the two of them with no way to communicate with the natives. Also, if they didn't recuperate in the next day, she'd not be able to let them know about Decker and the others.

Alice went to the leader of the village and explained to him what Sam had told her. If she did have to leave before Sam and Ted recovered, at lease Chief Mongusu, would be forewarned and be on the lookout for the two evil men still out there who could be a threat to the tribe She also asked—should there be a need—if Chief Mongusu would draw the men a map to where Decker and his team had gone, or at least, take them back to the falls so they would know where to go.

There was no way of knowing if the cave was a backdoor to the lost city as Decker had determined it might be. If it wasn't, and they had taken another route, Alice would no longer be of any help to Sam and Ted. All she could do now was wait and see if they would shake off the sickness quickly and regain their strength.

Sam's sickness went through the night. Ted, even though he had looked the worst of the two, seemed to be faring a bit better. By early morning, Ted had pushed himself into a sitting position and was eating one of his packets of food, though he was still feeling nauseous.

Alice entered with a cup in her hand. "How is he?" she asked.

"He seems better. He stopped thrashing anyhow and looks like his fever may have broken."

"What's your name?"

"Ted. Ted Bingham." He stretched his hand out to her, grateful for how she had stepped in to help them. She certainly must be an angel, he concluded.

Feeling Sam's forehead, she replied, "I think you're right. He feels cooler and isn't so restless."

It was her touch that woke Sam. His eyes fluttered open, and it took a few minutes to focus in on her angelic face. Briefly, he forgot where he was. When he searched the room and saw Ted, everything came hurtling back into reality.

"I'm still alive, go figure," he groaned, every muscle in his body rebelling.

200

"Here," she said, pushing the cup towards his lips. "Electrolytes. You need to rehydrate as much as possible. So down the hatch!" She said forcefully. Her brows were woven into a frown, trying to look intimidating, but it didn't work with Sam.

Sam smiled. "You're a spitfire, I've got to say."

"I can be. Now drink it." She pushed the cup toward him. "And then we'll tend to that broken thumb of yours."

There was something in the cup that had a nasty smell as well as a foul taste. The smell turned Sam's stomach. Plugging his nose, he tipped the cup and took several gulps of it down. His eyes rolled back and his face scrunched in revolt. "What the devil did you put in this? Animal dung?"

"You'll live."

"If you say."

"You'll live. Come on, drink it," she insisted with a disarming smile.

Sam turned to Ted. "Hey buddy, how are you?"

"Couldn't be better," he lied. "Thankfully, we survived, that's the good news."

"You're right, it could have been much worse. It was our good fortune the natives found us and sweet Alice came to our rescue." He smiled at her, truly appreciating her help. "Do they intend to let us go?"

Nodding, she replied, "Yes, I explained what happened to the two of you to Mongusu, the head chief of the village. He understands you mean them no harm and they'll send you on your way when you're strong enough."

"What would they do to us if you weren't here to speak for us?" asked Ted.

"I think maybe they'd have you for dinner," she replied humorously, recalling Callie's irrational fear.

Ted chuckled but hiked his brows, unsure if she meant it or not. "I'm not all that tasty anyhow."

Alice laughed. "Now that you're both lucid, I guess I can update you."

"Update us?" Sam repeated.

"I met Decker, Callie, Carson, and Manuel," she informed them and watched surprise animate their faces. "They were brought here, much like yourselves, by the natives. The natives had no intention of harming them, but they wanted to make sure they weren't going to victimize anyone in the village."

"Are they okay?" Sam pressed her. His greatest fear was something had happened to them since they'd not had any contact with them.

"Carson was sick for one evening like you two but was doing fine the next day."

Knowing they were doing all right brought a sigh of relief from Sam's lips. He tipped his head back, eyes closed and he breathed in deeply. "At least something's going right," Sam replied, feeling as if a weight had been lifted from his chest.

"You probably walked right by where they departed," she told them.

"Which was where?"

She saw Sam's excitement. "The falls. Decker thought the water falls could be a backdoor to the lost city."

"The falls?"

"Sorry," she apologized. "Right behind the falls, there was a recessed area that looked like a substantial cave. Decker thought they should explore it and see what they could find. However, I haven't seen them since, so I don't know if they found anything or not."

"In other words, if it didn't lead anywhere, they would have gone on their original route," Sam said almost to himself.

"Afraid so," she agreed. "I don't suppose you know what route they were going to take?"

"Not without the GPS and the coordinates," he conceded. "All we can do is what we have been doing, looking for evidence that shows their path—broken branches, a footprint, etcetera."

"Sorry," Alice sympathized.

"Not your fault."

"I'm leaving tomorrow," she told Sam. "If you need to come back, the natives will show you hospitality, but there won't be anyone here who can interpret for you, I'm afraid."

"I can't thank you enough for your help, Alice. Truly, you've been an angel in disguise and also for our team it appears." Sam was grateful.

Sam imagined he looked a fright. He hadn't shaved in days, his hair was matted with sweat and dirt, and his clothes were soiled. He hadn't given much thought before, but with Alice standing in front of him, he had suddenly grown self-conscious about his appearance. He had to admit, she was an attractive woman.

"I told the chief about the two other men who had held you prisoner," she told them. "If you give me their descriptions I can tell the chief so he knows ahead of time they have evil intentions and they can see them back down river to the proper authorities."

"I'd appreciate it," Sam let her know. The last thing they wanted was the villagers having to contend with the two miserable thugs. Sam wouldn't wish that on anyone. They were contemptible snakes and needed to be locked away for the rest of their life. If there was any justice, the wild animals would have them for dinner.

"We really need to head out and see if there's any chance of catching up with the team."

"Nice meeting you both," she smiled. "You're sure you're up to this?"

"Not really, but it's imperative we find the team.

Alice stretched out a small bag to Sam. "Here, I'm sending along some extra water, protein bars, and some antibiotics. You really should continue to take them."

"No question you're a nurse," chuckled Sam. "But we're grateful for everything you've done for us."

"Best of luck," she smiled and held out her slender fingers to shake their hands.

"We owe you," Ted told her.

"You owe me nothing. Find Decker and Callie, and make it home safely," she replied tenderly. "Now, for your thumb…"

Chapter 25

Decker and the team followed the passageway deep into a large cavern. The farther they went, the wider the cave became. It appeared they were going down and some of the places were quite steep. In one particular area, they were forced onto their back sides and scooted down a section, fearful of losing their footing. Reaching his hand back, Decker caught Callie's fingers and helped her slide to the next level.

The floor continually sloped downward and eventually formed a wide chasm. Where they had been on a solid surface, they were now forced to walk on a ledge that jutted out from the right wall. Manuel slung a couple of rocks over the side periodically to determine the depth of the rift. It was becoming deeper and was rather daunting as they only had three feet in width to walk on.

"Watch your step," Manuel warned. "If you slip it's a long way down."

The temperature had increasingly dropped, the chill forcing them to stop and dig out light jackets to keep warm. It was somewhat welcoming after having been out in such intense heat for so long.

From time to time, Decker paused and motioned for the others to stop. He couldn't see or hear anything, but he had a sense there were eyes fixed on them. His intuition had proven right so many times in the past, he tried not to dismiss his feelings, no matter how trivial they might seem.

"What's up?" Carson probed, looking around the cavern curiously. His fingers twitched nervously by his holster where his revolver was sheathed, preparing to pull it if necessary.

"Search me. I have an overwhelming sense we're being watched."

"That's not good," Carson replied.

Ganigi raised his lantern and looked around the cavern. He was not a perceptive man but having been alongside Decker over the past couple of weeks, he knew Decker definitely was. Being the last one, Ganigi looked behind him over and over again, fear beginning to take hold of him. He couldn't see anything. The only thing evident was the continual dripping of water and occasional small rocks sliding off the edge and clattering to the bottom.

Hesitantly, Decker continued. "Even though we can't see anything, I'd like us to be prepared." He slowly pulled out his revolver and cautiously, evoking the others to pull out their weapons as well. His suspicion was all it took for them to become keenly aware of their surroundings.

Manuel squatted. His fingers ran along the floor as if looking for something specific. He brought his fingers to his nose, turning his attention to the others and said, "I believe we're in a jaguar's den."

"That's not what I wanted to hear right now," Carson said, feeling the hairs on the back of his neck stand taut with apprehension.

Unease filled the air. Even though there were none to be seen, it was reasonable to assume, if the jaguars were surveying them, the team would not be welcome. And if there happened to be cubs hiding out in the various recesses, their motherly instincts would be understandably territorial and aggressive. Their eyes began to survey the surroundings, looking up at the berms and flashing their lights into the dark alcoves.

"Move along," Decker encouraged them.

Once more the ground angled downward sharply, and the ledge they were following was growing narrower by the minute. Not only was the thought of jaguars foremost in their minds, they also had to pay close scrutiny to their footing. If one of them stepped on a loose stone, they could easily topple to their death.

Manuel motioned for the team to stop and pointed. "A section of the ledge has broken away from the wall, making it impassable. "Unfortunately, we'll have to make some decisions about how we'll make it over to the opposite side."

Decker was beginning to think he had made a terrible decision but turning back now didn't make much sense. "What if I connect the steel rock climbing claw onto the end of the rope, throw it across the gap, and with any luck, I can snag it on the rock over there? We can connect our carabiners and work our way across using what small projections there are to stabilize ourselves."

"Works for me," Carson jumped in, always ready for a challenge.

"Me too," Callie agreed.

Ganigi didn't know anything about the procedure, but he was not going to stay behind, for sure. He'd rather chance plummeting down the canyon then be torn to shreds by an angry jaguar. Gathering his courage, he nodded. "Okay, we can do this."

"If anyone doesn't feel comfortable tackling this, I understand," Decker told them. "Either we all go, or we all turn back."

"I think we're good," Manuel was the last to speak. His voice was the last vote and the most important vote as he was the hired guide. If he deemed it was too risky, it would be his duty to call a stop to them proceeding.

Standing back from the drop off, Decker swung the rope over his head. When he released it, it sailed across the chasm striking the boulder but did not catch. He pulled the rope back hand over hand and once again began swinging it overhead like a cowboy roping a calf. When he let go of the rope, it soared over the break, the claw catching the stone. Decker yanked several times to ensure the rope was secure, and when satisfied, he clamped himself to the rope.

"I'll go first," he told them. "My idea, so if anything goes wrong, I should be the one to bear the consequences."

Callie remained silent, but there was a small knot in the pit of her stomach. Decker was good at what he did and was skilled at climbing and yet there was always a slight risk. She tried her best to look confident about the whole situation, but she was not sure who was buying into it.

"It all looks good," she reassured him. "Be careful."

Decker clipped himself to the rope and tugged a few more times to test the line. Feeling confident it would hold, he started out onto the small ledge and eased himself across. There was a short two-foot gap where he had to extend his leg over to reach. As his foot caught the edge and he started to pull his body over, his foot slipped. His body slid against the cold stone, raking against his flesh. He winced. He'd not even healed up from the last brutal scraping. He hung there briefly to gain his composure, then finding a protrusion, he was able to pull his body upward, his foot swinging over to reconnect. With brute strength, he pulled himself back up onto the small ledge and manipulated himself slowly to the other side of the gap.

Callie sighed with relief, her heart fluttering and was more than happy when Decker took his last step, completing the task at hand. She felt a hand on her lower back pressing her forward to be next. She hooked herself to the line and nimbly began her trek across the flat face of the rock. She felt her arms shake as she held her body as close to the cold surface as possible. When she came to the gap on the ridge, she inhaled deeply, swung her foot over and caught the edge. She relaxed somewhat knowing she had made it over the most difficult section.

When she was within an arm's length away, Decker bent over and clasped her shirt and reeled her in, thankful to have her in his arms. They waited while the other three managed to draw themselves across, and there were high fives at the end, their hands slapping together echoed in waves throughout the enormous chamber.

"Whew, what an awesome experience," Carson said, exhilarated by the challenge. "I could do this all day."

Decker shook his head and smiled. "You're hopeless, Carson."

"Learned it from you, Hayden."

"Let's get cracking."

The cave appeared to be endless. They kept expecting to find an opening, but one track led to another. Manuel looked at his watch. It was difficult to discern what time of day it was because the cave was so dark, but it was growing late. They had gone quite a distance, and his aching muscles told him it was time to settle in for the night. They searched the perimeter until they found a leveled off area where they could spread out their bedrolls.

As they sat in a semi-circle, they laid out their food and water sources to take stock of what they had left. While they shuffled through the items, they removed their head lamps and attached them lower on their hips so they didn't blind one another.

Digging through the packs, they pulled out their meal packets. As they ate, they went over the map again and used the compass to make sure they were on a direct course and not veering off in the opposite direction from where Leonard had discovered the lost city.

"I vote we take turns watching over our camp tonight," Decker announced, finishing off his stroganoff meal and discarding the package. Everyone could still see he was on edge. If indeed there was something lurking in the shadows looking for an opportunity to take them unaware, it would be to their advantage to be on the lookout. Plus, everyone would sleep better for it.

"Not going to hear me complain," Ganigi snorted, wiping his mouth with the back of his sleeve.

"I'll relieve you," Carson offered, experiencing the same feelings that something was hiding beyond in the dark niches just watching. He had strapped his tactical knife to his thigh and had unsnapped the security strap on his gun for easy access. He did not take the sensation of being watched lightly and did whatever he could to be prepared in case of an abrupt attack.

"I wonder if what we're feeling are the ancients," Manuel said, his eyes searching the corners of the cave. "Those who have come before us whose spirits are left guarding what belongs to them." Everyone's gaze lit on him and a long stretch of silence followed.

Decker and Callie did not give credence to spiritism, but there was a cold chill that rode along their spine. It was the same sensation Callie experienced when she'd gone off to summer camp, and all of the girls would sit around the campfire exchanging ghost stories. When it was time to go to bed, they'd all hide under their blankets through the night scared to death something would get them.

"Whoa, that's crazy!" Ganigi reacted instantly, his eyes wide as half-dollars. His whole body shuddered, and he began looking all around as if expecting a spirit to come and overtake him.

Manuel glanced over at Ganigi, then in a quiet voice said, "The Chorotega people who lived in the Honduran jungle had many gods. There is a story that's been told for hundreds of years about a *Urus*, the native name for monkey and translates into *'sons of hairy men,'* had abducted some of the tribes' women and lay with them. It was said that their children grew up to be half-man and half-spirit and that these spirits roam throughout the jungle today."

210

Ganigi released a nervous laugh, but the story had given him the jitters. "That's the most ridiculous story I've ever heard!" Even though Ganigi had lived in Honduras all of his life and was raised a Garifuna, he'd never heard of such things.

However, Manuel was not laughing. He took these stories quite seriously. A part of him dreaded going any farther into the interior. He had seen the curses effects on villagers over the years, and he often wondered if Leonard and his team had been victims of this curse because they had entered the forbidden city of Ciudad Blanca.

Ignoring Ganigi's comments, Manuel continued. "They're said to have walked upright, not living in trees like a monkey, but walked the land and looked like great hairy men. I have even heard they were as much as nine feet tall."

"Sasquatch," chuckled Carson, spooning a forkful of food into his mouth.

"Really Carson?" Decker said, shaking his head.

"C'mon, you have to admit, that's what it sounds like."

"I think everyone's imaginations are running wild and that a bit of bed rest would do us all wonders," Callie tossed in and took to her feet. "Good night."

Every small noise that evening was like a shattering resound to those trying to sleep. Manuel had certainly pricked their sensibilities. As much as they wanted to shove those stories to the back of their minds, the images came back to plague them and steal their sleep. It was interesting as none of them outside of Manuel were superstitious, but his intense beliefs seemed to have heighten their apprehensions.

By morning, which was only determined by their watches because of the lack of any natural light, they pulled their camp together. They all felt tired and restless and had wanted to discover a fracture in the rock that would enable them to get out of the cave. Their nerves were strung taut, and it was clear the expedition was beginning to take its toll.

What was worse, they came to another split in the passage. Frustrated, they were forced to make a random decision which way to go. Decker looked to Manuel thinking he had a better sense of the situation than he did. He'd made a wrong choice the first time and thought someone else should make the next call. Without his GPS, which had long since quit working, he was quite inept at making any decisions which way they should go.

Manuel smiled. "We could pick straws or flip coins," he said jokingly, and yet none of them seemed quite up to being humorous this morning for lack of sleep. "I say we go left this time." Of course, it was as much a guess to him as it would be to any of them, but at least it was decided.

"Mark our route if you will," Callie jumped in.

Decker bent over and grabbed several rocks which he piled one on top of another at the entrance of the tunnel. They had their fingers crossed they wouldn't have to turn back if it turned out to be a dead end. It was a sobering thought, and one none of them hadn't already contemplated.

They had descended deep into the bowels of the cave, and now it appeared to be gently sloping upward which was a good sign. At least the pathway had broadened out making their passage much easier. As they continued to climb, the muscles in their legs were beginning to tighten with exertion. They could feel the temperature beginning to rise, and they began to peel off a layer of clothing to make it more comfortable. All signs pointed to the fact they were getting closer to the end of the tunnel.

After an hour, there was a great rumbling sound, and they felt the rock shifting beneath their feet. Manuel, who was leading, was thrown off his feet and struck his head on a protrusion. The others, trying to gain stability, stretched out their palms against the wall. Several rocks dislodged and crashed down around them. Just when they thought it had run its course, the ground shuddered again. The rolling motion caused more rocks to be dislodged and threatened to shut off their route.

Once the ground beneath them became stable, they rushed over to Manuel to see if he was all right. His body was limp, and there was a cut above his eyebrow. Blood poured down his cheek. Quickly, Decker opened his pack and dug for the medical kit. He pulled out a handkerchief and wiped the blood from the wound to see how deep it was.

"I need to stitch this, it's pretty deep. Also, we need to wait it out here until he wakes up to see how severe the injury might be." Decker's hands worked with expertise as he sewed up the gap in Manuel's brow, who still remained unconscious. Wadding up his shirt, Decker made a pillow for Manuel's head and took some of his antiseptic cloths to wipe the wound clean, then injected an antibiotic.

"Now what do we do?" Carson asked growing weary of all the setbacks. It was clear they were in a rather precarious situation.

Decker coughed from the dust and debris the quake had created within the tunnel. "We're going to have to wait it out for a short time and hope Manuel is able to go on." He dug for smelling salts and waved it under Manuel's nose. With the jerk of his head, his eyes fluttered open.

"W-what happened?" he said, looking disoriented.

"Minor earthquake it appears," Decker told him.

"The curse," he trembled. "It's the gods keeping us from going on."

"Nonsense!" Decker said, wanting to put a stop to all of the gibberish about walking hairy monkeys that were ten feet tall. He quickly changed the subject. "How are you feeling?"

"I have a terrible headache."

"I stitched up your forehead. You had a nasty gap but I think you'll be fine," said Decker. "We're going to pull some of these rocks free and try to form enough of an opening to climb through. You rest and we'll take care of everything."

213

One by one, they began removing the rock that sealed the tunnel. It was slow and tedious, but it was the only avenue, save turning back and wasting two more days. Their hope was to dig out an area large enough for them to shimmy through, at the same time, taking every precaution to prevent another rock slide.

The light from Decker's headlamp reflected through the hole they had created. There didn't look to be any major disturbances so far as he could see.

"Okay, let's get on through before there's another mishap," he said, boosting Callie through first.

Ganigi and Carson grabbed Manuel under the arms and helped him to his feet. He swayed unsteadily for a moment and when he had gained his composure, they maneuvered him through the narrow gap to the other side. Once everyone was through, Decker followed.

"Are you able to go on?" Decker asked Manuel.

He nodded. "Thank you, by the way, Decker." His dark eyes were filled with appreciation.

Covered in a layer of sediment, they began their trek across the rock. Fifteen minutes later, they heard pebbles falling from above, clattering against the cave floor. They froze, wondering if they were having another tremor. A split-second passed before they saw a shadowy form leap from the shelving above. A piercing scream followed. A rare, black jaguar was now on top of Ganigi.

Decker pulled his revolver from his holster and took aim but Ganigi's back was to him. No sooner had the black jaguar sprang from its perch, that another rocketed several feet in the air above them and landed a foot in front of Callie. Callie slowly backed against the rock wall, her heart pounding with fear as her fingers fumbled for her gun.

Without hesitation, Carson lunged forward, knife extended in his hand. The jaguar whirled around, its fangs glinting threateningly in the illuminating lantern light. Its paw swung a

214

wide path, its claws raking into his arm. Spots of blood popped to the surface of his flesh and rushed down his arm, staining his shirt and jeans, but it did not stop Carson from advancing on the beast fearlessly. He studied the powerful muscles in the jaguar's legs for any slight of movement to anticipate when it might spring forward for its kill.

Decker fired a gunshot into the air, spooking the jaguar viciously ripping Ganigi's flesh apart. The jaguar twisted back its head, its black eyes looking almost demonic. With blood dripping from its fangs, it sped off down the passage and slipped into a fissure out of sight. The jaguar that had Carson in its sights, turned as abruptly and fled.

It all happened so fast they stood stunned, frozen to the spot. Gaining his composure, Decker turned and hurried to Ganigi. He bent down on one knee, checking for a pulse. Ganigi was unresponsive, his neck torn wide open. "Let's gather some rocks and cover his body," Decker said. "He's dead."

Callie felt nauseous as she stared at Ganigi's lifeless body, mangled and bloody. It dawned on her suddenly, that it could have been her lying there in a pool of blood had Carson not stepped in.

"I'm heartsick about Ganigi," she said, her face pale. "And Carson, thank you. Your quick response saved my life."

"Ah, it was nothing," he smiled.

They gathered the loose rocks near the area and piled them on top of Ganigi so the animals couldn't get at him. Now, more than ever, they had to be on the lookout for any more jaguars.

Manuel looked over at Decker with haunted eyes. "It's the curse, I tell you. The gods are angry with us."

"No, it's merely happenstance," Decker said. "An unfortunate accident. The jungle is full of potential hazards. We knew that when we came, and surely you know that first-hand since you've orchestrated multiple expeditions into the jungle."

"Not this far in," he said. "There is evil here."

The series of events had taken its toll on Manuel. Fear was etched on his coffee-colored face and he looked as if he would bolt at any given moment. It was a dilemma. They had no GPS, and if Manuel left them they would be on their own in a city of vines, trees, and jaguars.

"What do you want to do?" asked Decker.

Manuel stayed silent for an excruciatingly long time. "I won't leave you. You hired me to see you to Ciudad Blanca, and I want to honor my word."

"I appreciate your integrity," Decker said with relief. He caught sight of Carson out of his peripheral vision. His shirtsleeve was shredded from the jaguar's sharp claws and blood oozed from the scrapes. "Let's see the damage."

Decker was happy Carson's wounds weren't deep enough to warrant stitches, but he did see the need to clean the wounds to prevent infection. He dug through the medical kit for antiseptic and what things he would need.

"Ouch!" Carson yelped when Decker dabbed on the antiseptic.

"Quit crying like a baby," Decker chuckled.

"I'd like to see you take on a jaguar bare-handed, then we'd see who cries."

"You boys need to get serious," Callie said. "There are still jaguars in this cave, and we are at the top of their food chain right now, so if I were you, I'd hurry up and get us out of here."

"You've always been the sensible one, Callie," Carson said. "You're right, though. We need to hightail it out of here."

"Okay," said Decker. "Let's head out."

Chapter 26

Adrián and Javier wondered if they were going in circles. Everything looked the same. They had been following what they believed to be Sam and Ted's trail by inspecting the foliage that had been obviously sliced through with the machete. How they had ever opened themselves up to be overtaken by Sam and Ted was a bit mystifying and humiliating as well.

They were desperate for water and had no weapons to safeguard them from wild animals. Regrettably, they were exposed to whatever befell them along the way, and they needed Sam's skills to see them through, as well as Ted to help pack their rucksacks. They were stuck between a rock and a hard place, and Adrián wondered if they'd make it out alive.

The heat was nearly unbearable, and the flies were tormenting them. Both men were swollen with red bites on their faces and up and down their arms from both the flies and the mosquitoes. They had used the last of their repellent and had cut their rations in half for fear of running short.

Adrián grabbed Javier's shirt. "Listen!"

"To what?"

"It's the sound of a rushing river or a waterfall."

"Yeah. I hear it."

Desperate for water, they quickened their steps. The roar of the falls increased, as they moved closer, taunting them. They stumbled forward, breaking through the thick underbrush and vines that tangled around their shoulders with their bare hands. As they pulled back some tree fronds, Adrián shoved Javier to the ground and covered his mouth. He put his finger to his lips telling Javier to keep quiet. He pointed his finger, then removed his hand.

Peering through the broad leaves, they spied Sam and Ted swimming across the large pool of water beyond. They pulled themselves out and onto a ledge to the left of the waterfall. Curiously, they ducked in behind the tumbling cascade of water and did not come back out.

Adrián laughed and slapped his thigh. "It's a cave!"

"About time we got a break, and I'm dying for a drink."

They gave them a few minutes head start before the two of them ventured out into the water, taking large swallows to replenish what they'd lost and then refilled their canteens. They already felt better as they slid themselves up onto the embankment outside the falls. They listened carefully to make sure Sam and Ted were on the move. They could not afford to be seen.

***

Sam saw a marking at the left passageway and released a long sigh. "Will wonders never cease," he grinned. "If they hadn't marked the passage we'd have had to go through both passages. This saves us a heck of a lot of time!"

Ted nodded in agreement. "We're already at least a day behind the team. It was fortunate when the natives took us captive; we had Alice as our voice. Have to say, she was a godsend."

"Seems miraculous, doesn't it?"

"Well, we certainly can use a few miracles about now," Ted replied.

They dug through their pack and pulled out their head lamps. Without them, they wouldn't be able to see the tip of their nose. It was pitch black. They began their trek down the long passage and spied multiple slides of rocks along the way. They had sensed a tremor earlier and wondered if the rocks had shifted with it. Thankfully, the passage was wide enough for them to follow. They quickened their steps wanting to close the gap of time between them and Decker's team and at the same time, pay close attention to their footing as the rocks were unstable.

After a distance, they entered an enormous cavern filled with spires of stalactites and stalagmites. Their headlamps danced off the tiered steeples that reflected brush strokes of pastel colors.

The trail they followed plummeted at their right side, and there was only a narrow walkway that slanted nearly at a forty-five-degree angle making it difficult not to slide to the bottom. Their fingers clasped the slick, cold side walls searching for small rock projections to grasp hold of to help stabilize their footing.

Ted stepped forward, his foot slipping on loose rocks. He slammed into Sam, who lost his balance as well. The two of them were sliding precariously close to the cliff's edge. Sam stretched out his hand fighting for something to cling to before they plunged over the side. Thankfully, his hand caught a large bulbous stone that stopped him abruptly and even though Ted's body hammered against him, Sam was able to maintain his hold.

"Sorry," Ted sputtered, his heart racing.

"Yup," Sam replied. "This is one steep slope. I hope it improves along the way."

"You and me both."

They were relieved when they managed to reach the bottom of the rocky pathway and were thankful it had widened out. They could hear water rushing below them as they pressed forward and assumed there must be an underground river.

Going deeper still into the cave's bowels, Sam could have sworn he heard a landslide behind him. There was no doubt in his mind, it was the rush of rocks tumbling into the deep crevasse. The sound echoed throughout the cave. For a moment they wondered if the rocks might have blocked their access.

***

"Dang, watch it, Javier!" came Adrián's sharp voice, though somewhat hushed so Sam and Ted wouldn't hear them.

Javier's foot had caught the edge of a rock and tripped. He fell headlong down the narrow path they were on, smashing into the backside of Adrián. Fortunately for Adrián, he had already made it to the bottom, and when Javier slammed against him, he fell backward over Javier. A small bank of rocks dislodged from the edge and banged noisily down into the dark void.

"Not like I meant to," he snapped back, dusting off the dirt and pulling up the side of his shirt to see his flesh raked up across his ribs. "I'll be so happy when we're finished up with this. I'm sick of the jungle, the heat, the bugs and mosquitoes, and tired of those blasted flies that act like vampires!"

"Don't you have anything better to do than gripe and complain?"

"Well, do you like them?"

"That ain't the point, now is it?" Adrián sneered, curling up his lip with disgust. "The point is, when we reach the end, we'll both be rich men. It's worth all the rest."

Javier remained silent. He wasn't so sure it was all worth it. His body looked diseased from all the mosquito and fly bites he'd received over the past week, and his stomach churned and gurgled as if there was some creature thrashing around in his guts. He had vomited twice already and the day wasn't even over yet. Apparently, the natives fared well in this climate, but it didn't suit him at all.

They hurried their steps, not wanting Ted and Sam to out distance them, especially since they had headlamps. Adrián and Javier were only in possession of a couple LED penlights to see them through the otherwise black cave. The last thing they wanted was to take a wrong passageway and lose Sam and Ted. Becoming separated now would be certain death. They would never find their way back out.

They stopped short when they came to a narrower passage than what they were already on. In the distance, they could hear Sam's voice ring out clearly, so they knew they were within a stone's throw. Adrián straight-armed Javier to keep him from running into him again and to warn him they were on the back doorstep of entering Ted and Sam's quarters.

They flicked off their lights and crouched behind a boulder to keep out of sight and watched as they prepared to make a camp. All they needed to do was wait it out. It wouldn't be long.

***

Sam had found a great spot to settle down for the night. He had wanted to keep pressing forward, but they were exhausted and decided to take a short nap, then they'd continue. All they needed was a couple hours of shut eye, and that would re-energize them enough. With some amount of luck on their side, they might even be able to catch up with Decker and the team before too much longer.

It took awhile before their breath was heavy in sleep. This was the opportunity Adrián had been waiting for. As quietly as they could, they slipped behind several large rocks to conceal themselves, taking care with each step not to awaken them. One of the rifles was perched on a rock near Sam. If only he could manage to go around to the other side without disturbing them, he could grab the rifle and take them by surprise.

One foot in front of another, carefully planting each one, they closed the gap. Adrián reached out his hand and slipped his fingers tightly around the butt of the rifle. Gently, he slid it from its place.

Javier had rounded the other side and saw Ted's rifle leaning up against a large rock, inches from him. Quietly, he stretched his hand forward catching the barrel and eased it towards him.

No sooner had Javier had the gun in his grasp, Ted turned over, his eyes flickering open. "W-what the…" his words were dashed as Javier used the butt and struck him on the side of the head. Ted slumped back against the rock like a rag doll.

Sam's eyes flew open at the sound and found himself looking down the barrel of a rifle. He pushed his arms up in surrender and moved into a sitting position. He could scarcely believe these two had overtaken them once again. He looked over at Ted. Concern rose as he saw his limp body.

Adrián had a humored look on his face. "Well, well, what have we here?"

Sam moaned in disbelief. The situation was more than his mind could take in. Briefly, he wished they'd killed them when they had the chance. Now here they were, yet again, prisoners of these maniacal men who had not shown one ounce of compassion.

"And here I was missing you," Sam said sarcastically.

"You need to get your friend to his feet or we'll leave him for the jaguars to eat for dinner," Adrián growled, his rifle pointed squarely at Sam. "We don't have time to rest."

Sam crawled on all fours and began to shake Ted, to see how he was. He had a gash on his head, and a stream of blood trickled down over his eye and across his cheek. "Ted," he called out, "Ted, can you hear me?"

222

Ted moaned and rolled to his side. His hand instinctively went to his head, blood seeping through his fingers. "What happened," he muttered, fighting to sit upright, and then saw the faces of Adrián and Javier and everything flooded back to him.

"On your feet!" ordered Adrián. "Quit dawdling. We need to catch up to the others."

Sam grabbed Ted's arm and helped him to his feet. It took a moment for Ted to steady himself, but, even before they could gather their wits, Adrián was pushing them forward without a single concern for Ted's head wound.

"How are you holding up?"

"Been better," came Ted's weak reply. It didn't matter if he was or wasn't. They would force him to move or shoot him. It was all the same.

It was a dilemma when they discovered the ledge was too narrow to cross. Sam and Ted had to try to figure out a way across. They didn't have a rock climbing claw as Decker had, only a couple of ropes.

"We're going to tie a rope around you," Adrián told Sam. "And you're going to have to find the footholds to see us to the other side and tie one end of the rope to one of the boulders over there."

Sam looked dubious. There were not a lot of projections for him to cling to and if his fingers or his foot slipped, he would come slamming back into the rock wall. And then there was the matter of his broken finger. It was a dilemma but what could he do? Adrián was calling all of the shots.

"What are you waiting for?" Javier decided to jump in and at least sound as if he had some say-so over their plight.

"It's going to be really difficult trying to cross over from this side to the next," Sam tried to explain. "There aren't many fingerholds."

"Not my problem," Adrián responded without the slightest concern. "Oh, and by the way, I'll have a gun pointed at your

223

friend's head all the while. If you think to do something stupid once you're over there, I'll have to put a slug in his head, and before you can make a move, you'll have a bullet through you too."

Sam had no doubt he would do it. Not thrilled with the idea, he strapped the rope around him, and rubbing his palms on the floor to coat them with sediment as a substitute for chalk, he stretched out his arm to find a lip large enough for his fingers to clasp onto. He moved his foot out slowly searching for something of substance to step onto. Once he had, he caught sight of another ripple formation for his other hand to catch and began a slow crawl across the face of the rock wall.

As he progressed, his arms began to quiver. His fingers were taking the brunt, holding the weight of his body and they were losing their strength rapidly. He had but four more feet to go. A trickle of sweat meandered down his forehead and into his eyes. He blinked several times trying to clear the stinging droplets. He grunted as he pulled himself along, sliding his chest a few inches at a time. For a fleeting moment, he thought his cramping fingers were going to slip out of the notch, but he managed to hold fast in spite of the intense pain. Right before his fingers threatened to give way, they caught hold the jagged edge opposite of him, and with what little stamina he had left, he heaved himself up onto the shelf. He lay there for a brief time breathing deeply and trying to gather enough physical strength to continue the task at hand.

Tying the rope around the large rock opposite, he pulled it several times to make sure it was going to hold, he hurled the rope back across the gap and motioned for Adrián to secure it. When Adrián finished tying it off, he pushed Javier forward and hooked him to the rope.

"Move it," he said gruffly.

Javier took a deep breath and leaned out in an attempt to find the same notches Sam had used that got him safely across. His

224

muscles shook as he made a slow trek across. He was not as agile as Sam. Sam was much taller and had a longer reach than he did. He strained to grab hold of the small flanges protruding from the face and grunted with exertion. His crossing was taking twice the time of Sam's, and Adrián's impatience was palpable.

"Come on, you slow cow," Adrián goaded him.

Javier sputtered something under his breath, fed up with Adrián's perturbing insults. He'd been sick for several days from bad water and food. Even now, he felt as if he could vomit but dared not for fear of falling.

Making it to the other side, Javier swung his leg up and rolled over, and reached his arm back quickly to clutch the leather strap that held his rifle. He removed it from his shoulder to keep Sam from trying to take it from him again. In one swift movement, he pushed himself to his feet and pointed the barrel at Sam. Last thing he needed was for Sam to think he was a coward, even if he was unable to stand his ground with Adrián.

It took another half hour for the other two to make it across. With guns pointed squarely at them, they began their tense progression to find the others. A short time later, they came across a recent rock slide. There was still a dust cloud swirling in the air.

"Looks like they had to move the rocks aside to get through," Adrián said. "They aren't too much farther ahead."

Each of them crawled on all fours through the opening and moved on. When they came to a pile of stones with a piece of material hanging out, they stopped. There was a span of time Sam and Ted merely stared at the heaped stones. They could only imagine what happened—another rock slide, a snake bite— It was all supposition, but they wondered who lay buried underneath?

"Doesn't matter who it is," Adrián barked. "Let's go."

"Have some respect for the dead," Sam said.

"What for? Their dead."

Taking several more steps, they saw a pool of dried blood. By the amount crusted on the rock floor, it was clear something traumatic had happened.

Sam knew their captors had to be getting tired, after all, they hadn't slept. At least he and Ted had gotten a bit of sleep before they'd been overtaken. Even the twenty minutes had given them a renewed vigor. And Sam was not a fool. He knew they couldn't keep going at this pace, or eventually, they'd collapse.

"Aren't you going to rest?" he urged Adrián.

"Why, do you need your beauty sleep?"

It was as if Adrián was possessed and refused to stop no matter what. "I can't imagine you going at such a grueling pace without some rest."

"Don't bother me. There's a pot of gold at the end of this journey and ain't stopping for nothing."

Moving on, they discovered another passage. There was a stack of rocks to mark the route Decker and the others had taken. At least they were on the right track. It seemed as if they had been walking for an eternity. Sam's legs felt like rubber. He wondered how Ted was faring after having been struck on the head, his eyes looked drowsy and a bit glazed. He hoped he'd be able to continue at the rate Adrián was pushing them.

It was beyond Sam how this could have happened to them twice. *What were the odds,* he deliberated? But when he recounted the strange coincidences they'd encountered thus far the whole scenario was beyond bazaar.

Coming to a steep decline, scattered with small pebbles, they carefully began a descent, their feet sliding. To keep from falling Sam and Ted leaned into the solid rock wall their fingers grabbing at whatever edges they could find to keep them from hurtling over the side. Each step made their nerves crackle with anticipation.

Halfway down the slope, Javier lost his footing. He went tumbling forward, his shoulder grinding against the sharp-edged

226

rock beneath. Unable to keep his balance his body rolled to the side, his feet dangling over the edge. Not thinking clearly, he held fast to the rifle and was unable to keep his body from sliding farther. Frantic, he began trying to dig his fingers into the ledge to hold him, but it was too late, there was no protrusion to grasp, and he kept slipping.

Sam got to his knee and reached out his hand. "Grab hold, Javier!" he yelled.

Javier let go of the rifle and swept his hand upward with a frantic attempt to clasp Sam's hand. His fingertips latched onto a piece of Sam's sleeve, his face twisted with raw fear. Bulging eyes looked desperately into Sam's—a look that revealed he knew he was going to die.

He made one last attempt to hold himself to the cliff edge, but to no avail. With a scream of terror, his body wrenched free. With arms and feet spread wide, he tumbled end over end, his cries echoing through the black cavern with a blood-curdling intensity. There was a splash, and then absolute silence.

Sam, Ted, and Adrián stood like stiff statues. They could not seem to move for fear of falling themselves. What they had witnessed was surreal. It was not until Adrián shouted at them to continue, that they got their bearings and began the slow descent once again. None of them spoke. It was difficult to know how to feel at that moment. Even though his death was beneficial in that they only had one captor to contend with, Javier's death was horrifying to watch.

Chapter 27

Bruno paced the floor. He was perplexed he hadn't heard anything from his men. There was a plaguing suspicion something might have happened to all of them, and he'd be without leverage. He'd not let a fortune slip through his fingers, not a chance. With that reeling in mind, he grabbed the phone and called one of his other hired hands, Benito Vasquez.

"Benito," he bellowed. "I need to see you right away. Bring along Cayo and Rico."

"What's up?"

"I'll explain when you get here," Bruno told him. "And make it quick!"

Benito could hear the urgency in Bruno's voice. "I'll be there in short order," he assured him. Benito was good to his word and walked through Bruno's door within the hour with Cayo Reyes and Rico Vasco; all of them had worked for Bruno for nearly twenty years. They reasoned it must have great importance for Bruno to insist they all come. After all, they knew Adrián and Javier were already out on orders from Bruno.

"What's up, boss?" Benito inquired as he took a chair opposite Bruno's desk.

"I've lost all contact with Adrián and Javier as well as Ganigi," he said with annoyance.

"I give them a simple job and look what happens." He spread his hands out, palms up. "I'm at a loss. They already botched things up once and I gave them another chance because I'm a fair man. I could have easily blown their heads off, right? And this is my reward for being a nice guy."

Benito stared at him. Nice guy? Well, he knew better than to dispute that. "Yeah, don't know what they were thinking." He sidled up to Bruno, knowing that was the best course of action. He knew Bruno's temper all too well, and he was not going to push it.

"I have a job for the three of you," he told them. "The *Jade*, Haydens yacht, is moored in the bay. I've learned Leonard's wife and Decker's father are on board. I'd like you to overtake them and bring them here."

Benito's brows rose in surprise. "There are other crew members," he reminded Bruno. He had it fresh in his mind that the last time they tried to take the *Jade* when they were on course for Trujillo, they'd lost one of their men. It had not been an easy target.

"You scared of an old man and woman?" Bruno goaded him, knowing exactly how to challenge a man and his pride. Bruno had years of learning to manipulate others. In this case, if gentle coercion didn't work, his revolver was tucked at his side. That was always persuasive.

"No," he muttered, seeing the combative flash in Bruno's eyes, daring him to defy him. "No, not at all, Bruno. When do you want us to do this?"

"Nothing like the present."

"How can we lure them off the yacht without calling attention to us?" he inquired, having his doubts about accomplishing such a feat.

"You're a smart man, Benito," was his dispassionate reply. "I'm sure you'll figure it out." He tipped his head toward the far wall, which was equipped with an assortment of rifles, Smith and Wesson Revolvers, AR-15's, CZP-07 Urban Grey with suppressors, and shotguns. It was only a simple matter of choosing whichever one Benito felt most comfortable with from Bruno's extensive arsenal.

When he had looked the guns over, Benito stood and selected for himself the CZP-07 with an extended capacity magazine. He motioned for the other two to join him and select their firearm of choice.

"We'll wait until after midnight when they go to sleep," Benito informed him. "Where do you want us to hide them once we have them?"

"Out back in the shed. They can yell like wild banshees if they want and no one will hear them. We'll hold them until we have the map," Bruno said confidently. He tucked his hands behind his head, leaned back in his chair and smiled wickedly. It was a perfect plan!

Once they had their weapons and ammo, Benito and his two cronies strutted out the door, leaving Bruno's booted feet propped on the desk, and a Cuban cigar dangling from the corner of his lips. Bruno had set a challenge before them that would not be easily accomplished, but they had the element of surprise on their side. They hoped for a good outcome, and not lose any more men in the process.

***

Holly leaned against the railing aboard the *Jade*. She gazed out over the water thinking how utterly peaceful it was. Long spears of golden light shimmered across the tumbling waves from the full moon. She felt as though she could stay there forever. The velvety black sky was magnificently waxed with twinkling stars, and a light breeze stirred, lifting the strands of dark hair from her face. She closed her eyes and tilted her head back, relishing the coolness of the evening.

"What thoughts are whirling in that pretty head of yours?" Garrett's deep voice broke through her contemplative mood.

Holly turned her head and smiled warmly. "I was thinking what an amazing evening it is. Listen," she said, and when both of them stood quietly, all they heard was the gentle lapping of waves on the yacht's hull.

The salty sea air filled Garrett's nostrils, and he breathed in deeply. Like Holly, he savored the moment. He gazed at her beauty, a flutter of excitement flooding his senses. He'd not felt these kinds of feelings since his wife Anna had passed away from cancer years ago. He never thought he'd ever recover from the loss, nor did he ever anticipate another woman would affect him the same way.

Holly was kind, compassionate, and put her needs aside to help others. Her selflessness touched him. Boldly, he slid his hand to the small of her back and was thankful he didn't feel her tense, or worse, step away. Instead, she turned to him a big smile on her pink lips, and her hand reached out to touch his cheek.

"I'm so glad I came," she admitted. "I'd never have come to know you."

He was surprised by her candor. He had kept a conscious distance out of respect for her grieving, realizing how much she had gone through. He realized she'd need time to come to grips with the atrocious events that had taken place. She had suffered greatly, and yet, she was innocent.

"Likewise, Holly," he admitted, reaching his hand up to cup hers. "You're an incredible woman."

She sighed. "I never spent much time with Leonard over the past four years," she admitted. "He was always gone. I went on a couple of expeditions with him thinking to rebuild our relationship; even then, we never seemed to spend any intimate time together."

"I'm sorry," Garrett said with genuine compassion.

She smiled cocking her head to the side. "I'm not complaining," she quelled any thoughts to the contrary. "I loved him dearly. I'll forever hold our memories close to my heart. He was my first love, and when we were married, I believed it would be forever. Fate has a way of changing that, doesn't it?"

He looked her squarely in the eyes. "Yes, I'm afraid it does."

"Tell me about her."

He looked a bit surprised, but then how could she not know there had been someone special in his life when all she had to do was look at Decker. "She was dazzling," he told her, a few tears touching his eyes. "I suppose I'll always love her. We had many great times together, dancing, boating, fishing…" He looked distant for a brief time, recollecting the years they had shared. "I never thought I could ever look at another woman with the same passion I had with Anna." He knew it was time for honesty even if it caused Holly to withdraw from him. He had held the emotions inside for too long, and he was bursting to tell her.

"She must have been a wonderful woman," admitted Holly, lowering her eyes.

Garrett cupped her chin and raised her face upward so he could gaze into her dark eyes. "She was," he agreed. "But so are you, Holly. You've brought joy back into my life."

There was surprise written on her face. "I have?"

"When I said I never thought I could look at another woman with the same passion, I meant it—until I met you."

Tears gathered in her eyes. "I'm so glad, Garrett. I've never felt closer to anyone than I do right now with you. Not because of all the horrible situations I've gone through, but because of who you are."

He placed his palms on either side of her head and bending forward, gently kissed her. All the emotions he had been stifling now rose to the surface, and he gathered her into his arms and held her.

As Phil stepped out on deck, he interrupted the moment. "Sorry," he apologized.

"That's all right, Phil. What do you need?"

"Actually nothing," he replied. "I made some ice tea and have some orange-cranberry scones. Thought you two might want to have some."

"How could we refuse your extraordinary culinary delicacies?" Holly complimented.

"Why thank you, ma'am, I aim to please," he laughed heartily. "Would you prefer to eat in the dining hall next to the galley, or up here?"

"Up here would be nice," Garrett told him, taking Holly's hand and leading her across the deck to a small round table. He pulled her chair out for her and then walked around the other side to seat himself.

Phil brought out the white linen table cloth and spread it out, then set down two large glasses of iced tea, a sprig of mint dancing on the ice cubes. The scones were beautiful and looked scrumptious. Alongside the scones, he set out two small bowls, one was lemon curd he had made himself, and the other was a blackberry jam. Either would be perfect with the scones. He always knew what to serve.

With their feelings out in the open, Garrett felt a weight had been lifted. He'd been reluctant, unsure if this was the right time to express what he'd been grappling with for quite some time. His heart had leapt like a school boy's first kiss the moment he had set eyes on her. Now, there were no more pretenses, and he was free to court her, but ever so slowly because of how much she had suffered through.

The two of them shared old memories, ate scones, laughed and simply enjoyed each other's company. Garrett was thinking how good it was to have everything laid out before them. No guesswork. They were excited about where this newly founded relationship would carry them.

It was nearly eleven at night when they made their way to their cabins. It would be a night to remember. Both retired starry-eyed and felt somewhat sedated by the turn of events. Relaxed as they were, they ventured they'd sleep like babies.

Phil, Shane, and Polly stayed in the dining area playing poker. They each had a glass of bourbon, a rolled cigar, and a bowl of snacks off to the side. They were tired of endless days of waiting for the team to return and looked for games or anything that might amuse them. In the back of their mind, they mulled over the circumstances. They still couldn't figure out what happened to Sam and Ted's communications system.

Sam was proficient in what he did. Their equipment was working fine, so why Sam's sat phone was unreachable was perplexing, to say the least. There was a moment when they'd considered forming their own team and going after them, except it would mean the *Jade* would go unmanned, and Decker would not be very supportive if they left their posts. He was a stickler about his crew following orders, and they did not want to break that trust with him.

Unless they heard otherwise, they would stay where they were told. However, that being decided, they agreed if they didn't hear anything from the team within the next week, they'd be forced to go to the authorities and try to convince them to send out officers to find them. It was unnerving to be kept in the dark.

"A flush!" Polly rolled with laughter, sweeping in the pile of plastic chips.

"You must be cheating," grumbled Shane.

"Sore loser," Polly roared, releasing a cloud of gray smoke from the cigar.

"Put a pipe in it, Polly."

Polly poured them more bourbon from the bottle while Phil shuffled the cards and dealt them another hand. Even before he looked at his hand, Phil tossed out a few chips to the center of the table; the others followed suit. Polly tossed two cards out and waited for Phil to give him two more. He grinned and shoved in more chips.

"Seriously!" Shane yelped. Polly's confidence was beginning to annoy him. "I'll take three cards."

Phil replaced his three cards and waited to see what he was going to do. Shane was pondering whether to continue or fold, but not wanting to give Polly the satisfaction of winning again, he did his best to bluff his companions. He shoved out two piles of plastic chips and set his face to look confident.

"I'm staying in," Phil cooed, "And I'll raise you."

Polly arched his brows, staring down his poker partners to see if they were bluffing. He shoved out his chips. "Call you." Spreading out his hand he revealed a full house. He looked a little smug.

Laying down his hand, Phil said, "Two pairs, dang!" he told them.

Shane laughed. "Tell you what, Polly, you're one lucky sucker."

He scooped up all the chips a big grin on his mouth. Snuffing out his cigar, and taking a large swallow of his bourbon, he slapped his glass down and informed them he was finished for the night. He'd had one drink too many, and he was feeling its effects. Nothing a good night's sleep wouldn't cure.

"Yeah, I think I'm ready to retire as well," Shane said, taking to his feet. "I'll see you guys in the morning."

"Good night, y'all," Phil yawned.

Chapter 28

Benito waited it out. He would not make his move until he was sure everyone on board was settled down for the night. He and his two companions sat around a table at the local bar having a bottle of Salva Vida beer. It was nearly one o'clock in the morning. As his eyes searched the swells of the bay for signs of life aboard the *Jade*, he could see nothing but one light on deck. Taking his last sip, he took to his feet and motioned for the other two to follow him. He tossed a few coins onto the table and then strode out onto the sandy beach.

Once on the docks, they climbed on board a small boat with a three and a half horse powered motor. The boat was old with paint chipping off the sides, but it would suffice. An SUV was awaiting them close by for when they brought their captives back. It would be risky should anyone see them on their return, but that was Bruno's plans, and they had no choice but to follow it through.

Nearing the *Jade*, Benito shut off the motor and took to rowing, so they could come alongside the *Jade* with as little noise as possible. As their boat rubbed against the dive platform, he leapt onto the *Jade* and secured the lines to keep the small boat stable until they returned. The other two men stepped out, being as quiet as they could, and climbed the ladder to the deck.

Peering out, Benito didn't see anyone, so he motioned for the two men to follow him.

They had their guns prepared and hoped they'd not have to use them yet, if at all. The men went below deck, trying to determine where the cabins were. It would be a guess as to who was sleeping where, so they'd simply have to start with the first cabin and work their way down the companionway.

When they encroached on the first room, Benito twisted the handle slowly, cracking the door slightly to peer inside. Against the far wall, he saw two bunks, both occupied. Stepping inside, Benito walked quietly across the wood-planked floor. He placed the barrel of his gun at the base of the man's skull, and he gave a quick shake to his shoulder, while the other held a gun aimed on the upper bunk.

Phil stirred as he felt a sudden jostling of his body. He rolled over to face the barrel of a gun, and he sobered immediately. His hands slid upward to show he did not have a weapon. "What do you want?" he spoke in a raspy voice.

"I want you to shut up," Benito told him coldly. "Slide out of the bed and move over there where I can see you."

Phil slid out from the covers dressed only in his striped boxers. He walked hesitantly over to the chair and sat down while one of the men began binding his hands and feet, then watched helplessly while one of the men stirred Polly from his sleep.

Polly grunted as he sat up, wiping his eyes. Groggy, he hadn't comprehended what was taking place, and when his eyes focused in, he saw Phil strapped to a chair. His head was a bit cloudy from drinking, but he gathered they were in a rather bad predicament. There was nothing he could do except follow their instructions.

"You need to hop on down from there and over to the other chair," Benito ordered him, holding his gun even with his head.

Polly was not going to argue and leapt down from his bunk, arms raised high over his head. Taking a seat, one of the men grabbed his arms and yanked them back behind him. He could

237

feel the ropes cutting into his flesh. He winced. After his hands, they pulled his feet together and secured him to the chair at the bottom. Taking out handkerchiefs, they placed one in Phil's mouth and one in Polly's and tied them tightly to keep them from yelling out.

Garrett had heard some noises and had gotten out of bed. He slipped into the companionway and padded down the hall. He spied someone rounding the corner and had ducked back into one of the vacant cabins to hide. When he saw the men had gone into Phil and Polly's cabin, he rushed down the hall in the opposite direction to wake Holly.

Her eyes widened with fear as Garrett's hand covered her mouth to prevent her screaming. He placed his finger over his lips to warn her not to make a sound. "There are some men on the boat, we need to hide," he whispered.

She climbed out of the covers, grabbed her light housecoat and followed Garrett out of the room and quickly toward the stern where there was another exit. Her heart was beating fast as she stayed on Garrett's heels. As they slipped out onto the deck and rushed to the side, they saw the intruder's boat moored at the stern.

"I think we can swim to shore from here," he said, not knowing what else to do at the moment. "Do you think you can make it?"

"I think so."

They climbed down the ladder and eased themselves into the warm waters of the bay. Both of them were good swimmers and hoped they'd be able to make it that far without being spotted by the intruders.

They kicked hard, their arms beating at the water, carrying them farther from the *Jade* and nearer to the shoreline. Streamers of golden light stretched out across the bay from the quaint bars dotting the shoreline.

Garrett figured they could find help once they made it back. He hoped that the men would not harm Phil, Polly or Shane. He was not even sure if these men were the same ones who'd been following them all along or if they were thieves. Either way, if one of the crew chose to rebel against them, the men might possibly take sport in killing them.

Shane too was more than a little surprised when he was wakened to see three men standing over him with their guns leveled at his head. The men led him down the narrow hall to the other cabin and tied him to another chair beside Phil and Polly. Presently, they were all disabled and couldn't help Garrett or Holly. Frustration boiled to the surface as they struggled against the bindings.

The men left the room and began searching the other cabins looking for Garrett and Holly. When they'd gone through every room, they hurried to the deck.

"Where on earth could they have gone?" Benito mumbled, knowing that if they allowed them to escape, Bruno would have their heads.

"Search the deck, and I'll go search the galley," Benito told them.

Every place they thought someone could possibly hide, they searched. Unable to find them, they met on deck and tried to decide what to do next. This was not a part of their strategy. What they thought was a well laid- out, detailed plan was failing miserably. Already Benito was trying to figure out what he would tell Bruno. It was not going to be a pleasant task.

Certain Garrett and Holly were not on board, they headed back to their boat, not caring whether the men they had tied up ever got free. Their only concern now was finding the other two.

As they headed back for shore, one of the men shouted and pointed. "There! They're going to shore!"

Benito turned the boat in their direction. They were bearing down on them fast. As they closed the gap, they saw Garrett and

Holly crawl out of the waves and stagger to the sandy beach. They glanced back and saw the boat nearing the shore. Garrett grabbed Holly's hand and pulled her in the direction of the town.

Determined they'd not have the chance to elude them, Benito jumped over the side, slogged through the small waves and took to a dead run after them. Water flew in every direction. He held his gun in his hand as he continued his sprint, knowing he was young and had much more energy and perseverance than they did. He could see he was gaining ground on them and pumped his arms even harder to close the distance.

Aiming his gun left of them, he popped off a round as a warning. The ground in front of Garrett and Holly exploded into a spray of sand where the bullets had struck. It was a frightful realization that the man might possibly shoot them. That thought brought the two of them to an abrupt standstill. The last thing they wanted was a bullet in their back. Standing stationary, hands up, they waited for him to catch up.

"Over there," he directed them.

Turning, they saw a black SUV parked alongside the road. They trudged slowly toward it, chilled to the bone. Their clothes were soaking wet, and with the cool night air, they shivered, their flesh rising into goosebumps. Garrett draped his arm over Holly's shoulder and drew her near to help warm her. Every instinct in him wanted to turn and pounce on the man, but he was fearful something would happen to Holly if he did. For the time, he'd try and follow their instructions, but he would continue to look for an opportunity to get away.

By the time they got to the vehicle, the other two had caught up with them. Still having strands of ropes with them, they secured Garrett and Holly's hands and pushed them inside the vehicle all the while making sure no one had seen them. This late at night, the beach was deserted, although had they made it to one of the bars farther down the beach, the two of them could have sought help because they'd seen the flicker of lights coming from one of the establishments. Unfortunately, that was not the case.

Once inside the vehicle, one of the men put black sacks over their heads, so they were unable to see where they were being taken as Bruno had instructed. The ride was painstakingly long. Garrett tried to memorize the twists and turns they were making, in case they found an opportunity to make a getaway.

Chapter 29

Back at the *Jade*, the men battled the ropes. They were tight, and no matter how hard they fought to free themselves, it was a losing battle. Worse, they were unable to communicate with one another because of the gags over their mouths. Since they had not seen Garrett or Holly, their worse fear was that they'd been kidnapped. But their biggest concern at the moment was, if they couldn't free themselves, they'd starve or die of thirst. No one would think to look on board, so they were on their own.

Polly was the brawniest of them. He figured if anyone was able to overcome the bindings it was him. His mind whirled trying to come up with some ingenuity that would help to free them. He struggled against the harsh hemp cords but to no avail. He purposed not to give up no matter what. Garrett and Holly needed them.

Polly started rocking back and forth until he had enough momentum to topple the chair, gaining the attention of the others. He landed with a thud, his shoulder driving agonizingly into the floor. He moaned and scrunched his face from the knife-sharp pain. As the sting subsided, he motioned for Phil to do the same.

With a crash, Phil struck the floor. He understood what Polly planned to do and used his feet to propel him in a circle so that he was back to back with Polly. Close, they began working their fingers at each other's bindings. Polly could feel the knot loosening as he tugged and pulled at the twisted fiber. Their struggle went on for a time until he felt the rope give on Phil's wrist and fall away.

Phil brought his arms around and unfastened his feet and removed the gag, then started removing Polly's. When both were free, they moved swiftly to Shane. Their wrists were bloody, but at least they were unharmed. Their first impulse was to see if they could find Garrett and Holly. If this was a robbery, they'd find them tied up in another room.

Polly sprinted out of his cabin and down the hallway, breaking through the door like a bulldozer. His countenance fell when he saw Garrett was indeed gone.

Phil had gone to see if he could locate Holly and felt his heart plummet when he saw she was not in her cabin. In hurried strides, Phil made his way towards Garrett's quarters and ducked inside where he found Polly. His face spoke for itself. Their worst fears were confirmed. They all stood there looking at one another, trying to figure out what to do next.

Dawn was breaking when Polly and Phil prepared to launch the dinghy. They decided Shane needed to stay with the yacht and they'd go to the authorities and file a missing person's report. After that, they'd do some snooping on their own to see if anyone had any information about the incident. They needed to catch a break. Possibly someone might have seen them once they came to shore and give them a lead.

They gave the description of the three men to the police as well as Garrett and Holly's, but the police did not appear too distraught over the matter. The chief of police assured them they'd be on the lookout for the men but told Polly his description looked like most of the town's people.

As they walked on the beach, they stopped several people and showed them photos of Garrett and Holly. There was a possibility someone might recognize them, but after several hours, they didn't have much luck. Next, they went to the beach and inquired at some of the local bars near the docks.

Polly strode up to the open-aired bar and motioned for the bartender to come speak with him. He was a pleasant fellow with a neatly trimmed mustache and a black mop of hair with straight-cut bangs. He wasn't very tall, and Polly had to look down at him as he spoke.

He walked over to Polly with a wide smile, "Hola, Señor," he greeted cheerfully. "How may I help you?"

Polly laid a picture of Garrett on the table. "Have you seen this man?" he asked.

The bartender studied the picture for a time and then shook his head. "Don't recognize him. Sorry."

Polly picked up the picture and stuck it inside his shirt, disappointment creasing his face. His hand rubbed his reddish beard which was usually well kept, but since he had been at sea for a time, he had neglected to trim it, and it had become quite unruly, lending him, even more, the appearance of a Viking.

"Did you see three men here last night sitting together? They would have been here probably until one in the morning." Polly described what he remembered about the three.

"Sorry. I wasn't here last night Señor."

"Do you know who was?"

"Montego, he'll be here this evening if you want to speak with him."

"Thank you for your help."

"What to do now?" Phil piped up, feeling a bit helpless.

"What do you say we rent a vehicle and drive around some," Polly replied. "Who knows, it's possible we might see one of the men. Can't hurt."

Renting a beat-up, olive-green jeep without a top, the two of them began to scour the city. They drove along various back streets and down alleys, their eyes peeled for anyone who looked vaguely familiar, but with no luck. They kept in contact with Shane to let him know what their plans were. The last thing they wanted was for Shane to think something had happened to them.

It was later that evening when they went back to the bar and located Montego. He was a large-bellied man, somewhat balding, with a black mustache that was waxed and curled up at the ends. He was quite accommodating, giving them each a beer while he spoke with them about their missing friends.

"Come to think of it," he began, "there were three men here last night, right there where you are sitting. They were not drinking much. If I remember correctly, I think they only had one beer each. They left around one in the morning."

"Do you know who they are?"

He shook his head. "No, I think I may have seen one of them before, but I don't know any of them personally."

"Did you see what car they were driving?" Phil asked.

"No, sorry." He started to walk away then stopped short. "Wait a minute. It was around two or two thirty when I was closing up; I thought I had heard a gunshot outside. A few minutes later, I went out with the garbage. Over at the far parking lot, near the boat ramp, I saw a dark SUV. Could have been the same men I saw inside the bar. I also heard a woman's voice calling out, though I couldn't hear what she was saying. It's unusual to have much going on that time of night, at least around here."

"Anything else?" Polly asked, thinking the man might remember something else to help them.

"That's all I can tell you."

"Thanks, you've been helpful," Polly answered wearily. He tucked the photos inside his back pocket trying to decide what to do next. Unfortunately, they were back at square one, though having a description of the vehicle would be helpful.

"I hope you find your friends."

"Thanks again," Polly said and waved goodbye.

Except for driving around, there was not much else they could do. However, they did make a quick stop-over to the police station and told them about the dark SUV, but without a license plate number or more information on the men, they had nothing else to go by. For the time being, they'd have to go back to the boat and keep checking randomly, with hopes they might see the vehicle or the men.

Chapter 30

Decker spied a cone-shaped spear of light in the distance. He felt a lift in his dampened spirit. They had been moving from one passage to the next, and he had long since lost his excitement and wondered if they should concede and throw in the towel.

"I see it," Callie said. More than anything, she wanted out of this cave and back into the sunlight. Always in the back of her mind was the horrific jaguar attack, and chances were the longer they remained in the cave, the more risk there was of another brutal attack.

They all rushed forward and came to a fissure in the ceiling. "Do you think we can squeeze through it?" Carson questioned, thinking it looked a bit small for their large bodies.

"Hard to say," Decker responded. "I'll have to climb up there and see for sure." Taking his steel claw, he swung it upward to catch the lip of the crack and began climbing the rope. Once he made it to the top, he saw there was no chance they'd make it out. The crack might possibly allow for Callie's slim body to squeeze through, but for the rest of them, it didn't look promising.

Decker dropped back down. "Sorry," he apologized. "Too tight."

Frustration shadowed their faces, but they shrugged, knowing there was no way to change the situation and they'd have to move on. They were all tired and began to wonder if they would ever make it out of the cave.

"Well, okay," Callie tried to sound chipper. "Let's move on."

They pushed forward once more. The passage got narrower the farther they walked until their shoulders were touching the walls. Decker was at a place where he turned sideways and was thinking this was going to be the end of the line, but he pressed himself and nearly fell forward as he made it through to the other side. As he advanced, he found himself in a large cavern. To his delight, there was a stream of light coming from across the chasm.

"Eureka!" he yelled, as the others squeezed through the gap.

Callie's headlamp lit on something bright off to the side, and as she went to explore, she realized it was piles of skulls, one on top of another, measuring four-foot high. Most of the skulls appeared to have a wide crack in the parietal bone as if something had struck them hard. At the base of the skulls were piles of bones. She called the others over to take a look.

"This is amazing," she said with excitement ringing in her voice. "What do you make of this Decker?"

"The bones will have to be examined to determine their age," he responded. "But peculiar. I suspect these people, at some point in history, performed sacrifices. That certainly would account for the skull fractures."

"Do you think the culture practiced cannibalism?" Callie inquired, finding that a reasonable conclusion as well.

"Possibly," Decker shrugged. It was mere speculation. Right now, he was trying to put the pieces of the puzzle together to form a conclusion.

Callie came across more bones as she walked through the cave. "Decker, you have to see this!" she exclaimed, digging out a brush from her pack and brushing off sediment from the bones. "This man must have been over eight feet tall." She could scarcely believe her eyes.

Decker was astounded as well. Bending down on one knee, he began to examine the bones without disturbing them. This discovery was monumental. Taking out his measuring tape, he began to line it up with the bones and shook his head in disbelief. "The length of the skeletal remains measures eight foot, three-inches in height!" he spouted. "This is extraordinary."

Manuel stood off to the corner overcome with fear. These were burial grounds and being there meant their lives were in danger. He did not take the curse lightly. These were sacred places, and man should never tread here. His first thought was to bolt and put as much distance behind him as possible but going alone without adequate supplies would be sure death. He recalled the stories of the giants who had lived here, half man, half monkey. He trembled with uncertainty, not knowing what they would encounter once they went outside of the cave. He believed the jaguars were there to protect the heritage of the natives who had once dwelled here.

"Are you recording this, Callie?" Decker asked as he saw her jotting something down on a small notebook.

"You bet I am—I feel like a schoolgirl on her first date," she said, "This is more than I can take in."

He chuckled at her exuberance, but he also was experiencing a pitched enthusiasm. This discovery was even more magnificent than the cave they'd discovered in France. The implications were staggering.

While Decker poured over the bones with utmost fascination, Callie and Carson made use of the time. They discovered lithographs along the walls painted in red, depicting a wide range of animals, many unrecognizable. But they did make out the shape of jaguars, several species of birds, and a few crude drawings of men and women with what looked to be feathers on their bodies and heads. The natives had used some sort of dye which had seeped into the porous limestone that kept its integrity all these many years. Their ingenuity never ceased to amaze Callie.

Near the skulls were flint knives, spear heads, and broken pottery shards. Callie laid down on her stomach and put her camera up to the relics and took several pictures, careful not to disturb them. These artifacts belonged to the Honduran museum, to the people as a means to educate them about their cultural background. Their heart was never to plunder or disrupt their surroundings if at all possible.

After taking notes and snapshots of the remains, they continued their trek toward the hazy golden light up ahead. They knew they had to be close to the vicinity Leonard had marked out, according to the calculations on the map and charts they'd gone over prior to leaving Malibu. The cave was limestone. Leonard had made notes about it on the map and wrote that the cave was mere yards from his findings.

There was a new energy in them as they followed the path quickly, anticipating what lay ahead. The farther they walked, the brighter the light grew until they saw a large archway leading outside and into a new territory.

When they stepped out, they squinted and blinked several times trying to focus in on their surroundings. They had been in the dark for so long, the light was nearly blinding.

Decker was correct. This was a backdoor, and as they looked in every direction, there was evidence of a great metropolis; areas that appeared to be expansive gardens and stone pillars which stretched twelve feet high. There were rows of chiseled archways, and what appeared to be roads. One elaborate archway looked to be the main entryway, and it led into cobbled courtyards.

Off to their right and to their left were two massive rock pyramids. Though they were overgrown with vines, underbrush, and twisted trees, the handiwork of stone blocks was incredibly impressive. Decker figured the stones had to be around four feet by four feet in dimension, and each one was stacked perfectly.

Each one was finely shaped to near perfection and amazingly assembled by human hands. It was breathtaking.

It took several grueling hours, cutting away the tangle of bushes to have a closer look at the stonework. They got down on hands and knees and began a careful inspection of the area. They found ax heads and spears made of obsidian which they calculated came from Guatemala most likely, as there was no obsidian in this particular geographical area. The amount of antiquities they began uncovering were astonishing.

Overhead, the shrill screams of the Golden-Mantled Howling monkeys resounded. They could be seen swinging from one tree to the next, on long twisted vines, and their protests grew louder and louder. Acting aggressively, the monkeys began throwing down branches and whatever else they could find to try and threaten the intruders. Indeed, it was intimidating and ear-splitting.

Trying to shut out the warning screams, they distracted themselves by scouring the area more thoroughly, ducking from the debris raining down on them. As they identified the various relics they discovered, they recorded it on tablets and took several photos of each. There were many carved stone statues shaped like animals such as alligators, jaguars, snakes, and monkeys. Every step brought them to a new adventure.

To the front of one of the pyramids, they discovered an entryway that had obviously been cleared prior to their coming. No doubt it had been Leonard. Decker and the team fitted on their headlamps to cope with the veiled light inside. Decker was first to proceed. The entrance was not large by any means, and so they got on hands and knees and worked their way into the dark alcove. Decker broke through into the cavity and yelled for everyone to stop. Before him, he spied the remains of a Fer-de-Lance which had apparently been sliced in half and was decomposed. His eyes made a sweep of the area to make sure there weren't other snakes in the perimeter. When he didn't see anything, he signaled for the others to follow. The last thing he wanted was to step into a den of rattlesnakes, or worse, jaguars. Feeling a bit edgy, especially after what had happened to Ganigi, he slipped his gun from its holster and pushed himself to his feet.

Callie rushed to his side to find out what had held them up. "What was the problem?"

"It was a dried up, cut in half, Fer-de-Lance," he answered with a nervous snort. "I didn't want to take any chances. There could have been a pit of snakes somewhere in here, so please take your time when you're looking around and be on guard."

"Must have been Leonard," Callie said.

They followed a narrow passage a short distance and ducked into another cavity. After a couple of steps inside, they froze, their mouths agape. Everywhere around them was wooden chests overflowing with treasure beyond imagination. Their head lamps danced off solid gold plates, cups, and necklaces—jewels glittered brilliantly. Emeralds, chunks of rubies the size of a fist, and an assortment of turquoise jewelry set in silver were heaped knee deep in places. Dazzling opals and garnets overflowed one of the trunks and spilled across the rock hewn floor in a vivid display. There were headdresses inlaid with precious stones, statues carved out of gold, and chests brimming with handfuls of shimmering, golden-brown Sphalerite crystals. As the rays of light played off the minerals, a spectrum of colors licked like flames on the walls surrounding them. Everywhere their eyes lit they were met with heaps of gemstones of every size and color.

"I'm breathless," Callie gushed, her eyes transfixed on the indescribable wealth strewn out before her. There were no adequate words to describe the riches surrounding them.

"More than extraordinary," Decker said.

"I've never seen anything like it," Carson shook his head in awe. "All of this laying here untouched for centuries.

Off in an alcove near Callie, she spotted a layer of white bones neatly stacked one on top of the other. On top were two bleached white skulls, but unlike the others they had found earlier, their craniums were not cracked open. They speculated if the skulls belonged to royalty, the other bones might have belonged to their servants and that they were probably slain in order to attend to their royal masters in the next world, as cultures often practiced. A chilling thought, but that was how it appeared.

Decker dropped his hand on Manuel's shoulder. "Imagine what the people of Honduras will say when they see this amazing treasure trove of pre-Columbian culture on display at their museum."

There were tears in Manuel's eyes. "You mean you aren't going to take it?"

"Absolutely not," Decker told him. "We'll go back to the Honduran government and ask for permits to come return and excavate, but these relics don't belong to us."

"That's unbelievable," Manuel said, knowing anyone else would take possession of the jewels and whatever they couldn't carry out, they'd return for.

"We aren't treasure hunters, Manuel. We're archaeologists," Decker explained. "This isn't ours to take, but we are gratified to have the opportunity to return and uncover the past and give it to you and your people. It belongs to you."

"The gods will show you favor," Manuel spoke. He had dreaded the thought of discovering the lost city and what would be taken. Manuel believed if anyone took something that belonged to the city, they would face the curse and death would be the ultimate end. He stood awe-struck in the presence of these honorable people who chose to preserve his culture and weren't trying to benefit from what rightly belonged to the Honduran people. Somehow it gave him comfort.

They spent time walking through the interior investigating the hoard of riches. There were several carved statues that looked to be royalty of some kind. The highly technical skills of this people were awe-inspiring. What they had accomplished with their bare hands was remarkable.

Callie took pictures of various items that intrigued her most, then with a trowel in hand, she went out to the courtyard and began digging to see what else might turn up. The rest of the day the team moved in and out of the two pyramids. They took the time to cut away debris and brush off the stones to examine the artifacts before they headed back. They put together as much evidence as possible to convince the government to allow them to return to excavate. The photos spoke for themselves.

Chapter 31

Garrett and Holly were shoved into a room, hands tied behind their backs and hoods still covering their heads. A man stepped forward to untie their wrists and plucked the hoods off. They blinked several times from the light which hung in the center of the room by a black cord. A musty smell assaulted their nostrils as if the room had not been used for anything in years.

To the left of them was an old mattress tossed onto the floor with one blanket wadded up in the middle. There were no windows to speak of, and a small room off to the right which appeared to have a toilet and sink, but again, there was no window, and except for the one light that blinked on and off threatening to short out, the room was gloomy and dim.

"Welcome to your new home," Benito belched a devilish laugh.

Garrett leaned slightly and rammed his body full force into Benito. Benito stumbled backward, striking his head on the door as he fell. A flow of blood trickled down the side of his face. The two men with Benito grabbed Garrett solidly by the shoulders while Benito got to his feet.

"You son of a…" Benito's words were drowned out as he lunged forward fist doubled up and thrust it angrily into Garrett's stomach. Garrett grunted as the air was forced out of him. He slumped over, gasping for air.

"Garrett!" Holly screamed, making a move to help him, but Benito straight-armed her, refusing to give her the satisfaction of helping him.

"Leave her alone," Garrett thundered, his eyes narrowed with glowering anger.

"You're not in the position to tell us what to do," Benito growled.

"Why are we here?" Garrett demanded to know.

Benito's grin was twisted with deviltry. "You're our ticket to the biggest treasure known to mankind."

"What?" Garrett's voice cracked, not understanding what their intentions were.

"You'll find out eventually before you die," he laughed dispassionately. "For now, enjoy your room, you'll be here for quite some time."

When they left, Garrett and Holly heard the bolt being slid across the door to secure it from the other side. Garrett ran forward and rammed his shoulder into the door, but it didn't budge. The door was solid as was everything else in the room. Substantial as all of the walls looked, Garrett doubted if anyone would be able to hear them if they called out.

"You holding up?" he asked Holly, rushing to her side and gathering her in his arms."

"Me?" Holly was astounded that his concern was for her. After all, he was the one who had been used as a punching bag by that beast of a man. Please, don't try and be a hero on my account. These men are ruthless and will kill you for sure."

"I'll be fine," he told her, trying to assuage her fears. He scanned the room with his eyes to see if there was some way out of there.

"Where do you think we are?" she asked him, knowing it was a foolish question.

"I tried to imagine the roads we turned onto in my mind but lost track after several turns. I don't think we're in town anymore. At least, I haven't heard any horns honking or traffic for quite some time."

"Why do you think they abducted us?"

"My guess, they are using us as bait," he told her. "If Decker finds the lost city and if there's a treasure to be found, they can use us to make Decker give them the map. Once they have the map, there will be no need for us."

Holly shuddered, understanding what Garrett was saying. If these men received the information they were seeking, they'd have no qualms about getting rid of them. Unfortunately, they'd share the same fate of Leonard and his two guides. Holly lowered her head. "I should never have brought you and the rest of the team into this. This was my cross to bear, not yours or Decker's."

He saw tears in her eyes. "Please, don't blame yourself, Holly. This isn't your fault, none of it. You were put in a no-win situation, and you were alone. You needed help. We were all more than happy to rally around you. It's what we do, and there's always an element of danger."

"Not this much!"

"Let's see if we can't find some loose boards or vents we might be able to squeeze through," Garrett told her, thinking it would take their mind off what could happen to them in the next few days if they found Decker and the crew.

There was a small air vent in the floor of the bathroom, but hardly big enough for either of them to consider using it as a means to free themselves. They pushed against the boards throughout the room. If they found some that had dry-rot, or nails that had worked themselves out enough to dislodge them, there was a slim chance they could get out of there. When they realized there was nothing obvious, they stopped and looked despairingly at one another.

He led her over, and they sat down on the mattress as there were no chairs or other furniture to be had. "I guess all we can do is wait it out and look for an opportunity to make a mad dash," he told her.

Chapter 32

The following day, Polly and Phil went ashore and rented a jeep. They figured this was their only hope of finding Garrett and Holly. Their intention was to drive around town, linger in the bars and restaurants, and comb the streets with the purpose of eventually recognizing one of the men and follow them. They had no clues, and nothing substantial to follow, except that it might have been a black SUV they were thrown into.

So far, they'd gone to three different bars along the beachfront. They'd shown several snapshots of Garrett and Holly. And though it was a long shot, it was still worth pursuing. All they needed was to find someone who saw something unusual that evening, or who could identify Garrett and Holly. After several hours, they came up empty-handed again. And they still hadn't heard from Sam and Ted or the rest of the team.

Walking back to the jeep, Polly spied a dark SUV up the road from them in front of a small grocery store. They hurriedly climbed into the jeep and slowly drove in that direction. They veered off the road and pulled to the curb when they spotted a couple of men coming out of the store with bags in their arms.

They took a moment to recount the incident of the three men who'd come on board the *Jade* the night before and these two men fit the description perfectly.

"Hey!" Polly yelled.

Startled, the men turned their heads and ran for their vehicle, dropping their bags of groceries onto the ground. Food items were strewn across the road. It only took a minute before they squirreled out of their parking spot and sped down the road.

Polly had already punched the pedal to the floor and passed them. With the jerk on the wheel, the jeep whipped in front of the SUV blocking their way but that was not enough to stop them. The driver shoved the car into reverse and turned a complete circle. Gunning it, they headed off down the road.

"Dang!" sputtered Polly, cranking the wheel and doing a U-turn in the middle of the street. He slammed the pedal to the floor, the tires grinding against the hard ground then shot off like a rocket down the road. When he rounded one of the corners near the end of town, he was met with a small flock of chickens meandering across the road. Their wings flapped with excitement as the jeep barreled toward them and with loud squawks, they flew up into the air in front of them. Polly swerved, barely missing a couple of them, and adding to the drama, a shopkeeper came rushing out of the quaint little store, shaking his fist at Polly. His anger was evident as he shouted obscenities at them.

"Don't lose them!" Phil shouted.

"Really?" he shot back, a bit annoyed. He was doing the best he could. It was challenging trying to dodge all the obstacles, and he was sure Phil wouldn't do any better at the wheel than he was.

They headed toward the mountain area, dirt spiraling behind them. The jeep lurched to the side as it hit a pothole, tossing them forcibly around the cab. They could see they were in for a ride and fastened their seat belts. They didn't want to chance being thrown out of the jeep. Accelerating, they closed the distance on the SUV.

"Yahoo!" Phil shouted as if he was at a rodeo riding a bucking bronco. Polly suspected that if he had a cowboy hat, he'd be waving it over his head as well. It was clear Phil's adrenalin was pumping with wild excitement. It only took a moment for Phil to catch Polly rolling his eyes, revealing he wasn't amused.

They came to a split in the road, and the SUV headed off to the left. It looked like a route that would loop back toward Trujillo. Polly wasn't thrilled with the prospect. It was dangerous enough tailing them along the rutted dirt road, but it was worse in town trying to avoid running over a pedestrian or one of the farm animals scurrying unrestrained through the middle of the streets. Not only that, they had to avoid the local police, who, if they saw them racing through the narrow streets like a herd of wild steers, would not hesitate to drag their rears into headquarters.

They continued to speed along the crowded lane below. Polly swore under his breath. They were not making it easy for him for sure. The SUV dodged in and out of side streets and swerved into constricted alleys.

There was a narrow road to the right that the SUV sped down. People were having to dive out of the way for fear of being struck. At the end of the street, there was a donkey hooked up to a small, wooden, two-wheeled cart, overflowing with hay. The SUV hit the rear of the cart as it swung out into the adjoining street. The cart seemed to explode from the impact, hay and wood splinters erupting into the air like a volcano and came back full force into Polly and Phil's faces.

Polly spit stalks of hay out of his mouth and grumbled something under his breath. He cranked the wheel sharply to avoid taking out the donkey, the jeep sliding sideways, and coming to a complete stop. The angry cart owner and his companion looked as if they were going to chase them down as they ran out into the road with clenched fists. Polly revved the engine, then floored it and sped off down the road.

The SUV had out-maneuvered them and was nowhere to be seen. Agitated, they continued their search, but slowly now, moving from street to street to see if they could find the vehicle. No luck. Polly slammed his hand on the steering wheel, knowing these two men were their only avenue of ever finding Garrett and Holly.

Then as if from nowhere, the SUV came barreling up behind them. "Go! Go!" yelled Phil, bracing himself. The SUV slammed into the rear of the jeep, jerking the both of them backward. Polly shifted down, pushed the accelerator to the floor and blasted forward.

Astonished at the turn of events, they now found their situation reversed. They were now the ones being pursued. What a mess this had turned out to be, Polly thought, though he was able to maintain a narrow distance between them. As he glanced in the rearview mirror, he saw they were hot on their bumper. The jeep fishtailed on the loose sediment and gravel as they sped around sharp bends in the road leading back out of town. They both started coughing as they sucked in a mouthful of the dust swirling around them.

The SUV jolted forward, ramming them from behind, more forcefully this time. The jeep fishtailed but held fast to the road. Polly gave it more gas eager to get away from them, but it didn't look promising. There was another split in the road, and he sped down the right fork unsure of where he was going. Presently, it didn't seem to matter; he needed to shake them off his bumper.

"Here they come again!" Phil shouted, his head turned back and panic rising in him.

This time it struck harder, and Polly was unable to keep control on the wheel. The jeep literally flew off the road and soared through the air down an embankment. The front bumper caught on a swell of ground, flipping the jeep like a feather. It rolled three times on impact, then crashed into the bog below. Settled upside down in the mud, they were quite shaken, but neither were wounded except for a few cuts and bruises. They were thankful for the roll bar and that they'd put on their seatbelts earlier, as the jeep would have no doubt thrown them out or rolled on top of them.

Unhooking their belts, they slid down into the muddy quagmire. On hands and knees, they crawled to the slippery bank and climbed out. Weary, they flopped down on the long blades of grass and watched as the SUV sped off. They looked at one another, mud caked all over them and laughed. Their hair was plastered to the side of their heads, their faces were smeared with mud, and all that was visible were the whites of their eyes.

"Now, that was a rush. What do we do now?" asked Phil.

"Walk back to town."

"What about the jeep?"

Polly looked at it belly-up and shrugged. "I hope they have good insurance," he said, pushing himself to his feet. Exasperated, they began their long journey back to town on foot.

They had probably walked a mile when an old battered truck with wooden railings pulled up alongside of them. "Need a ride?" A man called out as he leaned out the window. He was wearing a wide straw hat, blue jean overalls, and a dirt-covered white t-shirt.

"You bet. Thanks," Polly yelled, running toward the truck, Phil on his heels.

The man looked at them a bit strangely. "That your vehicle in the swamp back there?"

"Yup," Polly said. He could only imagine what the local farmer must be thinking while observing their muddy attire.

"Sorry," the man sympathized. "Hop in back."

They climbed up on the bumper and swung their legs over the side and were greeted by several new baby goats and a couple nannies. The back was loaded down with bags of grain, and as they climbed over the goats, they came to rest on top of a couple of hay bales at the rear of the truck.

"We didn't gain a whole lot today," Polly moaned, shooing one of the goats away that was trying to chew on the tails of his shirt. Lifting up his shoe, he realized he had stepped in goat manure while getting in and it was ground onto the sole of his foot. He shook his head despairingly, wondering how much more could go wrong in one day.

"Could have been pigs," Phil tossed in, finding their situation a bit amusing. However, both of them were disappointed at losing the SUV. Their prospects of finding Garrett and Holly were looking rather dismal.

The driver let them off at the edge of town and no sooner had he sped off than a jeep carrying three policemen pulled up beside them. "Are you the two men who were driving the jeep through town a bit earlier?"

What could they say? Chances were, they had already been identified by the shop owners. And it was highly likely they'd have an extensive bill to cover all the damages.

"Sorry to say, it was," Polly offered, his heart sinking. The police were the last people he wanted to deal with right now.

"You're both under arrest."

One of the officers leapt from the truck his rifle pointed at them. They proceeded to handcuff Polly and Phil and helped them into the jeep then headed toward the station.

"We can explain," Polly said. "We found the men responsible for abducting our friends. The ones we reported as missing, remember?"

"Tell it to the judge."

Polly was not going to let the officers detached demeanor quell him and continued his forceful defense. "We only meant to follow them, but they turned on us, and came after us with a vengeance. And they ran us off the road. We can prove it! They are driving a black SUV, and by now it's fairly banged up after ramming us several times. Just find the SUV!"

The officers didn't seem to be listening. Instead, they marched them to the back of the jailhouse and thrust them into one of the cells. They removed the cuffs, and with a clang, they shut the barred door. One of the officers took a ring of keys from a hook and locked the door securely then headed off to the office.

"Hey!" yelled Polly. "Let us out of here!"

"Well, this has gone from bad to worse," Phil said wryly flopping back on the bed. "What the blazes do we do now?"

"Come on!" bellowed Polly banging on the steel bars. Presently, it was the only thing he could do—make a lot of noise and drive the officer's crazy.

"Don't think they're listening."

"Do you mind?" Polly snapped with frustration. "Hello, you guys are making a big mistake!" When he was exhausted from yelling, he sat down on the bunk alongside Phil. "This stinks."

It was several hours before an officer returned to speak with them. "Your vehicle was found in the bog outside of town. It's pretty mangled. We sent someone to pull it out, and we'll see it makes it back to the car rental for you. There'll be towing costs among other expenses."

"We'll pay for it," Polly told him.

"Yes, you will, and there is still the matter of endangering lives, and damaged property," the officer continued.

"It wasn't our fault, we were trying to catch the men who kidnapped our friends, and they were trying to elude us, then they ended up chasing us," Polly fought to explain for the umpteenth time, though the officer didn't appear sympathetic. "I want to make a phone call."

"What makes you think you're entitled to a phone call?"

"Because everyone is allowed at least one phone call," Polly battled.

"You aren't in America you know."

"Come on," he pleaded. "It'll be worth your while."

"Are you bribing me?"

Polly stopped short. Was he? Well, no matter, he needed to contact Shane. "Of course not," he replied, "I need to make a phone call to our boat so we can make bail."

Taking the keys from his pocket, he ushered Polly out to the office area and pointed to the phone over on the desk.

"Thanks," Polly said and dialed the *Jade*. He sighed aloud when he heard Shane's voice on the other end.

"Where the heck are you?"

"In jail."

"What?" he yelled. "Jail? What for?"

"Trashing a jeep and endangering lives," Polly tried to explain, though it was impossible.

"Are you kidding me?"

"Do I sound like I'm joking?" Polly asked. "We need you to come ashore and bail us out, Shane."

There was a space of absolute silence. "Okay, what do I need to bring with me?"

"Money," he stressed. "Lots and lots of money, and a change of clothes for Phil and I."

"A change of clothes?"

"I'll explain when you get here," Polly offered, wanting Shane to stop asking questions and hurry his fanny there so they could be released. He still had to wonder, that even when Shane offered to pay the bail if they'd be willing to let them out. This was their last thread of hope, and he was fairly sure it would not be an inexpensive endeavor.

Once Shane arrived, they spent more than an hour trying to persuade the officers to cooperate with them. As it was, there were still men out there who had kidnapped their friends, and they needed some kind of help from the police. After a lot of arguing and explanations, they did release them, but not before they handed over five thousand dollars in restitution.

"I'm not sure what our next move should be," Polly broached the subject again. "I'm pretty sure they won't rent us another vehicle.

"You think?" laughed Shane. "I'm going to have to settle up with them as well. Decker is going to skin us alive probably."

"All we can do is what we have been doing, and that's keep our eyes out for that SUV. It should be relatively easy to spot unless they switch out vehicles," Phil tossed in.

"Unfortunately, it sounds like something they might do," Polly agreed. "They won't want to risk being seen, especially now the police are involved. Changing out vehicles makes sense."

The only thing they had going was that they knew what the men looked like, and if they saw them again, they'd be able to stay under the radar and follow them without being seen.

Chapter 33

Adrián kept Sam and Ted going at a steady pace. They couldn't be too far behind, he reasoned. He was trying to figure out exactly how he would accomplish taking on five people by himself since he had lost Javier. There was a slim chance Ganigi was still with Decker unless he was the man lying under a pile of rocks in the last cavern. With two of them, they might have a fighting chance to overcome them. Worse, all of them were equipped with guns. At least he had Sam and Ted as hostages and could use them to his advantage. And when he got what he wanted, he'd eliminate them.

Well, he couldn't think about it, he decided. He needed to move forward and do his best. He had no intention of returning and explaining his failure to Bruno. He had done that once, and one chance was usually all you got with Bruno.

Squeezing through the narrow passage, they entered into a large cavern. They stared speechless at the skulls, stacked high against the far wall and the piles of bones. Adrián felt his skin crawl; the sight was gruesome. He hoped the bones were old and not fresh and that they would not make it outside only to find cannibals waiting for them.

Sam and Ted found the bones fascinating and pressed Adrián to let them look, but he was in no mood to dawdle, and he didn't want to give them an opportunity to catch him off guard. They had already done that once, and he was not a fool. Besides, he was thinking they weren't going to live long enough for it to matter if they inspected a pile of bones or not.

"Well, look at that will you," Ted roared, seeing the complete skeletal bone structure laid out a few feet away. "The man must have been close to eight feet tall!"

"Impossible," snorted Adrián, but as he studied the bones, he realized it was true. He began to wonder what they would find once they stepped outside the cave, which wouldn't be much longer because he saw a flood of golden light breaking through the dark cave a short distance away. He couldn't imagine the stories he'd heard over the years about giants being half human and half monkey were true. And yet, even the thought sent slivers of icy cold fear riding up his spine.

"This place gives me the creeps. "Let's go," Adrián ordered, wanting to be out of the cave.

The ground began to shudder, enough so that Sam lost his footing and tumbled to the ground. Adrián was able to catch himself on a large boulder opposite him. Several rocks slid down the walls and the cavity boiled with dust. They coughed, covering their nose and mouth with their hands trying not to breathe the fine particles of limestone powder, but it was difficult and their eyes burned. There had been several rumblings along the way, their intensity increasing each time. It would be to their benefit to head outside where the threat of the ceiling falling in on them was not an issue.

Pushing forward, they broke through into the light of day and squinted against the brightness. They had been in the dark for two days and stepping out into daylight was a welcome change. They were startled by what they saw before them. Two pyramids towering feet above them and arches which led into courtyards. There were statues of animals carved in stone and roadways. Briefly, all they could do was stare in awe. This was what they had spent so many insufferable days searching for. It was what Leonard had lost his life trying to protect. Sam knew if people

269

discovered its whereabouts, it would allure looters and treasure seekers alike.

To the right, they spied a couple of packs lying to the outside of one of the pyramids. It was all Adrián needed to point the way. They had caught up with the team, and now it would be a challenge for Adrián to keep them all corralled. There were only two men he needed to keep alive, and that was Decker and Manuel. He could easily take out the rest of them, and then it was a simple matter making their way back to Trujillo.

He urged them forward. "Make a sound and the first person I shoot is the pretty little lady in there."

They knew he would do it. As they had seen over the past few days, Adrián had no scruples at all. They didn't dare test him right now, but they were sure they'd have an opportunity to take him on. The numbers were in their favor. However, they resolved to do nothing rash and jeopardize Callie's life.

He walked them to the opening and ducked inside the chamber of the pyramid. It took a moment for their eyes to readjust, but with the headlamps of Decker and the team, there was enough light to discern the faces of the team.

"Sam, Ted!" Decker exclaimed before he had time to realize what was going on.

As they walked toward them, Adrián slid his arm around Sam's neck and pointed his gun at his head. "You need to drop your weapons on the ground," he ordered them.

It took a moment for Decker to discern what was happening but when he saw the long scar down Adrián's cheek, and the straggly hair to his shoulders, the pieces started falling into place. It dawned on him that Adrián had been one of the men tailing them ever since they arrived in Trujillo. No doubt, the same one who had chased Holly and Jeanette back in Los Angeles. It was also apparent he'd not hesitate to kill them if they didn't do as he demanded. Decker motioned for everyone to lay down their weapons.

270

"Gather up the weapons Ted," Adrián told him and waited for him to grab the guns and bring them back. "Splendid," he said, rather pleased the way things were going. Having the weapons, he shoved Sam forward. "Now, I'd like you to start putting all those gems and gold in the packs."

Manuel took a step forward. "You can't do that. You will anger the gods."

Adrián laughed. "Oh, shut up, you fool!"

"You can't do this!" Not thinking, Manuel rushed forward, and then a loud echoing blast shattered the air, and Manuel crashed to the ground, blood oozing from his chest.

"No!" Callie screamed and rushed to him.

Adrián swung his gun toward Callie threateningly, and Decker held up his hand. "I wouldn't if I was you," he shouted. "You kill Callie, and I'll do nothing to help you, and you'll die trying to make your way back to Trujillo. You would be lost soon as you left here and you'd surely be food for the jaguars or worse."

Decker tried painting the most gruesome picture he could to scare Adrián from following through. He could see the wheels turning in his head. After he had chewed on the prospect briefly, he knew Decker was right. He'd never make it in the jungle alone. Much as it galled him, he needed Decker and if it meant his wife stayed alive, then so be it.

Callie could barely feel a pulse in Manuel, and tears filled her eyes. She knew he was only trying to protect what belonged to him and to all of the indigenous people of Honduras. She pulled a bandana from her back pocket and pressed it against the wound to stop the flow of blood. She knew as bad as the wound was, and without a hospital, Manuel would probably not make it out of the jungle alive, but she would do whatever she could to help him.

"I have a medical kit and want to attend to Manuel's wound," Decker said forcefully, his blue eyes slit with outrage.

"You ain't doing nothing," Adrián said with a sneer.

Putting water to Manuel's lips, he choked, unable to drink. No matter how much pressure she used, it didn't seem to clot the blood. The wet, sticky stream flowed over her fingers. With a sputter, his body stiffened, and then he went limp. She tried giving him CPR, but it was too late, he did not respond.

Callie closed her eyes tightly, and a whimper tumbled from her lips. Her heart was broken, not only because she had grown fond of Manuel over the past couple of weeks, but because she had met his beautiful wife who would have to come to grips with his death. All because of greed.

"Now, like I said, start putting as much gold and stones in the packs as you can fit!"

"Where's your partner?" asked Decker.

"Now, ain't that kind of you to ask. "Slipped over the edge and into the black hole," he answered. "He was holding us back anyway. He didn't have the stomach for this. No loss, really."

The iceberg coldness in his eyes was disturbing. It was as if he didn't have a soul. Decker wondered how anyone could become so dead inside that life no longer had meaning. It perplexed him, and at the same time, it sickened him. He would look for the appropriate time to strike when Adrián was least expecting it. He knew the time would come; he needed to be patient and wait him out.

"We need to bury Manuel," Callie told Adrián, tears clinging to her lashes.

"Do what you want, but when you're done, start stuffing the packs full of those glorious gems!"

The team collected stones to cover his body, wanting to give him the respect he deserved and not leaving him to the animals. Without a thread of a conscience, Adrián would rid himself of anyone without value to him. Callie only became important when Decker refused to help him if he hurt her. Even so, when it was over, and Decker no longer served a purpose, Adrián would not hesitate to kill him.

Outside a storm was brewing. The dense, heavy cumulonimbus clouds were stacked like a New York high rise overhead. The ground shuddered as lightning struck the ground, seeming to tear the sky apart, then was followed by a deluge of rain. It only took a minute before the ground became rivulets and began rushing into the entrance of the pyramid. There was a near-blinding flash of lightning that sounded as if it had struck a tree close by and an ear-shattering crack!

The rain did not relent, and water surged into the room below the pyramid. They were now walking in three inches of water. Adrián continued prodding them to hurry, wanting to start back. He knew the packs would be heavy and their weight would slow them down considerably. However, he didn't want to risk leaving empty-handed either. Besides, no one would know if he stashed some of the items once they reached the river and he could return for them later.

"Come on…come on," he pressed them.

Adrián looked for Ganigi soon after he got there, and not seeing him, assumed he was the one buried beneath the piles of rocks back in the cave. No doubt the jaguars got hold of him, he reasoned. Or maybe he tumbled down the crevasse inside the cave like Javier had. But no matter now, he thought. He had gotten what he'd come for, and once this was all over, he'd live the rest of his life in luxury.

Waiting for the storm to pass, Adrián motioned for them to move all of the packs out into the open. Outside, the air was heavy with humidity, and the flies were unbearable. He determined to rid himself of at least one of them so they would know he meant business. Plus, he was badly outnumbered, which made him more vulnerable.

This was show time, Adrián thought to himself and aimed the gun toward Sam. As his finger started to press the trigger, the ground started shaking violently, and he was thrown off balance. There was a loud roaring coming from the caves all around them and underneath them. Rocks began tumbling down from the pyramids, bouncing off other stones and were catapulted into the air. They began to run in different directions trying to avoid being pinned under the gigantic blocks of stone and debris.

As the shaking continued, the ground began to split open, leaving wide chasms that continued to grow wider and deeper. Callie stumbled forward in an attempt to flee, but her foot slipped as the ground was swept out from under her. Her hands caught the edge of the fissure, and she screamed loudly.

Decker panicked when he saw Callie and dove to his stomach, grabbing her wrists to keep her from tumbling down into the dark abyss. He held tight and battled to pull her back up. The ground continued to shake with a mighty force. Using as much strength as he could muster, he began reeling her in, at the same time hoping the ground would hold until he got her back over the side.

"Hang on, Callie!" Decker yelled.

Callie pushed with her toes against the side, giving her some momentum as she clasped tightly onto Decker's wrists. She could feel herself being drawn upward, and when her body slid over the edge, she sighed with relief.

Decker motioned for the others to join them. They turned and began sprinting in his direction, the ground still quivering violently beneath them. Like an explosion, the pyramid to the right began caving in before their eyes, the ground seeming to swallow it whole. They saw parts of the earth folding in on itself, and they began to run in a panic.

The entrance of the cave they'd followed collapsed with an explosive roar, sediment bursting into a cloud that choked them. Coughing, they turned to go in another direction opposite the tunnel. They stumbled several times as the ground heaved beneath them but quickly scrambled to their feet wanting to distance themselves.

Adrián yelled at them to stop and when they didn't, he raised his gun to shoot. In an instant, the ground ripped apart, and he slipped downward, his hand clutching frantically at the ground above. "Help!" he yelled. "Help me!"

In spite of everything Adrián had done, Decker could not in good conscience leave him to die. He turned back and ran toward him, and dropping onto the ground, he thrust his hand down for him to reach. Panicked, Adrián grabbed his wrist. The shaking became extreme, and though Decker did his best to pull him forward, he couldn't hold his grip. Fingers slipping free, Adrián sprawled backward with his arms spread wide and plummeted into the dark gorge created by the quake. His screams reverberated through the gap as he fell into oblivion.

"Decker," Callie called out. "Let's go!"

They took off at a dead run when yet another loud blast resounded behind them. They twisted their heads back, horrified to see the second pyramid crumbling and being swallowed whole. Everything around them was collapsing in on itself and was closing in on them. They hurried their strides, fighting through the dense jungle thicket trying to distance themselves.

Once they were away, they all crumpled to the ground exhausted, their chests heaving, and sweat soaking their clothes. When the ground had settled, there was an eerie silence hanging in the suffocating hot air. They all looked at one another in complete disbelief. They had lost a good man, had suffered many setbacks, and had set their eyes on something spectacular that would never be seen again.

"I can't believe what has happened," Callie expressed.

"If I didn't know better, I'd be convinced there was a monkey god who watched over the city," Decker grunted, wiping the sweat from his brow. "And the curse Manuel kept warning us about."

"It's more than I can wrap my mind around," Callie replied. "Especially after witnessing an eight-and-a-half-foot skeleton in the cave. I wonder what else we would have found if we'd had the chance to excavate?"

"Man, it's good to see you, Sam and Ted." Decker got a chance to greet them without a gun pointed at his head.

"You know it," Sam said. "I thought we were done for a couple times. We thought something had happened to you as well. Seems Ganigi was working for whoever is behind this. Once they kidnapped us, we had no way to contact anyone."

"That became apparent," Decker responded.

"Unfortunately, Ganigi killed Webu rather than wait for help," Ted told them.

"We caught on to Ganigi when he showed up at the native village. His story didn't jive," Decker told them. "It has been a sad expedition. A lot of loss."

Carson smiled weakly. "But we have the packs full of antiquities to give back to the Honduran government, and we can show them photos of Leonard's discovery. If nothing else, Leonard will be issued credit for the find, and that should come as some consolation to Holly."

"There's still someone responsible for sending those goons," Callie reminded them.

"We'll get to the bottom of this when we return," Decker assured her. "Someone has to pay for the deaths of Leonard, his guides, Jeanette, Webu and now Manuel."

They sat for a time in silence, mulling over the deaths and everything that had gone on over the past weeks—the towering pyramids, the treasure beyond anything they had ever seen, and the quake that engulfed an ancient city. It was overwhelming; too much to absorb in the fleeting minutes of terror they had experienced only moments ago.

"I have to wonder if any of our equipment is still intact back by the river," Sam said, almost to himself.

Decker chuckled. "Of all the things to agonize about Sam, and you trouble yourself with your equipment!"

"My children," he shrugged with a half-smile.

"I guess there's only one way to find out."

They were forced to skirt around their original trail as the cave had fallen in. They still had a compass with them, and so they began heading back the direction they'd come, working their way out of the dark, dense jungle. It took several days battling through the heavy canvas of vines and trees,

There were some tricky places on their return, such as the sheer wall cliffs. They no longer had their climbing gear with them. Most of it had been swallowed up. There was one rope which they made use of and incorporated a few heavy vines. Exhausted beyond belief, they'd maneuvering down the face of the cliff, but it felt like they'd taken on Mount Rushmore.

Food supplies were next to none, and they were forced to find grubs and specific plants. Manuel had educated them on which could be used as a meal. Because they had lost their weapons, they sharpened sticks to make spears in case of a jaguar or boar attack. They also learned after every afternoon downpour, they could drink water droplets off the large leaves and gather as much as possible for their canteen.

An even graver dilemma was that they had no medical supplies, no insect repellent to stave off mosquitoes and black flies, nor did they have the luxury of anti-itch creams to slather on the red welts. Their circumstances had challenged them at every turn in a life and death game that they frequently thought they'd lose, but their tenacity had carried them through.

At last, they found themselves at the river. They were more than a little pleased to find that everything was still there, including the boats. If the boats had been missing it would have made their travel time-consuming and exhausting as they would have had to go on foot.

277

It wouldn't take long returning as they'd be going downstream rather than upstream. They'd cover ground more quickly and would be back to the *Jade* within a few days. They were ready to shower and have a good night's sleep on a soft mattress rather than the hard ground. Their clothes were soiled and caked with sweat. Their hair was plastered to their heads, and they figured if anyone met up with them, they might be overcome by their body odor. The only real bathing they had had was at the waterfalls. So, when they stood on the rivers bank, they couldn't resist jumping in to bathe. It was nothing short of pure bliss having the cool water rushing over their flesh, even though it was muddied from the torrential downpours.

They reached the Indian village Manuel had introduced them to, and though they were unable to speak the language, the villagers could visually see their needs. They rubbed leaves that had been ground on a stone and made into a paste, all over their bodies to ease the painful insect welts and saw they ate a hearty meal. When it was time to go, they sent them on with a bag of supplies to see them back to the *Jade*.

When they came to the rapids, they pulled the boats out and carried them overhead downstream until the waters were not boiling with white froth. They made good timing as the current pushed them along.

When they reached Barra Plátano, at the rivers discharge, they located Manuel's vehicle. The key had been slipped under the rubber mat inside. They all piled into the vehicle trusting their return would be easier than when they'd come. This time they had no guns to fend for themselves should they be held up again.

To their relief, they passed through the area without circumstance and the most they faced was another violent rainstorm. They pulled off the road for a couple hours not wanting to take the chance of sliding off into the mud again.

They had already seen two vehicles along the way that had slid off the road and down steep embankments.

They were happy when once again they got back onto the highway heading for Trujillo.

Chapter 34

The air was charged with excitement. It had been way too long since the crew had come together, and Decker and Callie were champing at the bit to see Garrett. Also, they were anxious to tell Holly all the details of Leonard's find and present the few relics they'd brought along so she could partner in his dream.

They hired a Garifuna man they'd come across along the docks in Trujillo to take them out to the *Jade*. The boat was weathered, its green paint blistered and peeling away from years in the tropical sun, but it would serve the purpose. The man pulled out the choke and yanked on the starter rope. The outboard motor coughed and sputtered then belched out a cloud of gray smoke and then roared into action. The wooden prow slapped the waves as they scudded across the bay. They closed in on the *Jade*'s stern deck, and Decker leapt from the interior onto the deck to tie off the yacht for the others.

His head twisted back when he heard a familiar shout from the deck. It was Polly, a huge grin plastered on his face. No sooner had he spied Polly, then Shane and Phil rushed out to greet them. They shimmied down the ladder where greetings and hugs followed. Decker looked around expecting to see Garrett running out. When he didn't see him, he looked at Polly with question in his eyes.

"We have a lot to tell you," Polly said. "Let's all go inside. I'll pour you some cold drinks and give you the scoop."

Decker didn't like the sounds of things, but without interrogating him, he followed Polly and the rest of the crew into the dining area off the galley. They settled down over a glass of lemonade, thankful for air conditioning after spending so much time in the sweltering heat. Even being able to relax against a cushioned seat was a relief. Every time they returned from an expedition they were reminded how fortunate they were when they settled back into the simple comforts afforded them.

"Okay, spill it," Decker said.

"The other night when we were sleeping, three men boarded the boat, tied us up and took your father and Holly," Polly told him. "Sorry."

"What?" Decker's face looked stricken.

"We went to ask questions along the beach, and we were told the men might be driving a dark SUV," he continued. "Phil and I drove around the town trying to find a vehicle that matched the description, and we did, as well as two of the men who had boarded the *Jade*."

"Did you catch them?"

Polly shook his head. "We tried," Polly assured him. "Boy, did we try. We chased them all through Trujillo, and then it became all discombobulated, and they began chasing us. Unfortunately, they rammed us, and we crashed the Jeep we were driving."

Decker's eyes widened. "You weren't hurt, were you?"

"No thankfully, even after flipping three times," chuckled Polly. "A farmer gave us a ride back into town, and then we were arrested."

"You're kidding," Decker could not believe what he was hearing.

"Wish I was," he admitted. "We tried to get the police involved, but they didn't seem too willing to help us. We couldn't give them a great deal of information because we don't know who these men are or who hired them."

Decker closed his eyes and sighed. "All we can do is wait it out. Chances are they'll contact me before long when they find out we've returned. They're going to want the map to Ciudad Blanca, which I have."

"Will you give it to them?" asked Phil.

"I'll hand it over willingly," Decker said.

"Does that mean you didn't find the lost city?" Polly asked.

Decker smiled. "We did, and it was amazing. However, there's nothing left of it."

"I don't understand," Polly said, wrinkling his brow.

Decker started from the beginning. "It was a wild ride. We discovered too late Ganigi was hired on as an inside man to keep tabs on us from the gitgo and unfortunately, killed Webu."

"What a shame," Phil said. "Webu seemed like a nice fellow."

"Once we'd discovered Ciudad Blanca, we were held up by Adrián—he was one of the men who had gone after Holly in LA. He had held Sam and Ted hostage, which was why you were unable to contact them, and when he caught up to us, killed Manuel."

"He was a good man," Callie said, tears springing to her eyes. "We'll have to locate his wife and let her know."

"Are you going to go back to excavate?" Polly asked.

Decker gave a short snort and shook his head. "Adrián held a gun on us and forced us to stuff our packs full of gems and artifacts. Out of the blue, we had a powerful earthquake…never seen anything like it in my life! The ground shook so violently we were thrown to the ground. We watched in awe as the pyramids came crashing down and the whole city was swallowed whole."

"Holy cow!" gasped Polly.

"So, even if they do get their hands on the map, it'll do them no good," Decker told them. At least they'd gain some satisfaction after what had happened.

"I'm going to go shower and change," Callie told them. "When I'm done, we'll pull out the artifacts and make a list of what we have. Once we have everything documented, we'll contact the Honduran Institute of Anthropology and History and see the artifacts are placed back into their hands."

"Wait up, I'll join you," Decker said, scarcely able to tolerate the build up of sweat on his body.

Callie felt as if she could stay forever in the warm shower. A couple of weeks of dirt washed away, and once again she felt refreshed and clean. Except for the many bites up and down her body, and the several lost pounds, there was little evidence of the jungle trauma she'd survived. She was thankful most of the team had survived the enormous challenges they'd faced, but she was having a difficult time putting the painful memory of Manuel and Webu's deaths out of her mind.

One thing she'd learned about the jungle was how outsiders were ravishing the land and destroying vital resources that kept the villages thriving. Manuel had helped them to see the sad truth through his passionate exhortation when they were traveling up the Rio Plátano River. It had been an extraordinary experience to see the rainforest through Manuel's eyes, and Callie realized that sometimes their eyes were veiled because of their own agendas. A lesson she'd not neglect in the future.

Now, there was one more thing they had to accomplish, and that was to find Garrett and Holly.

Decker and Callie had been so consumed with the expedition, and their safety, they had had little time for anything else. They stretched out on the bed in quiet reflection. It felt healing to lay wrapped in the warmth of each other's arms, they appreciated the fact they'd come through the ordeal almost unscathed.

Later in the evening, they met everyone back in the dining hall. Phil whipped them up one of his special meals—steamed fish he'd purchased fresh off one of the fishing boats, steamed vegetables, and grilled rosemary potatoes. After days of eating

283

food from packets, and grubs, the meal was a mouthwatering godsend.

They ate and talked and laughed. Being back together was a special moment for all of them. The fellowship drowned out some of the chilling events that had happened over the past few weeks, and they happily embraced their friendships.

After dining, they began going through the packs and pulled out the assortment of relics Adrián had forced them to take. In hindsight, all of it would Have been left behind had Adrián not insisted they stuff the rucksacks. It would take bulldozers to excavate the lost city as it was presently. Everything was buried deep underground; they held the only remains. The snapshots they took of the skeletal remains and measurements would be their only proof that at least one giant of a man lived there.

Sam and Ted studied the photos, while Carson had the others looking at the gems and gold plates. It was all impressive, and they were excited to share it with the museum in Honduras. Even the small amount they gleaned made them overjoyed that all wasn't lost.

It was the following morning when a phone call came in for Decker. He'd been expecting it, and as he answered, he was met with a gruff, menacing voice. "Decker, so glad you have returned."

"Cut to the chase," Decker replied coldly. "Where's my Father and Holly?"

"Not so fast." Bruno refused to answer. "I'm disappointed none of my men came back alive. After all, they were paid handsomely."

"Not my problem."

"Now, now, Decker," he laughed shortly, sarcasm dripping in his voice. "I'd think an apology would be appropriate."

Decker hung up the phone. "Is this guy for real?" he growled, perturbed and not up to playing silly games with the man on the other end. He sat quiet waiting for the call he knew would come. The phone rang once more.

"Yup."

"I could kill your Father right now with no problem," the angry voice of Bruno erupted on the other end.

"You could, but then you wouldn't have the map," Decker challenged. "And that's what this little farce is all about, isn't it?"

He heard a sharp intake of air on the other end revealing Bruno's frustration with him. "It's time we meet," he said simply. "There's a warehouse at the end of town…"

"Give me the address, I'll be there," Decker agreed. Even though he was going to let Bruno make the plans, Decker knew he needed to stay one step ahead of him and be the one in control if they were to overtake these men and get his father and Holly back.

"If I see police or any of your team, I'll make sure you never see your father again."

"I expect to see my Father and Holly when we make the exchange," Decker told him firmly, making sure Bruno understood he'd not give him anything without seeing his father and Holly alive.

Bruno was agitated about Decker putting limitations on him, but he'd have to play it Decker's way if he was ever to set his eyes on the map. Besides, once the transaction happened, they would all be killed anyhow.

"I'll have someone with me to verify the authenticity of the map."

"It's authentic."

"And how am I to know for certain you even discovered Leonard's lost city?"

"I'll bring some photos with me which has the date imprinted on them, and I'll bring you one of the jewels Adrián forced us to bring back," Decker replied, his voice filled with disdain. He wanted this man to pay for what he had done and the lives that were lost because of him.

"We'll bring your Father and Holly with us, but I warn you, if anything should go wrong, my men are instructed to put a bullet through their heads."

"You'll pay," Decker informed him.

He simply laughed. "Let's say around eleven this morning?"

"Good as any."

"So, what's the plan?" Carson inquired as he hung up the phone.

Decker gave it some thought. Nothing was worth his father's life. At the same time, if they didn't pull the plan off, the man would surely dispose of them. "First, I want Ted to scramble over to the police department and advise them of what is going to transpire. I want them to know we'll be armed and ready to take his men down and that they need to be there no later than eleven thirty if they want to intervene."

"Got it," said Ted.

"I need Phil to go check out the warehouse right now and find a good hiding place so that when I give the signal, you guys can take out the sharp shooters. You can bet they'll plant at least one man in the rafters to take me out as soon as the exchange is made. I hope we'll beat them to it."

Phil nodded. "More than happy to. There's nothing more I want to see than this man to be taken out."

"Sam and Carson, I want you to go to the warehouse as well, but I want you to remain outside. Make yourselves invisible. He'll surely plant several men outside to guard the place. They're going to be on alert, so whatever you do, you need to be crafty and silent as a puma readying for a kill. They'll out man us, and they'll no doubt be toting AK47's. What more can I say."

Carson slapped his arm. "No need to say more, we know what we have to do, and we'll make sure it's done."

286

"Callie and Shane, you stay here on the boat. If anything happens to us, you need to pull anchor and go."

"Decker…"

"No argument this time, Callie."

She saw he was dead serious and thought better than to argue with him over the matter. He wanted her safe, and she understood that but at the moment she felt helpless, and the thought of staying behind frustrated her. At the same time, someone had to stay with the *Jade* to make sure the hoodlums who had come on board before would not try again. She and Shane would see to it.

Taking a deep breath, he looked at his watch. Nine o'clock. They would have to move quickly and invisibly. He began putting a couple of photos in his shirt pocket, rolled up the crude map Leonard had sent to Holly and determined what relic to part with. All the while, he kept wondering if they would be able to pull it off without any of his team being harmed.

They figured they'd be watched, so they'd have to sneak into town, blend with the people then make their way to the warehouse all without being seen. It would be a challenge.

As it neared time to go, Decker moved to Callie and took her fingers into his hand. Her fingers looked so tiny and frail in his. He raised them to his lips. "I love you, Callie."

"Stop it," she said sternly. "You're acting as if you won't see me again." Tears sprang to her eyes.

"I don't want to leave without saying it," he told her. "I want you to know how important you are to me. But, I do intend on coming back with my Father and with Holly. You can't get rid of me that easy." He smiled, then drew her close to him and held her tightly.

Inhaling deeply, Callie pulled back and forced a smile to her lips. "It's time to go."

"Take good care of her Shane," Decker said as he went aft in long, confident strides.

"You got it, Decker!"

"What about me?" Polly asked, looking somewhat dejected because Decker had not given him an assignment.

Decker smiled. "Walk with me, Polly, and I'll tell you what I'd like you to do."

"Well okay, that's more like it."

Ted had gone to the police station to inform them of what was taking place and had returned in the skiff. He tossed keys to Decker, and said, "It's a red Mustang. I figured you might as well drive first class."

"Always looking out for me, aren't you, Teddy," he winked and patted his upper arm.

Decker drove to the warehouse. When he arrived, he saw a banged up dark SUV which he assumed was the one Polly and Phil had tangled with. There was another black jeep parked beside the SUV. This was it. He took a deep breath before he got out of the rental car. If everything didn't go according to plan, there was no telling what the final outcome would be.

The warehouse was a two-story, dilapidated building constructed of variegated metal which had turned a rusty orangish-brown from years of neglect. There was old lumber strewn around the perimeters and corroded equipment dating back at least fifty years. A couple of sections of tin had been torn free from the roof and lay a distance from the building. Windows had long since been broken out. Red paint on the south side of the building had peeled back from the metal, much of it piled near the foundation.

Outside the door, three men were posted, two of them toting AK47's and one with a rifle pointed directly at Decker. The man's eyes darted from left to right surveying the surroundings to make sure there was no one else with Decker. He wore dirty jeans frayed at the cuffs and a white, tattered t-shirt. His black hair hung to his shoulders, and he sported a Fu Manchu mustache which drooped an inch below his square jaw. Much like the other men who worked for Bruno, this man too bore a cold, calculating glare.

One of the men strode over to the rental car and began searching the interior to make sure no one was hiding out inside. He blasted the trunk with his rifle, the sound of tearing metal shattered the otherwise stale air. The trunk flipped open, and Decker was glad he'd not tried to smuggle someone inside the compartment.

Entering the warehouse, he saw Bruno, three men, his father, and Holly. He walked toward the middle of the warehouse and stopped when Bruno put his hand up. "Far enough, Decker," he said.

In front of him was a small card table with three chairs situated around it. Bruno walked forward with one of the men and stopped at the table. He made a sweeping gesture with his hand for Decker to come and sit down.

Decker noted there were two men at the door and four inside the warehouse. He knew they were outnumbered, but he counted on Phil's marksmanship to take out at least two of them. Though he was unable to determine what was going on outside, he had to trust they'd gain the upper hand and make it out alive. The odds were certainly against them.

One of the men who had walked alongside Bruno had a black patch over his right eye. He left Bruno's side and walked over to Decker. "Hands up," he said. Decker did as he was told and the man began to pat him down to make sure he wasn't carrying a weapon. When he was satisfied, he moved back.

"Sit down," Bruno said, as he too, took a seat. His charcoal-black eyes raked over Decker with mocking amusement. He looked fully confident he had outsmarted Decker, and that he would walk away with a fortune.

Decker sat down. "So, you're the brains of this operation," he snorted sarcastically.

Bruno grinned, exposing a row of discolored teeth. He bit off the end of his large, brown cigar, popped it into his mouth and struck a match. The smell of sulfur and smoke floated in a gray cloud around his head. Bruno was used to being in control, and he wasn't going to let someone like Decker have leverage over him, nor would he let his insults ruffle him. Once he had the map and everything was settled between them, they would die anyhow, so what did he care?

"The photos," Bruno said, reaching his greedy hand outward.

Decker slid his hand into his shirt pocket and pulled them out. He slapped them soundly on the table. He could see Bruno's eyes round with greed as he saw the pyramids and the expanse of the lost city. He also gazed at the treasure that lay sprawled on the floor of the stone pyramid. The subterranean room glimmered brilliantly from the jewels that had spilled out over the sides of stone-inlaid boxes; there were silver and gold plates, goblets studded with rubies and jade statues. His jaw dropped with disbelief. It was exceedingly more than he could have ever dreamt.

Decker pulled out one of the stones which was as the size of an egg. Its value would no doubt be in the hundreds of thousands, if not more. "There are trunks of these, all you have to do is release my Father and Holly," he told him.

"The map!" he inquired, holding out his meaty hand.

From inside his loose Hawaiian shirt, he pulled out the crude map Leonard had drawn on the back of the heavy wrapping paper which also included the coordinates. He dropped it in front of Bruno and watched his face take a covetous twist.

Outside, Sam had made his way to the side of the warehouse. He peered around the corner and saw three of Bruno's men guarding the door. One of the men had started walking in his direction. There was a bushy plant Sam ducked behind, waiting for the guard to come around the corner. He pulled his knife from its sheath which was tied around his thigh and waited until the man's footsteps had fallen past him.

With a lightning quick movement, Sam's arm flung around him, his hand cupping his mouth. With his other hand, he ran the cold blade across the man's throat, and he slithered to the ground. Sam dragged his body behind the fragrant bush, then crept back to the corner of the warehouse.

He knew he'd have to distract the other two men long enough for Carson and him to sneak up from behind and overtake them. Beside Sam was a fist-sized rock. Grabbing it firmly, he catapulted it past the men into some bushes off to their right side where he knew Carson would be hiding. As he intended, the men's heads jerked around and cautiously walked toward the brushes, at which time, Sam took advantage of the diversion and hustled to the other side of Decker's rental car.

Carson flung his knife with expertise, driving it deep into one of the guard's chest. He dropped like the ship's anchor. Carson sighed with relief. Two down.

Sam darted forward before the other man could comprehend what was happening. He brought his rifle quickly around the man's throat and applied pressure. The man struggled violently to break Sam's hold on him, his face turning scarlet and his eyes bulging until his body went limp. Sam and Carson dragged the man behind some piled lumber and secured his hands and feet with rope and placed a gag over his mouth in case he woke. Lithe strides carried them over to the closed entrance. Quietly, Carson cracked the door ever so slightly in order to monitor what was happening inside. There were several men with guns holding watch over Decker.

Directly above, in the rafters, Phil was hunkered down waiting patiently for a shot. He was trying to map out how he could take on the four men below with Bruno by himself when he spotted another man stretched out a distance from him on the upper level of the warehouse, rifle-ready. It was clear once the

291

deal was consummated, the shooter would try and take out Decker. Phil realized he'd have to be the first one to take out. His nerves were taut with anticipation.

Carson got on his stomach and crawled through the door, moving behind a rusted barrel off center from where they were seated. His eyes roamed throughout the room trying to see if there was anyone else hiding out who could take a shot at Decker. It wasn't long before his legs were burning from crouching, but he knew it would be a deadly mistake if he revealed himself and so he remained steadfast. He was ready, his finger resting on the trigger. Sam remained outside ready to rush the door when there was a need for him and to make sure no other men came.

Both Bruno and the other man studied the map. They looked at the coordinates and then compared the longitude and latitude with an updated map of the Mosquitia area. When both of them looked satisfied, they nodded to Decker and pushed themselves to their feet.

"Let my Father and Holly loose."

"Sure," Bruno said and motioned to Benito and the men behind him.

Benito raised his gun, and it exploded before anyone anticipated what he was doing. Decker flew backward and crumpled to the floor, a moan escaping his lips. As he went down, he could hear Holly's mortified scream.

Phil didn't hesitate to retaliate. He opened fire on the sniper, who was stretched out on the planks opposite. He heard a grunt and the man slithered from the rafters falling headlong to the cement floor, his head splitting from the impact.

Carson took aim and got off a shot, taking down the one-eyed man beside Bruno. The blast threw him backward onto the floor, blood pooling around his body.

Bruno ducked and ran back in the direction of where Garrett and Holly were being held. As he got to them, another gun blast exploded in the room, and Benito crumpled like a rag doll onto the cement floor with a large hole in his chest.

Two other men ran for cover and opened fire on Carson. Bullets whizzed overhead, splintering the wooden beams he had taken shelter behind. Realizing how vulnerable he was, Carson rolled across the floor and found cover behind an old tractor. Bullets zinged off the machine with a loud metallic ring nearly breaking his eardrums.

There was a short span of silence, and it became obvious to Carson the man had run out of ammunition. Taking the advantage, Carson rushed the man, slamming the butt of his gun into the side of his head. The man slithered to the floor. Without hesitating, Carson dropped to his stomach and rolled for cover to avoid the last man's bullets whizzing past his head.

Decker felt pain shooting through his shoulder as he struggled to his feet. He started to move forward but stopped when Bruno put his gun to Garrett's head. Holly was panicked but was unable to move because she was secured to a wide beam. She struggled against the ropes but to no avail. She was held fast, and all she could do was watch helplessly.

"Stay back, or I'll kill him," Bruno threatened. "Move aside."

Holding his shoulder, Decker staggered out of the way. Blood seeped through his fingers. He began to feel light-headed. There was no way he was going to let his dad go out the door with this maniac, he reasoned.

Bruno darted behind Garrett, slashed the ropes, and then used him as a shield. He began pulling Garrett toward the door; his one arm looped around Garrett's neck, the other held a gun to his temple. He was determined not to let Garrett loose. He was his ticket out. He had the gem, and the map, all he needed was a few more men, and it would all be his! This was not over.

As Bruno closed the distance between him and the door, the sound of a motor roared loudly outside, startling them. Without warning, a car crashed through the front door. Wood planks soared into the air, and the shriek of metal and wood colliding thundered through the warehouse. The windshield glass crumbled as a post drove through the front of the vehicle, thankfully missing the crazy, Viking-looking man behind the wheel. Everyone scattered like a shotgun blast.

The interruption was enough for Bruno to throw Garrett aside and make a mad dash for his SUV. Bruno jumped inside, revved the motor, and the tires burned against the dry, hard-packed ground. The rear end fishtailed as he gunned the engine and sped off down the road.

Decker ran out of the warehouse. Throwing the door open on the rented sports car, he followed suit and spun the car in a circle. The engine whined as he slammed the gas pedal to the floor—the spinning tires spit dirt and rocks in a spiraling cloud around him.

It didn't take long before he was on Bruno's tail at seventy-five miles per hour. The road began to twist like a snake, and with each corner the rear of the vehicle pitched back and forth, sliding on the loose dirt. Decker stuck like glue to Bruno, refusing to let him get away. Blood soaked his shoulder, and he knew he had to force Bruno from the road before too much longer.

Phil took out the last man at the warehouse. Seeing Polly was still seated in the smashed jeep he was driving, Phil sprang into action and leapt into the front seat opposite Polly. "What are we waiting for? Let's go, buddy!" he yelled.

Polly threw the car into reverse, the smell of smoke and rubber filling their nostrils as he punched the accelerator. They knew Decker was in no condition to be chasing Bruno and they were determined to catch up to them. As they sped down the drive, they could hear sirens in the distance and knew the police would be at the warehouse any moment.

The jeep was veering dangerously around the sharp corners, barely holding to the road, but Polly continued to push the pedal as far as he could, fearful Decker would pass out from the loss of blood. Adrenaline pulsed through him as he closed in on the two vehicles.

"Watch out!" hollered Phil, as a mule driven wagon entered onto the road.

Polly slammed on the brakes, and the jeep spun in circles, sliding all the while. Both men yelled as the jeep nearly missed the side of the wagon and roared to a stop, a cloud of dirt circling them. For a moment, Polly thought his heart stopped. He turned his head toward Phil whose eyes looked as though they might pop out of their sockets.

As Polly straightened out the car, he could hear the man in the wagon cursing at them. He certainly didn't blame the guy. If he'd been in the same situation, and a jeep come hurtling at him like a runaway tornado, he'd have responded the same way.

Decker was feeling weaker the farther they went. He fought against the dizziness. Thrusting his foot to the floorboard, he moved inches behind the SUV, and with a surge, he struck the rear end of it. There was a deafening, high-pitched squeal as the two bumpers clashed. He was thrown back hard, a burning sensation driving through his neck. Again, he slammed into the rear of the SUV and watched it squirrel wildly in both directions.

Bruno pulled away again, his heart thumping. He would not be taken down without a fight, he reasoned. He had the map. He had lost several men in his quest to obtain the treasure, but they could all be replaced. Like-minded men with greedy hearts were easily recruited. He'd pick up where he left off once he rid himself of Decker Hayden.

Decker fumbled under his seat until he withdrew his PX45 Storm compact Berretta and aimed it out the window. Doing his best to hold steady, he popped off four rounds of ammunition through the back window of the SUV.

Decker watched as everything around him seemed to happen in slow motion. The SUV swerved, the tires striking the abrupt

295

edge of the road which caused it to flip like a rotary blade. It soared outward over a deep ravine and then flipped end over end crashing against boulders and snapping off trees on its journey down. When it struck the bottom, there was a loud explosion, and a ball of fire erupted like a volcano.

Decker, weak from the loss of blood, felt his head swirling dizzily, then as if someone pulled a bag over his eyes, everything went black.

Polly and Phil watched on with astonishment as Bruno plummeted to his death. They were thankful it would be the last time they would ever set eyes on him again. He was a cold, ruthless tyrant, and the world would be better off without him in their opinion.

No sooner had they watched the fireball below than they turned to see Decker's vehicle veer off the road and crash into a tree, the sound of tearing metal and breaking glass resounded from the impact.

Polly gunned the Jeep. Upon reaching the crumpled red sports car, he slammed on his brakes, nearly flying out of his seat in a panic, Phil at his heels.

"There's a crowbar in the back," Polly yelled frantically. He fought to open the door, but the side was crushed in, and Decker was not responding. Phil handed him the crowbar, and while Polly tried to pry the door open on the driver's side, Phil tried shimmying through the passenger side. At the same time, Phil called the hospital for an ambulance.

After a lot of ratcheting and tugging, Polly managed to open the door enough to pull Decker from the vehicle. He could hear the sirens coming on fast; he hoped it wasn't too late. Decker had a deep gash on his brow, and blood streamed down his face. Polly dabbed at the opened wound and applied pressure to his shoulder where the bullet had lodged.

Once the ambulance came, and they had loaded Decker, Polly and Phil rushed back to the warehouse to let the others know what had transpired.

"That's three rented vehicles we have terminated since this all began," Phil said.

"I don't think Decker will pay much mind to that after everything we've been through," Polly chuckled.

They spent nearly an hour going over the details with the police when they returned and were happy to find Garrett and Holly in good shape. However, they were stressed about Decker, and they wanted to get to the hospital as quickly as possible.

The police made it clear they had been wanting to take down Bruno for a long while. Bruno had preyed on the community way too long, and though they were well aware of it, he'd always seemed to cover his tracks, and they never had enough evidence to hold him. In the past, Bruno had paid several officers handsomely to turn a blind eye to his evil deeds. The department was not disappointed he was gone and figured he'd gotten his just reward.

***

The team piled into the jeep and headed straight away to the hospital. They placed a call to Shane and Callie to let them know what had happened and when they arrived, Callie was already at the hospital at Decker's side. They were relieved to find the bullet had not done too much damage. It had lodged in the bone, but they were able to remove it without and problems. The doctors assured them he would recover in a few short weeks, and the gash on his forehead had only needed some stitches.

"I can't believe you got shot," Callie said.

"Well, as you can see, I'm going to be fine," he comforted her.

"Don't you ever do that again, Decker Hayden," she scolded, but with a smile.

Holly and Garrett stepped into the room and rushed to greet the two of them. She threw her arms lovingly around them, relieved they'd made it safely out of Bruno's snare. They knew it could have made an ugly twist and gone a different direction.

Thankfully, their team worked together like a tapestry. Each of them was like a thick cord woven together in the fabric that formed a strong union.

"I can't wait to show you what Leonard discovered, Holly," Decker said. "It's an amazing find. We have photos, and some wild stories to tell you."

"I can't wait either," she said, her eyes lined with tears. "But more than anything, I'm thankful everyone's all right. Thank you. Leonard would be very proud of what you did for him and for me."

"I'd do it again for you, Holly." Decker smiled.

Back at the *Jade,* they arranged to see the relics back to the Honduran Institute of Anthropology and History, as well as notified the Ambassadors Fund for Cultural Preservation. It was important they turn over everything they had so it could remain in the country, especially in honor of Manuel. They also saw Leonard would be accredited as the one who discovered the lost city. Whether it was Ciudad Blanca or the Lost City of the Monkey God as some called it, they would never know. Lingering in the back of Decker's mind after everything he'd seen, he had to wonder if it wasn't more than a legend.

Once the details had been dealt with, they began making plans to return to their home in Malibu. They stood on the deck of the *Jade* looking out over the bay. The horizon was washed with pastels of pink and gold. They were thankful they'd survived the inhospitable jungle and the brutal men who had pursued them. They had accomplished what they had set out to do, in spite of the impossible odds. A bit bruised, but certainly ready for the next adventure.

Thank you for reading The Monkey Idol. I hope it was a fun and exciting read for you. If you enjoyed it, be sure to read SHARK EATER, book two in the Decker & Callie Adventure Series.

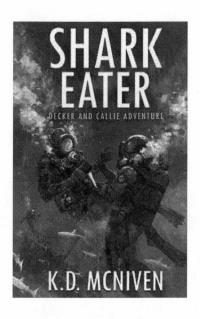

Archaeologists, Decker and Callie Hayden, pair up with salvager, Dax Drake, to investigate what appears to be one of the galleons from the Spanish fleet that was shipwrecked after the 1539 hurricane off the Turks and Caicos Islands. In their search, they discover more than what they had bargained for and ultimately puts the entire crew of the Shark Eater's lives in jeopardy. Filled with action-packed adventure on the high seas, Shark Eater will keep you turning pages.

If fictional romantic adventures are what you like to read, pick up a copy of the soon to be released, Sheba's Treasure, A Sam Carter Adventure, on Amazon Kindle this June.

Sam Carter begins a journey through the African bush looking to find peace and solace. What he finds is an old acquaintance, Alice Peterson, and a whirlwind of intrigue that could cost them their life.

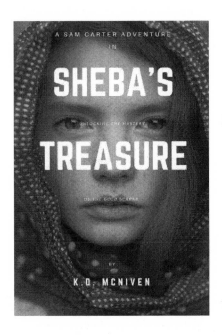

K.D. McNiven also is working on her third book in the Decker & Callie adventure Series, due to be released by the end of 2018, and is also in the process of writing a new series with one of the characters from Shark Eater, **India Dymond in Cypher.**